FATAL CARNIVAL

FATAL CARNIVAL

Charles O'Brien

This first world edition published in Great Britain 2006 by
SEVERN HOUSE PUBLISHERS LTD of
9–15 High Street, Sutton, Surrey SM1 1DF.
This first world edition published in the USA 2006 by
SEVERN HOUSE PUBLISHERS INC of
595 Madison Avenue, New York, N.Y. 10022.

British Library Cataloguing in Publication Data

O'Brien, Charles, 1927-
   Fatal carnival
   1.   Cartier, Anne (Fictitious character) - Fiction
   2.   Women teachers - France - Fiction
   3.   France - History - Louis XVI, 1744-1793 - Fiction
   4.   Detective and mystery stories
   I.   Title
   813.6 [F]

   ISBN-13: 978-0-7278-6403-1
   ISBN-10: 0-7278-6403-3

All Severn House titles are printed on acid-free paper.

Typeset by Palimpsest Book Production Ltd.,
Polmont, Stirlingshire, Scotland.
Printed and bound in Great Britain by
MPG Books Ltd., Bodmin, Cornwall.

Acknowledgements

I wish to thank Andy Sheldon for his skill on the Internet and for various computer services. I am grateful also to Gudveig Baarli for assisting with the maps, to Jennifer Nelson and Deborah McCaw of Gallaudet University for helpful advice on matters pertaining to deafness, and to the professionals at Severn House who produced this book. My agent Evan Marshall and Fronia Simpson read drafts of the novel and contributed to its improvement. Finally, my wife Elvy, art historian, deserves special mention for her keen editorial eye and her unflagging support.

Cast of Main Characters

In Order of First Appearance

Anne Cartier: *wife of Paul de Saint-Martin and teacher of deaf children*

Paul de Saint-Martin: *Provost of the Royal Highway Patrol for the area surrounding Paris*

Georges Charpentier: *Saint-Martin's adjutant*

Jean Lebrun, aka Leblond: *escaped convict from Toulon naval prison*

Jacques Duclos: *master cabinetmaker, murdered, 1768, in Marseille*

Pierre, Comte de Maistre: *Commandant of Nice*

Beverly Parker: *Anne Cartier's cousin and wife of Thomas Parker*

Thomas Parker: *wealthy British merchant*

Janice Parker: *young deaf ward and niece of Parker*

Jack Grimshaw: *amateur archaeologist and steward at Parker's villa*

Jeremy Howe: *soldier, gambler, companion of Louise, Comtesse de Joinville*

Douglas McKenzie: *elderly, retired Scottish physician and year-round resident of Nice*

Mario de Maistre: *son of the Comte de Maistre*

Louise, Comtesse de Joinville: *Paul de Saint-Martin's cousin and Captain Howe's companion*

Abbé Gombert: *elderly Marseille priest*

Gabriella Rossi: *manager of winter visitors' rental property*

René Barras: *Marseille police officer*

Henri Duclos: *stepson of Jacques Duclos*

Cécile Duclos: *Jacques Duclos's widow, mother of Henri Duclos*

Catherine Galeta: *Gabriella Rossi's maid*

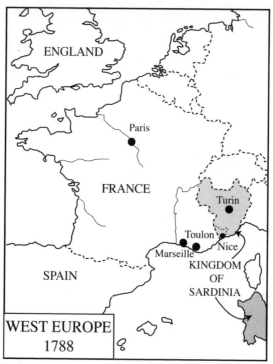

ENGLAND

Paris

FRANCE

Turin

Toulon
Marseille   Nice

SPAIN   KINGDOM
OF
SARDINIA

WEST EUROPE
1788

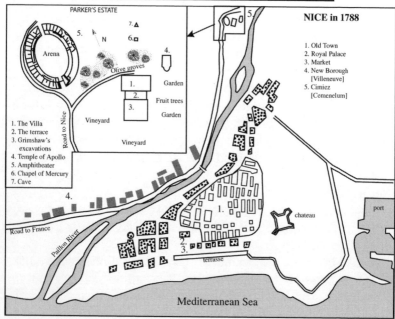

PARKER'S ESTATE

NICE in 1788

5.   7. △

6. □

Arena   4.

Olive groves

1.   Garden

2.   Fruit trees

3.   Garden

1. The Villa
2. The terrace
3. Grimshaw's
   excavations
4. Temple of Apollo
5. Amphitheater
6. Chapel of Mercury
7. Cave

Vineyard

Vineyard

1. Old Town
2. Royal Palace
3. Market
4. New Borough
   [Villeneuve]
5. Cimiez
   [Cemenelum]

5

1.

chateau   port

4.

Road to France

Paillon River

2.
3.

terrasse

Mediterranean Sea

One

A Fugitive

'The Marseille strangler is still at large,' said Paul de Saint-Martin, handing his wife Anne a letter. 'Georges writes that he can't find him in Paris.'

Anne Cartier set aside her coffee and took the letter with a mock show of displeasure. Under a mild January sun, she had been enjoying breakfast on the terrace with a view of the distant blue Mediterranean.

'Do you mean that escaped convict, Jean Lebrun?'

'Yes, Georges asks if anyone has found traces of him here in the County of Nice.'

Anne recalled the bits she had heard over the past few months. Magistrates in Marseille had convicted Lebrun, a journeyman, of robbing and strangling his employer Jacques Duclos, a master cabinetmaker. They sentenced him to life in the naval prison at Toulon, a large port seventy-five miles west of Nice. In early November, after twenty years in chains, he escaped and was still at large. He might have fled back home to Paris, where he still had family.

Paul took a chair next to Anne. 'Lebrun has inspired many false alarms, been sighted all over France, even in northern Italy.'

Anne scanned the letter, then asked, 'Why so much interest in him? He hasn't strangled anyone else in twenty years.'

'Many masters believe that he sets a bad example for other journeymen.'

She returned the letter to Paul. 'If masters treated journeymen fairly, there would be fewer murders. What can you do for Georges?'

'I'll talk to the commandant, the Comte de Maistre, since he's in charge of the local police. The authorities in southern France have surely warned him that Lebrun might pass through Nice if he flees to Italy. When I visit the naval prison in

1

Toulon, I might interrogate a few of the fugitive's comrades.'

Anne frowned. She thought Paul should instead remain in Nice, rest, relax, soak up the sunshine, fill his lungs with fresh air.

Anne and Paul had come to Nice for his health. The cold, damp, and infected air of Paris and the stress of work had brought on a debilitating, hacking cough and chronic fatigue. Conscientious to a fault, he hadn't taken a vacation from work since becoming provost of the Paris region's highway patrol four years ago.

His patron and superior, the Baron de Breteuil, had insisted that he spend the winter months in Nice. He would be at a safe distance from his work, not only four hundred miles from Paris, but also in a foreign country where he would have no authority or responsibilities. The County of Nice was in the Kingdom of Sardinia – if just barely. The French border was only a few miles to the west. An elderly, retired colonel would serve as Paul's nominal substitute as provost of the highway patrol. Paul's veteran adjutant, Georges Charpentier, would remain in Paris and do the bulk of the work.

Still, Paul wasn't to be entirely free. The baron, who often used Paul as an investigator, requested brief weekly reports on conditions in Nice and the surrounding area. When Paul felt well enough, he should also unofficially visit Toulon's naval prison and Marseille's police administration and report on whatever seemed worthy of note. The baron's oversight as a royal minister of state included these southern cities, the French kingdom's chief ports on the Mediterranean. He and other enlightened government ministers were discussing possible reforms.

Recently, the baron had written that unrest was spreading throughout the city. A conspiracy was suspected at the Palais-Royal. Paul had grown anxious, felt that he should return. But Anne had reminded him that the country was in crisis before he left and would continue to be in crisis for the foreseeable future. The royal government was virtually bankrupt. In any case, he wasn't responsible for policing the city, only the countryside. He should stay in Nice and repair his health. He agreed that he hadn't fully recovered. And Georges, back in Paris, appeared to have things under control.

This winter vacation had thus far been nearly perfect. As the sun warmed the terrace, Anne closed her eyes, brought up images from her memory, and enjoyed them a second time. She and Paul had left Paris in early November and travelled leisurely by coach and boat to Toulon, thence to Nice along the Mediterranean coast in a felucca, a small, narrow boat propelled by lateen sails and the muscles of several sturdy oarsmen. The stern was partially covered by a roof of canvas but shelter wasn't necessary. The sun shone gently, the wind was favourable, the sea moderate. So, for two days, they sat on the open deck and enjoyed the rocky beauty of coastal Provence.

Anne's older cousin Beverly Parker had invited them to live with her in a palatial summer villa near the village of Cimiez, two miles inland from the city of Nice. The villa was situated on a high plateau and surrounded by olive groves, fruit trees, gardens, and the ruins of the ancient Roman city of Cemenelum. Like many of the winter visitors, Beverly suffered from chronic shortness of breath and could not tolerate the cold, damp English winter.

Fortunately for her health, she had married a rich London merchant, Thomas Parker, who had made a fortune in sugar and slaves. He could afford the lease of the villa and its estate, as well as the other high costs of wintering in a Mediterranean climate. An avid collector of Roman antiquities, he found an outlet for his passion in the ancient ruins scattered throughout Provence and northern Italy. In particular, Cemenelum caught his fancy. Off the beaten track, it was less encumbered with tourists than Naples or Rome. Promising sites were only a stone's throw from the villa's terrace. His excavations yielded ordinary artefacts and weapons, common pottery, bronze figurines, a few coins, and simple jewellery. This was a modest harvest but sufficient to pique his interest. He hoped eventually to find greater treasures.

In late October, Mr Parker had brought his deaf niece Janice into the household. Sixteen years old and asthmatic, the young woman suffered severely in London's damp, gloomy weather. Parker put her in his wife's reluctant care. Defiant and moody, as well as deaf, the young woman threatened to fly out of control. Back in November, when Anne arrived in Nice, Beverly was already desperate and asked Anne for help.

3

Anne in turn asked, 'Has she always been difficult?'

Beverly sighed. 'From infancy Janice has been a bright, lively, headstrong person. Her parents indulged her every whim. She was ten, and thoroughly spoiled, when they died. Mr Parker became her guardian and put me in charge of her upbringing. A thankless task! For two years she resisted my efforts to teach her how a proper young lady should behave. Then she lost her hearing due to complications from a severe scarlet fever. I was frankly happy to hand her over to Mr Braidwood.'

Anne knew Braidwood, head of a school for deaf children, where she had once worked for several months. The school taught Janice how to read lips and to sign, as well as how to utter words that she could no longer hear, but failed to teach her how to behave in respectable society. That task fell again to Beverly.

'Ungrateful girl!' Beverly exclaimed. 'She resents whatever I try to do for her.' Beverly seemed close to tears.

To comfort her Anne had promised that she would try to win the young woman's trust, and to improve her articulation of words. Anne had said, 'If Janice were to speak better, she would feel more comfortable with the people around her and less unhappy with herself.' Since leaving Braidwood's institute a year ago, the young woman's speech had begun to deteriorate. She noticed that people sometimes couldn't understand what she was saying, or they stared at her because her inflection sounded monotone or a bit odd. So, for the past few months, Anne worked with her almost every day on speech as well as on signing. They developed a friendly relationship, and her speech improved, but her attitude toward Beverly remained hostile.

Anne opened her eyes, glanced at her husband sitting next to her, dozing, his head bent over an open book. For Paul, after the dark grey skies of Paris, Nice was almost like heaven, enjoying warm dry air and clear blue skies nearly every day. A couple of months in this paradise had begun to work a cure. The lines of fatigue that had come with him from Paris had vanished. His hacking cough was gone.

Many other winter visitors came to Nice hoping for similar improvement to their health. Some four hundred British men, women, and children, together with a sprinkling of Swiss,

Germans, and French, gathered apart from the local people and rented houses in the new, western district, called New Borough or Villeneuve, that stretched along the road to France. The visitors found the old quarter of the city much too noisy and crowded.

Preoccupied with their health, without the bustle of society, business, and politics, these wealthy, civilized visitors created an isolated seaside village that was remarkably quiet, restful. At least on the surface, Anne thought. Her scepticism was born of bitter personal experience. Among human beings things were never quite what they seemed. Pride, greed, lust, and the other evil passions must be stirring in New Borough as in more lively places, such as London or Paris.

Early in the afternoon, Anne was reading in her room. Suddenly, she heard the clatter of horse's hooves in the court-yard below. She rushed to the window. The Commandant of Nice, the Comte de Maistre, and several of his men had arrived on horseback, armed with sabres and muskets. Anne hurried to the ground floor. A servant had already opened the door, and the count stood in the foyer, a stern look on his face.

A moment later, Mr Parker arrived, his eyes wide with consternation. 'What, may I ask, is going on, sir?'

'A criminal investigation,' replied the count. 'This morning I received word that the escaped French convict was hiding somewhere on your estate. My source is reliable. I must conduct a thorough search.'

Anne guessed that the promise of a reward must have brought one of the servants forward. It would be an odd coincidence, she thought, if the convict were to be caught here on the very day when Georges's message arrived.

'I'm pleased that you've come,' said Parker. 'Otherwise, we would never again enjoy a sound sleep. The villain might cut our throats. My steward, Mr Grimshaw, would be happy to accompany you. He knows every nook and cranny of this place.'

Grimshaw was summoned. He frowned at the startling news, but readily agreed to assist in the search. The count's party divided into several pairs, some searching the villa, others the farm buildings. After an hour's vain effort, they spread out across the estate, searching the archaeological excavations, the vineyards, the olive groves, and the desolate hillside at the far edge of the estate.

At the end of the second hour, the count met with the Parkers in the foyer. Beverly asked Anne and Paul to be present.

The count sighed with frustration, then began, 'I'm quite sure that the convict was here yesterday. My informant described him accurately in specific detail: bald, slim, average height, light complexioned, blue-eyed. For a week or more, he did odd jobs, slept in the barn. Mr Grimshaw, however, couldn't be certain that any of the day labourers he hired fitted the convict's description.'

'If he was hiding here, he must have left overnight for Italy,' remarked Paul.

Mr Parker agreed. 'We're too close to France. He would have known that he might soon be recognized and handed over to French authorities.'

The count looked sour, shook his head. 'Somehow he saw us coming and has escaped again. We've searched everywhere else in Nice and its vicinity and are confident that he's not there. I'll report our efforts to the naval commandant at Toulon. We'll continue to be on the lookout for the fugitive.' He bowed to the Parkers. 'Sorry to have disturbed you. Good day.' He joined his men outside.

As Anne watched them ride away, she struggled with nagging questions. Later, as she and Paul sat in the shade of an orange tree, he gazed at her and asked, 'What are you thinking, Anne?'

'I'm trying to recollect the recent day labourers. They were mostly small, wiry men, dressed in ragged clothes, some dark-skinned, others light. Several of them I saw only from a distance. I don't recall one who would closely match the fugitive's description.' She paused, stroking her chin. 'If he really was here, I wonder who could have warned him?'

Two

A Loyal Spouse

Paris, Monday to Thursday, 28 to 31 January

Georges Charpentier stood at his office window and looked out over the garden. Its trees and flowers were largely beyond his ken. He knew none of their Latin names. In the spring and summer, he enjoyed their colours and scents, but now, on a grey, damp, cold winter morning, the garden reminded him of a cemetery: barren trees, dead leaves, rotting plants. In fact, the garden expressed his own present mood. The search for Jean Lebrun, murderer and escaped convict, had come to a dead end after weeks of wasted effort.

Before leaving the dismal garden scene, Georges indulged in a flight of imagination that he was in Nice with his superior, Colonel Paul de Saint-Martin, and his wife, Anne. Her latest letter described eating freshly picked oranges from the villa's orchard. The sky was blue, the sun warm. The city was looking forward to a festive carnival of lively music and dance, exotic costumes, abundant food and drink, and the freedom to be silly, outrageous, or foolish for a few days. Georges put himself in the picture, savoured it for a minute, then returned to his desk.

He opened the convict's file for a last look before writing a final report for Thiroux de Crosne, the Lieutenant General of Police. Lebrun had done the nearly impossible, escaped from the naval prison in Toulon on the Mediterranean, more than four hundred miles away. It had seemed likely that he would make his way to Paris, where he grew up and had family and friends. Georges and his colleague, Inspector Quidor of the Paris Criminal Investigation Department, interrogated everyone with a connection to Lebrun, placed several of them under surveillance, offered a reward for information.

There was strong pressure to recapture Lebrun, for he was a convicted murderer, a journeyman artisan who had robbed his master and strangled him. It was the kind of crime, Georges reflected, that must have inspired anxiety and fear in the minds of masters throughout the country.

The lieutenant general took a personal interest in the search, summoned Georges to his office, and gave him carte blanche to pursue the fugitive wherever he might have gone. But the search came to nothing. Lebrun might have tried to leave the country. Georges had mentioned that possibility to Colonel Saint-Martin in Nice. Even though he was on leave, recovering his health, he could still keep his eyes open for a murderer passing through the city.

A servant entered the office. 'Madame Lebrun wants to speak to you, sir.' He stood at attention awaiting a response.

'Show her in, and bring tea and biscuits.'

Well! thought Georges. What could this mean? The faithful wife of the escaped convict had been Georges's primary target in this investigation. He had intercepted her mail, questioned everyone who knew her, planted an informer among her household servants, had her followed every time she left her house. Georges fingered a thick file of reports on her. He knew her better than any woman he'd ever met. At first, she had irritated him – she had obstinately refused to cooperate, remained silent or replied in monosyllables. When she realized an agent was following her, she cleverly confounded him.

Georges understood that she was expecting contact with her husband and began to think of his struggles with her as a game of cat and mouse. He learned to respect her, then to like her. He even sensed that she might reciprocate his attitude. Fool! he said to himself, recalling that he had often misjudged women in matters of the heart.

Georges then glanced with despair at the untidiness of his office. He cleared file boxes off the tea table and chairs by the window, brushed the wide red cuffs of his blue uniform, and smoothed his bald pate.

As she entered, an odd, apprehensive feeling struck him. Why would she come uninvited to his office? She was a small, slender, comely woman, nearing forty but looking ten years younger, thanks to a clear complexion, straight white teeth, and erect posture. Her husband's shame had not humbled her. Her eyes met Georges's evenly.

'Good morning, Monsieur Charpentier.' She addressed him

8

respectfully but a little hesitantly. Something was weighing on her mind.

He returned the greeting and directed her to the tea table. The servant poured tea and offered the biscuits. When he had withdrawn, Georges asked, 'What can I do for you, Madame?' 'That remains to be seen. For weeks, as you know, I've been waiting to hear from my husband.' She paused, drew a deep breath. 'I know now that I've waited in vain. He is dead.' 'Oh,' said Georges softly. 'And how do you know that?' 'In a dream last night I visited his grave. It was a deep, dark place. His body was decayed, clad in rags.'

Georges paid attention to dreams, though they were difficult to interpret with any accuracy. So he encouraged Madame Lebrun to continue.

'For twenty years we wrote to each other without the police ever knowing. If Jean were alive, he would surely have found a way to reach me. He must be dead.' She drew a small packet of letters from her bag and placed them on the tea table. 'Monsieur Charpentier, I've come to know you through this investigation and I've also made enquiries. You and your Colonel Paul de Saint-Martin are known to pursue justice wherever it may lead.' She touched the packet. 'These are the words of a man, my husband, who was unjustly condemned. Would you read them?'

He nodded, though his best instinct urged caution.

'I'll leave them with you. Tomorrow, I'll come back and ask two favours of you: First, clear my husband's name, and, second, find his body and return it to me.'

For a moment, Georges stared at her, incredulous. Her strong, clear-eyed conviction had taken him by surprise. Perhaps truth and justice were on her side, though too late for her husband.

After she left, Georges returned to his desk and lay the letters before him. A reluctance to become involved in what promised to be a very difficult and perhaps unrewarding enterprise held him back. For a minute or more he stared at the letters, marvelled at their closely written, tiny script, then read them through from first to last. They concerned chiefly Lebrun's experience as a journeyman in the master cabinetmaker's household.

9

Georges wasn't surprised to read that the journeyman resented being poorly treated, having wages unpaid and the like. What caught his eye were quarrels within the master's family, the stepson demanding that the stepfather retire and turn the business over to him. The journeyman overheard the stepson and his mother plotting to kill the stepfather. The plot didn't seem serious enough to report to the police until after the fact.

At the trial, held in secret and without defence counsel, Lebrun accused the stepson and mother of the murder. A majority of the magistrates rejected his argument and laid the blame on him. But a minority were clearly unhappy with that decision. The court therefore agreed on a life sentence rather than capital punishment.

When Georges put down the last letter, he could understand why Madame Lebrun believed that her husband's name should be cleared. Even after twenty years, a new investigation might shift guilt to the stepson and mother, especially if one of them could be persuaded to testify against the other. Unfortunately, any such investigation would require the lieutenant general's approval, by no means certain. And the courts that had condemned Lebrun would be reluctant to change their judgement.

Finally, Georges had to admit, the letters could be a clever attempt to shift blame for a crime away from her husband to someone else. Madame Lebrun could have written the letters herself or selected from his correspondence those letters that demonstrated his innocence.

The next morning, Madame Lebrun reappeared, a hint of anxiety on her face. She sat facing Georges again at the tea table. He returned the letters to her, suppressing his doubts.

'I have made copies of them. They have the ring of truth. Justice sometimes fails in our courts. Higher authority, however, limits what I can do. All I can promise is that I'll study your husband's case and bring it to Colonel Saint-Martin's attention immediately.'

'That's all I can ask. I have no one else to turn to.'

'As for his body,' Georges continued, 'if it is found, I'll do what I can to have it returned to you, rather than see it burned.'

She rose to leave. At the door, she thanked him with a wan

10

smile. For an instant, she seemed about to collapse, as if she had suddenly lost her inner reserve of courage and hope. Georges felt powerfully moved to take her in his arms and comfort her. But she quickly recovered before he could help. She gave him a lovely parting smile.

After she left, Georges stood at the window, staring into space, hands clasped behind his back. In his mind's eye, the slender figure of the widow Lebrun dressed in black approached him. Her eyes were downcast. He met her and put his arm around her shoulder. She looked up and smiled sadly at him. Out in the garden the porter's dog barked. The vision vanished. Georges sighed.

He went to his writing table for several minutes of reflection, pen in hand. As the influence of the woman's seductive presence diminished, his sceptical instincts reasserted themselves. True, Lebrun might have been wrongly condemned, and he might also be dead by now. But he might just as well be alive near Marseille, waiting for the search to wane, preparing to wreak revenge on his murdered employer's stepson and widow, the authors of his misfortune, and on the magistrates who wrongly condemned him.

With renewed ardour, Georges wrote a report to the lieutenant general on the failed Paris search for Lebrun and a description of his wife's visit. In conclusion, he asked permission to travel post-haste to Marseille to investigate the questions raised by Lebrun's enclosed letters. Georges summoned a clerk. 'This must go immediately by courier to the lieutenant general.'

Late the next morning, Georges was called to de Crosne's office at police headquarters. The lieutenant general was waiting at his writing table, an expectant expression on his face. He nodded Georges to a chair facing him. Georges felt awkward. De Crosne was no stranger to him, but he always seemed distant and aloof. His bright searching eyes, his thin lips, his large nose reminded Georges of a ferret.

'I'm pleased, Charpentier. Your report is thorough and convincing. It doesn't matter that Madame Lebrun may be trying to throw us off her husband's tracks. My handwriting expert read the letters she lent you and is satisfied that they are candid and meant for her eyes alone. Her husband's account of the master cabinetmaker's death rings true. Therefore, we should take another look at the case. I'm disturbed that an innocent man might have been convicted and imprisoned. As you know, I've had some experience with judicial error.'

'Yes, sir. I'm familiar with the Calas case.' De Crosne was responsible for clearing the name of Jean Calas, wrongly executed twenty-five years earlier in Toulouse for the murder of his son, who had in fact committed suicide. News of the atrocity reached the far corners of Europe and greatly discredited French justice.

De Crosne leaned forward, arms resting on the table. 'You say that you want to go to Marseille. What can you do there that you can't achieve with a letter?' His eyes fixed on Georges's. 'The local authorities will doubt your competence, resent your presence. After all, you are a stranger from Paris, threatening their professional reputations. Shouldn't the initiative for the investigation come from them?'

'Everything you've said, sir, is true. But during the twenty years that Lebrun has been in prison, the local authorities haven't done anything to correct a possible injustice. Nor have they stirred in the three months since he escaped. A letter from Paris would simply be filed away. A new investigation into the cabinetmaker's murder must be led by a person enjoying the trust of the royal government and the respect of the local authorities. He must also have at his side someone who is familiar with all the circumstances of the case.'

'And whom, may I ask, do you suggest for the task?'

'Colonel Paul de Saint-Martin, sir. He's already in the area and will shortly be in Marseille. True, he's on vacation to recover his health. But I understand that he's fit now. I would assist him, and supply all that he would need to know.'

De Crosne's thin lips broke into a smile. 'I like your plan, Charpentier. I'm going to give you a broad commission to investigate the circumstances of Lebrun's conviction as well as his escape. You will take with you instructions for Colonel Saint-Martin, to be used according to his best judgement. He is authorized to act on my behalf in dealing with royal officers in Marseille and Toulon as well as with officials of the Sardinian government in Nice. If appropriate, he can reopen Lebrun's case and set in motion the procedure for a new trial.'

He smiled again and said, 'That will be all.' Then he had an afterthought. 'A word of caution, Charpentier. Don't allow sympathy for Lebrun or his wife to distract you. He might be guilty as charged. Your goal should be justice, as best you can determine it.'

The following morning, Georges set out in a private coach for Marseille, hoping to arrive at about the same time as Colonel Saint-Martin, who would be coming from Toulon. In his portfolio was his commission from the lieutenant general, as well as the colonel's papers.

He leaned back, closed his eyes, and recalled Madame Lebrun's dream. Was her husband really dead, or was he hiding? If he were alive, he might kill one of his enemies or do something equally desperate or criminal, and hopelessly compromise himself. Georges shuddered. What then would be the point of investigating a past injustice against him?

Three

Trouble in Paradise

Nice, Monday, 4 February

Anne Cartier walked leisurely through the main city market with her husband Paul, admiring oranges stacked in golden pyramids, smelling fresh-cut herbs. While Paul stopped at a flower stall to buy a few red roses, Anne continued on for a short distance to an open space where a crowd had gathered. Suddenly, she heard loud voices raised in anger.

Jack Grimshaw stood shaking his fist at a younger man with a woman on his arm. Their backs were turned toward Anne. The older man's face had become livid, his eyes bulged with passion. He cursed the man through gritted teeth.

The local people nearby could not understand his English, but they recognized his fury and gave him a wide berth.

The pair turned their backs on Grimshaw, and Anne recognized them. The woman was Janice Parker, the young deaf house guest at the villa where Anne and Paul were also staying. Her escort was Captain Jeremy Howe, a tall, athletic, handsome soldier in his thirties, the Lothario of the British community at Nice. The captain had a smirk on his face. His young lady looked up at him with admiration. He cast a word or two over his shoulder. Grimshaw flinched, and they sauntered away.

For a moment, Anne thought that Grimshaw, fists clenched, would pounce on the pair. He took a step, but men from the gathering crowd rushed forward and held him. He protested in the local dialect, but the men did not let go until the objects of his wrath were out of sight.

By the time Paul caught up with her, Grimshaw was standing alone staring down at the pavement. 'What could have provoked such anger?' Anne asked Paul, after describing the incident.

Paul replied, 'Mr Grimshaw evidently thinks he has prior rights to Miss Parker. I've noticed him hovering over her in the villa. He appears protective, paternal, gives her advice that she hasn't asked for. He's a widower approaching fifty. She's only sixteen and probably regards him as ancient or decrepit.'

'And a tiresome nuisance,' Anne added. An uneasy feeling came over her. She sighed. Her cousin Beverly, mistress of the villa, had more than enough to worry about, without having violent disputes in her household. Anne looked up. Mr Grimshaw was walking toward them. His long, craggy face was set in a morose expression, his eyes fixed on a dark inner vision. He walked past without seeing them.

In the early evening, the sun hung low above the horizon. Anne and Paul sauntered from the market to the beach. Waves rolled in gently, splashed upon the pebbles, and retreated. The pebbles glistened like precious stones. Long rows of brightly painted fishing boats rested on the beach. Nets were stretched out to dry. A light breeze came off the water and cooled Anne's face.

Anne eagerly grasped this precious moment and glanced at Paul beside her. His countenance had brightened with pleasure. He gave her the roses to smell. Inhaling their fragrance, she felt a rush of tenderness and took his hand. For several minutes they stood linked together, their faces uplifted to the sea, breathing in deeply its gentle, healing air.

Then they left the beach and wandered up to the seaside stone terrace. It was crowded with people on promenade. Most remarkable to Anne's eye were the women in colourful local costumes displaying themselves and their entourage of young male admirers.

This evening, the terrace was even livelier than usual, reminding Anne that this was Shrovetide, the days leading up to Lent. When she was growing up in Britain, she had celebrated at family gatherings with traditional pancake suppers, followed by singing and dancing. Here in Nice, in a short while, she and Paul would attend a similar party at the home of the British Consul, Mr Nathaniel Green, who was about to return to Britain on business.

From behind the terrace in the old city came the rousing sounds of drums, fifes, and horns. As Lent approached, the local people were in high spirits, anticipating Carnival. Bands of musicians marched up and down the narrow streets, followed by men and women in masks and fantastic costumes, hooting and shouting. Anne imagined wine flowing freely, though without the drunkenness she had witnessed at similar celebrations in London.

Shortly after dark, Anne and Paul joined a dozen other guests at Mr Green's table. It was a mixed party, though mostly English-speaking. Across from Anne and Paul was an elderly gentleman, Douglas McKenzie, a kindly retired medical doctor from Edinburgh, one of the few British visitors who remained in Nice throughout the year and had a fair grasp of the dialect. He was a mine of useful information and a good friend to Anne and Paul.

At the end of the table next to Mrs Green, the consul's wife, sat a darkly handsome young man, who spoke fluent English with a distinctive, pleasing Italian accent. There was a wild, reckless air about him, though now restrained by the presence of older adults. Anne recalled seeing him in the city, lounging in cafes, one among several rich young men with no useful employment.

'Who is the young man?' Anne asked Paul.

'Mario de Maistre, son of the commandant.' Paul nodded toward the Comte de Maistre seated next to his son. 'Mario's a bright fellow, badly spoiled. His father nonetheless has high hopes for him, would like to send him to England for training in commerce.'

Hmm, thought Anne, the count was a sanguine father. The young man appeared more inclined to a gambling den or a bordello than to a business office. She whispered to Paul, 'Mario will have to fight off the young ladies.'

'Takes after his father,' Paul remarked softly. 'The commandant is an amiable, lusty fellow, a courtier more than a professional army officer. His position in Nice is recent, fragile, and temporary. He's just occupying the post until another man is ready to take it.'

Pierre, Comte de Maistre had introduced himself to Paul shortly after he and Anne had arrived. A courteous, middle-aged man, he was the Sardinian King's officer in charge of public order in Nice and commanded the small garrison. Fluent in French and cultivated Italian, he didn't speak English, and had little personal contact with the winter visitors. He had come tonight to introduce himself and his son to leaders among the English-speaking visitors.

While a chilled plum soup was being served, Anne leaned over to Paul and whispered, 'Have you noticed that Intendant Spinola has been paying special attention to Mario this evening? I detect displeasure in his eyes.' At the far end of the table next to Mr Green was the intendant of Nice, Marco de Spinola, the central government's chief financial agent. He reported on all aspects of the county's administration.

Paul had come to know him through a mutual love of court tennis. They played several times a month in a hall of the royal palace, outfitted for the purpose. A large block of a building in the city's eighteenth-century quarter, it served as the seat of the county's administration and the governor's residence.

'The intendant,' Paul replied, 'is usually very discreet, but even his patience has limits. A few days ago, in the heat of a tennis match, someone mentioned Mario's name. He had taken part in a riotous dispute in a notorious wine tavern in the old city where smugglers gathered. Spinola exclaimed, "He'll be the ruin of his father." He immediately regretted the outburst and asked us not to repeat it.'

Prudent as ever, Paul had studied the commandant, the inten-

16

dant, and the other Sardinian officials in charge of Nice. Before leaving Paris, he had gone to the ministries of defence and foreign affairs for insight into intrigue and influence at the Sardinian court. The British and French Consuls in Nice also shared their view of conditions in the city with Paul. He included the main points in his reports to the Baron de Breteuil. One of the guests mentioned the escaped convict Lebrun and turned the table conversation toward the Comte de Maistre. Dr McKenzie asked him, 'Is it true that the murderer who escaped weeks ago from the naval prison in Toulon is now believed to be hiding in the south of France or even in Nice?'

The commandant nodded. 'The French government alerted me to his escape shortly after the event. My men have been watching for him. Recently, the French police shifted their search from the Paris area to this region. For weeks, my men have been circulating his description, asking anyone who recognizes the fugitive to come forward. There's a reward offered for his capture. We have checked several sightings, including one at the villa – all of them false.' He cast a knowing glance toward Anne and Paul.

A buzz of discussion ensued about the dangers that the convict posed to life and property in the county, only a couple of days' journey away from the prison. It was a notorious school of crime, where hardened recidivists instructed newcomers in every sort of evil craft. Should one of them escape he was likely to pass through Nice on his way to a new life in one of the larger Italian cities, such as Naples.

'The fugitive was a brutal murderer to begin with,' said the count. 'Twenty years at Toulon haven't made him a better man.'

A small orchestra distracted the guests from these fears and anxieties, while servants removed the soup bowls. The musicians were recruited from the visitors' households, mostly servants with a musical talent who had accompanied their masters to Nice for the season. With more enthusiasm than skill, they played several simple jigs and airs.

At a signal from the consul, an attractive young woman joined the orchestra. Her skin was fair, her eyes blue, her hair thick and black. She bowed with modest grace, gave the guests a lovely, winning smile, and sang a sequence of familiar ballads in English and in French.

'A lovely voice,' remarked Paul to Anne. 'Who is she?'
'Mary Kelly,' Anne replied. 'Irish. I've met her often in the flower market. She's a maid in the consul's household. Came from England shortly before we arrived. Lived here as a child and knows the dialect.'

The evening's entertainment was well underway, when a servant approached the consul with a message. He excused himself to read it. His brow creased in a frown. He rose from his chair and faced his guests. The orchestra stopped. A hush came over the table.

'The Comtesse de Joinville, unfortunately, shall not join us this evening.' Mr Green paused, glanced at the message again. 'She has injured herself in a fall. Let us hope that she will soon be well.'

The consul signalled the orchestra to play, and conversation resumed at the table. Anne turned to Paul. His expression had grown sombre. The countess was his distant cousin, a rich, attractive woman of deeply flawed character. Anne frankly detested her, but treated her with respect. Paul expected that of Anne, though he felt the same as she.

Dr McKenzie leaned toward Anne and said softly, 'Since the countess arrived in Nice with a certain Captain Howe, weeks ago, we have seldom seen her. Injured in a fall?' The doctor shook his head. 'I've heard neighbours say that he beats her.'

Anne passed this news on to Paul.

He whispered in Anne's ear, 'That may be why she has avoided us. I must nonetheless pay her a visit as soon as possible. The Baron de Breteuil is concerned about her and will certainly enquire. Her behaviour hasn't improved since she left Paris and settled here for the winter.'

While the obligatory pancakes were served, together with strawberry preserves, Anne probed the doctor. 'Do the neighbours say *why* he beats her?'

'Most recently, according to the servants, the countess accused him of stealing her money and running after other women. He laughed at her, called her a silly whore. She became wild, grabbed a knife, and attacked him. He disarmed and beat her. Shortly afterward, they reconciled in a passionate embrace. For whatever reasons, they are drawn to each other.'

Anne asked herself, had years of debauchery undermined

the woman's common sense? She was acting like the devil had taken hold of her.

In the carriage on their way back to the villa, Paul remarked, 'I must see Louise tomorrow morning, if that can be arranged. Granted, there's little I can do to help her, other than inform the Baron de Breteuil of her situation.' Paul gazed at Anne. 'Would you come with me? I value your opinion.'

A visit to Louise, Comtesse de Joinville was second in pain only to extracting a tooth. Anne preferred to avoid her. Bitter memories came to mind of insults to Anne's simple, middle-class background and to her years as a music-hall entertainer. The malice behind Louise's barbs still rankled. Worse by far was an incident involving Paul's young cousin Sylvie de Chanteclerc, who had been assaulted and subsequently felt socially stigmatized and outcast. Louise had gone out of her way to taunt the young woman and had driven her to an attempted suicide.

Nonetheless, for Paul's sake, Anne agreed to help, but she added, 'This is trouble that Louise has brought on herself. She chose an unsuitable companion for this trip, then provoked him beyond endurance. Or, so it seems. I see little hope of a happy ending.'

As she changed into her nightdress before retiring, Anne fell to thinking about the evening's table conversation. Much of it was little more than fear-mongering and had made her uneasy.

She asked Paul, 'What do we know about the escaped prisoner from Toulon? Was he truly dangerous to others?'

'We know at least this much,' he replied. 'A court in Marseille has convicted him of murder, and the Parlement of Aix, the supreme court of Provence, has upheld the verdict. Many reasonable persons would conclude, perhaps erroneously, that he has a bad character and that prison life has made him worse.'

'Can we be certain that the French court was more just than the English one that convicted me of lewd solicitation, public drunkenness, and assaulting a gentleman?' She stared at Paul, her eyes expressing her pain. Two and a half years ago, a lecherous bully, Jack Roach, had assaulted her, late one evening, near her cottage in Islington. While defending herself, she had injured him. At a farce of a trial, Judge Hammer had condemned *her* rather than him, had pounded his gavel and silenced her protests. At the last minute, friends saved her from a shameful public punishment. But the injustice and humiliation still angered her.

Paul knew her story. Now he took her hands and drew her to him. 'You were treated cruelly. I often think of you when I examine suspects, lest I be hasty or unfair. When I'm in Toulon and Marseille, I'll keep an open mind on the fugitive's case. It's a fact, and not only in your case, that judges can be incompetent, corrupt, or biased, and cause great harm.'

Four

Secrets

Tuesday, 5 February

Breakfast on the villa's terrace was one of Anne's favourite pleasures. She shared it this morning with her husband at the table beside her. The fresh, cool, gentle breeze, together with the coffee, gave vigour to her spirit for the demands of the day ahead.

On today's agenda were preparations for Paul's trip to Toulon and Marseille. He would leave tomorrow, be in Toulon by Friday, then on to Marseille on Sunday for eight days. If all went well, he would return to Nice on or about 19 February. That was a longer and more arduous trip than she thought wise. Without her to caution him, he might take on too much work, and undo the recent improvement to his health.

She had also grown accustomed to them confronting problems together. For the next two weeks she would be on her own. That made her uneasy. A crisis was brewing at the villa that she could hardly avoid. Her young student, pretty Janice Parker, was at the centre of it. Two strong grown men appeared ready to fight over her. Anne recalled their confrontation in the city market and shuddered.

20

'Is something the matter, Anne?' Her husband gazed shrewdly at her. He had grown uncommonly expert at divining her moods and feelings.

She raised her cup. He poured her coffee, then his own. 'Yes, Paul. I fear for Janice. If Grimshaw and Howe come to blows, she will be harmed. The Parkers seem unwilling or unable to care for her. That responsibility has largely fallen on me, the only person here who can really understand her.'

As their discussion wandered to less troublesome topics, Anne's gaze drifted over the Roman ruins and she gave her imagination free rein. In the early morning light the towering walls of the ancient Temple of Apollo appeared to have grown taller and more majestic. Surveying the site through half-closed eyes, Anne saw Roman Cemenelum awakening from centuries of slumber, its inhabitants leaving their brick and stone buildings to go about their daily business.

Grimshaw and earlier archaeologists had cleared part of the site to its level in the third century after Christ, exposing streets paved with stone, as well as the foundations and lower walls of buildings, previously concealed by vegetation. Until this winter trip, Anne had never seen such a landscape except in pictures.

Back in November, when she had just arrived, the ruins had saddened her, a reminder of the passing nature, the fragility of all human achievements. A flourishing city, the capital of a province, had once stood here, then had decayed, was sacked and abandoned.

Gradually, she grew curious about the things that the Romans had left behind. With mounting interest, she often watched Grimshaw from a distance. After much coaxing, she persuaded him to show her his recent excavations. He had dug up a large fragment of a Roman vase. 'I may find the other missing pieces,' he remarked. 'My work is like putting together a complicated puzzle, or gathering evidence to solve a crime.'

He was as much a puzzle as his fragments of ancient pottery, Anne thought. She had to find out why he was so protective of Janice Parker.

Anne had just finished her coffee when a servant arrived with a message for Paul. Earlier, he had written to Louise requesting permission to visit her. He read her reply aloud.

21

Yes, they could come late in the morning. She had letters to send to Paris in Paul's weekly dispatch to the Baron de Breteuil. The offer of that service was the ruse he had employed to win the visit.

'Did you see the countess?' Paul asked the servant, hoping to get an impression of her appearance.

'No,' the servant replied. 'I spoke only with her maid. But when I asked her, "How did the countess look?" she laughed and rolled her eyes.'

Promptly at eleven, Anne and Paul approached the large, square, two-storey building that Louise had leased for the season. It had been newly built on the road to France with winter visitors in mind. The plastered exterior was a soft yellow. The roof was covered with red tiles. Between the road and the house were well-tended beds of tulips in bloom beneath orange trees with ripening fruit. As they neared the door, a burly, suspicious gardener came around the corner, inspected the visitors, approved them with a salute, and disappeared.

A maid welcomed them and led them through the building. At a closed door, she knocked. A female voice called out. The maid let them into a small study. The shutters were closed, the room was dimly lighted. The countess rose from her chair to join them at a tea table.

She wore a white muslin gown gathered to her slender waist by a blue silk sash. Despite her excesses, her figure was still beautiful. Her hair was tied back in a chignon. The most remarkable thing about her appearance was her makeup. A thick coating of powder covered her face. Her cheeks were rouged, her eyes were shaded with a dark liner. Anne thought the woman looked grotesque, a female clown in a company of Italian street performers.

A servant came with tea and sweetmeats. A conversation ensued mainly between Louise and Paul concerning the dispatch bag he was sending to Paris and messages he could enclose for her. In March she planned to sail to Naples with Captain Howe to begin a four-month tour of Italy, stopping in Rome, Florence, and Turin, thence over the Alps to France and home.

Louise glanced occasionally at Anne but didn't include her in the conversation. Anne used this malign neglect as an opportunity to study the woman. Beneath the eyeliner and powder Anne detected swelling, evidence of blows from her companion, confirming the gossip. She appeared as arrogant as ever. The beating hadn't cowed her. Perhaps she gave as well as she took. Anne suspected that she might have marked the captain's face with her knife. During the incident in the market, he wore a small patch on his cheek.

Louise's financial situation was hard to determine on this brief visit. The room's furnishings were simple, worn, but decent. Probably supplied by the owner. So far, Anne had seen two servants, both of them local persons. There were probably a couple more, besides a cook. The winter visitors often complained that the servants, like the rents, were too expensive – dirty and lazy into the bargain. Anne thought that the visitors were wealthy and could afford to pay. For the most part, the local population appeared to be poor – indeed, some were destitute, to judge from their emaciated appearance and the rags they wore. The population had few economic opportunities apart from fishing and the export of olives.

When Paul had finished with his cousin, he nodded to Anne. They should leave now. He had letters to write before travelling to Toulon with his dispatch the next morning.

On the road up to the villa, Paul turned to Anne. 'Before Louise sails to Naples, I must more thoroughly investigate her situation and report to the Baron de Breteuil. We saw her bruises, and I smelled alcohol on her breath. The gossip about her has a basis in fact. She's in trouble. While I'm gone, I'd like you to keep an eye on her, help her if you can.'

Anne's heart sank even while she agreed. She didn't care to be involved with such a disagreeable person. But it was a way to win favour with the baron and that was always useful. Finally, Anne wanted to please Paul. He knew how she felt and wouldn't lightly ask her for such a favour.

Late in that afternoon, Anne and Paul dressed more formally than usual, she in a yellow silk gown and he in a buff silk suit. They joined a lively dozen or more guests in the foyer. On short notice, Beverly had arranged a festive farewell meal for her husband.

He would leave the next day for London with Mr Green. They would travel as far as Toulon with Paul. Parker's decision was sudden and mysterious. He had received a message from London only a week ago and kept the contents to himself. Anne suspected an urgent, serious, and unexpected business problem, for he was cutting short his winter residence in Nice by a couple of months.

After greeting the hostess, Paul whispered to Anne, 'Has her husband's sudden departure upset her?'

She answered also in a whisper, 'It did at first but not anymore. At least, she doesn't show it.'

In fact, Anne noticed that Beverly appeared to be in good spirits and enjoying the role of hostess. Her smile was gracious and warm, her brown eyes bright with pleasure. Male guests approached her like bees to flowers. Their women cast envious glances at her.

She had invited the winter visitors who knew Mr Parker, an amiable, gregarious man. Anne learned that the Comtesse de Joinville had been invited but had declined – she wasn't feeling well. But among the guests was Captain Howe. Recalling again the incident in the market, Anne felt a stab of anxiety. Would Mr Grimshaw also be at the table?

From the foyer the guests moved to the terrace and were served glasses of wine from the estate's grapes. The Roman ruins and the vineyard surrounding the terrace created a picturesque background for the festivities.

Several of the guests prevailed upon Paul, a generous, trustworthy man, to include messages to friends or family in Paris in his dispatch bag. He had let it be known that he was willing to perform that service.

While mingling with guests on the terrace, Anne took the opportunity to observe Captain Howe. His elegant pale green silk suit, embroidered in a silver floral pattern, advertised his expensive taste. An outgoing, witty fellow, he had a hard-eyed, calculating way of looking at people. She sensed that he would ignore the feelings of others who were of no use to him, not to speak of those like Grimshaw whom he disliked or hated. When Howe approached Thomas Parker, they greeted each other like bosom friends and were soon the centre of a small convivial group of men. Howe's anecdotes raised good-natured smiles and laughter.

Anne saw a need to make herself useful – no one was serving the guests on the terrace. Her cousin communicated poorly with the servants, nearly all local men and women. She knew little French, less Italian, and nothing of the local dialect. She often depended on Anne. A singer and actress, Anne had a good ear for language. At ease in both French and English, she had learned to converse with Italian music-hall performers at Sadler's Wells. After a few months in Nice she could also make herself understood in the local dialect and had made the acquaintance of the Parker servants.

Anne hurried to the basement kitchen and found the servants waiting for instruction. She directed two of them up to the terrace with Nice's famous little black olives preserved in brine, hard-boiled eggs, and more wine. The others should continue preparations for dinner.

When dinner was ready, Beverly invited her guests – twenty men and women – into the dining room and seated them, Paul at Mr Parker's right hand at the head of the table, and Anne next to Paul. The scholar Grimshaw was at Parker's left. Beverly was at the foot of the table with Janice at her right. Captain Howe was placed at a suitable distance from her, between two proper British ladies.

The meal represented the best of the local cuisine, beginning with sea bass grilled with fennel. Roasted lamb followed, served with a strongly aromatic red wine from the abbey of Lérins in Provence. Grilled aubergines, chard, artichokes and asparagus were served on the side. Dessert consisted of orange and lemon tarts.

During the meal Captain Howe and Janice carried on a secret conversation across the table with deft signs and gestures. Grimshaw watched them with a brooding hawk's eye. Parker seemed too absorbed telling anecdotes to Paul to notice what was going on. Beverly appeared annoyed but helpless.

The dinner lasted until early evening. By then, the air on the terrace had begun to cool. Anne nonetheless preferred to go outside rather than follow the others into the salon for brandy, cards, and games of chance. She stood with her back to a bower and watched the sun's rays slant across the ruined walls of the Roman city, casting odd shadows and creating a magical landscape. Suddenly, from the other side of the bower came hushed voices. Beverly was speaking to Captain Howe.

'I've heard that you and Janice were seen together in the

market today. That's not proper for a respectable young woman. Her reputation will suffer.'

'Harmless pleasures. Janice isn't a nun.'

'You are taking advantage of her gullibility. She's still young, and deaf as well. Aren't there enough women your own age in Nice to play with? The Comtesse de Joinville, to name one. You seem to have abandoned her.' Beverly's voice dripped with sarcasm.

'Thank you for the suggestion. Sometimes I need a less complicated playmate than Louise. Actually, she and I are still together, though of course we aren't married. Not that it should matter.' He paused. 'You would know better than anyone.'

'Bastard! You promised never to bring that up again.'

He chuckled. 'Sorry, I forget occasionally, conveniently.'

'If I must, I'll speak to Mr Parker. Janice is his ward.'

Howe's voice lowered to a threat. 'If you do, you will regret it.' He resumed his carefree manner. 'I'll try my luck at cards. Good evening, Beverly.' His footsteps receded. A door shut.

Anne had heard this exchange unwillingly, but thought it best not to interrupt. Now she wondered if she should make herself known to her cousin. Perhaps offer advice or support. But she couldn't predict how Beverly would react. She sniffled a bit, then left the terrace before Anne could make up her mind.

Anne remained on the terrace for a few more minutes, wondering. What exactly was the relationship between her cousin and the captain? When he said, 'You would know better than anyone,' what had he insinuated? Beverly and Howe seemed to have an understanding that Mr Parker was not supposed to know about.

It struck Anne that in this idyllic place of ripe oranges, bright sunshine, and blue sea none of the people she met seemed happy. Many were ill, she granted. But even so, they should count the blessings of this mild climate and beautiful setting. Instead, whenever they gathered, as tonight, they complained about the local people, or the lack of entertainment that they were accustomed to in London. Or they brought up old grievances.

Then, Anne reminded herself, there were also more serious issues around the young woman Janice. As Anne left the terrace, she found Beverly standing outside the salon, appar-

26

ently distressed. Anne drew her into the privacy of a small parlour and asked what was the matter.

'Please help me,' she pleaded with Anne. 'Mr Parker will most likely not return to Nice this season. I cannot cope alone.'

'I'll do what I can,' Anne assured her, at the same time trying to figure out what might be upsetting her cousin. 'I believe Mr Parker will leave affairs at the villa in the hands of Mr Grimshaw, who appears to be a competent steward as well as a scholar.'

Beverly hesitated, appearing to sort out her problems. Then she settled on the chief one. 'Janice is so difficult, I can't control her by myself. And Grimshaw is well intentioned but no help with Janice. She seems to respect you because you understand deaf people.' She shivered, hugged herself. Her gaze fixed on an inner place. 'I fear something dreadful may happen to her. Mr Parker is annoyed with me, says I'm neurotic, imagining things. But I have horrible dreams. I'm sure they portend disaster.'

The woman appeared to be at the end of her tether, alone and helpless in a foreign country. Anne could help her with the language and customs of Nice, perhaps even with Janice, but she didn't know what more she could do. Paul would help if he could. But he would be away for a couple of weeks.

Late that night Anne and Paul talked while preparing for bed. Sitting at a mirror and brushing her hair, Anne reported what she'd seen and heard that evening.

Paul stood behind her, gazing at her in the mirror. 'Mr Parker should pay at least as much attention to his wife as to his business and to his avocation.' He stroked Anne's thick blonde hair.

'What do you think of Grimshaw?' She took his hands and kissed them.

'As a person, he's well educated, reserved. He has no friends, male or female, that I can see. No one really seems to know him well. As a steward as well as a guide and tutor, he seems intelligent, competent. Parker trusts him with the villa and with the responsibility to bring Beverly and Janice back to England for the summer.' He leaned forward and kissed her neck.

'And Captain Howe?' She untied her bodice.

'An accomplished womanizer and gambler. As you've heard, he has a hidden grip on Beverly. Perhaps an indiscretion in her past.' He drew her shift from her shoulders.

'I sense a love-hate relationship between them.' She turned to him and they embraced.

'If I were Parker,' he whispered in her ear, 'I would be worried.'

Five

A Near Tragedy

Wednesday, 6 February

Shortly after dawn, Anne and Paul went to the beach to take leave of each other. Waves lapped at their feet. In the distance the rising sun cast a glistening grey sheen over the water. Nearby, dozens of fishing boats were setting out to sea amidst shouts of Godspeed and a bustle of activity. Paul's travelling companions, Mr Parker and Mr Green, waited a few paces away.

'I'll return in two weeks,' Paul said bravely. '*Deo volente*. Don't worry. The fishermen predict good weather at sea. They should know, they risk their lives there.'

'I'll miss you, Paul,' said Anne, as they embraced. Then he and the others climbed into one of the fishing boats that took them out to a large felucca for the voyage along the coast. Anne watched them sail south-westward toward France, until the ship left the Baie des Anges at Antibes and disappeared. Suddenly she felt a sharp attack of anxiety, such as she used to experience in the decade after her mother died and her stepfather moved away from home. Since she and Paul married a year ago, they had always been close together. Now, without warning, she realized how fragile their relationship was. His ship could sink, and he would be lost forever. She could not imagine living without him.

* * *

Off Antibes, Paul lost sight of Nice and began to miss Anne. They had been married first in her church in England, then in his in Paris. Twice blessed is how he felt. Did she? Yes, to judge from her parting loving smile. He opened his watch case. Inside was their friend Michou's faithful miniature painting of Anne's attractive face, framed by her blonde hair. Her blue eyes gazed directly at him, forthright and generous. The painting would be a silent partner on this trip.

Hugging the coast, the ship rounded the Cap d'Antibes and met contrary winds. While the oarsmen strained to make headway, the British Consul Green spoke earnestly with the ship's captain. Algerian corsairs had been reported in the area and had recently bombarded seaside villages in the Republic of Genoa. The threat to the felucca lessened, as it sailed ever farther to the west. Nonetheless, Paul cast anxious glances seaward for suspicious sails on the horizon.

When they had been at sea for an hour, Paul joined Thomas Parker in the stern. Though he had been Parker's guest for a little over two months, he didn't know the man well. On the surface he was convivial and usually wore a smile on his face. But he revealed his inner self to no one, not even his wife. He was equally reticent about his business affairs. So it was with some hesitation that Paul sought his opinion on the bad feeling between Grimshaw and Howe.

'Have you heard about the public quarrel Tuesday afternoon in the marketplace?'

'Yes, of course,' Parker replied readily. 'The news travelled fast. I believe it was a clash of two different personalities. Grimshaw is a man of reason and order, regular routine, and moral rectitude. He keeps scrupulous records. I trust him implicitly.'

Parker stroked his chin in a reflective gesture. 'Howe has the opposite characteristics – acts on impulse, indulges his lively imagination, enjoys adventure and taking risks. Women, young and not so young, fascinate him. However, he would rather win their love than honestly return it. For him love-making is a sport, a game. Is he a rogue? Yes, of course. Still, I find his company very entertaining, but I'd never hire him for a responsible position.'

'Both men appear to have taken an interest in your ward Janice. Is the young woman safe?'

As Janice's guardian, Parker could have taken the question to imply that he had been negligent. But he didn't object, perhaps because he missed the implication. He appeared immune to criticism.

'She's safe enough. Howe may appear to threaten her virtue. She's pretty, she's pubescent, and she's deaf. That combination of qualities fascinates him. Since he signs, he's able to communicate with her, flatter her. In turn, she welcomes his attention and appreciates his wit. But I'm not worried. Grimshaw imagines himself her watchdog and barks when she's in real or fancied danger.'

'I sense that your wife might be concerned about what other people think of Howe's relationship with Janice.'

With a wave of his hand Parker dismissed any such idea. 'Beverly claims he tarnishes the girl's reputation. I don't think so. This is Nice, not London. Winter visitors' gossip is like milk. It doesn't travel well, so it isn't carried far. In the view of "Society", we are out of sight, beyond the pale.'

In the evening the ship reached Cannes, an agreeable fishing village in Provence. The travellers found decent accommodation in a small rustic inn near the beach. After supper, Parker retired to his room. Paul and Mr Green lingered at the table over glasses of brandy. 'What draws you to England?' Paul asked. 'It's an arduous trip in the winter, at least north of Marseille.'

'Family business. Delicate issues in an inheritance need to be settled.' Green emptied his glass, then asked Saint-Martin, 'And your reasons for this trip?'

'An unofficial courtesy visit to the naval prison in Toulon.'

'Who are the prisoners, where do they come from?'

'Thieves, poachers, deserters, and a few more serious criminals from the south of France. Similar criminals from the northern provinces go to the naval prison at Brest.'

Mr Green ordered more brandy. Paul was still sipping his first glass. For a few minutes, they carried on a casual conversation. Then Green, now showing the effects of the drink and a day in the sun, leaned forward and asked in a low voice, 'Why do you think Thomas Parker is going to London?'

'He really didn't say. Something to do with his business, I presume.'

'I just received a letter from someone in London who knows.

To be sure, Parker will look into his business. But more important is the fact that his mistress has ordered him home. He's infatuated with her, jumps when she snaps her fingers, supports her in a fashionable establishment.'

'Does his wife know about this?'

'How can she not?'

'In the few months that Anne and I have lived with the Parkers at the villa in Cimiez, we haven't seen signs of discord. But they've been distant to each other.'

'Beverly Parker is a good actress.' Green stared into his empty glass, blinked. 'I've had too much to drink, and probably talked too much as well. Better go to bed.' He rose on shaky legs and wobbled out of the room, leaving Paul to wonder what other troubles he had failed to notice at the villa.

As Anne left the beach, she began to feel sorry for herself. So, once back at the villa, she sought a distraction. Janice Parker came to mind. It was nearly time for her to practise articulation. After a brief search, Anne found the young woman sitting on an ancient marble slab in the shade of an olive tree. She was staring at the ruins of the Roman amphitheatre a short distance north-west of the villa. Her shoulders shook. She appeared to be weeping. Anne walked a long detour to the arena and then back toward Janice, so as to give warning of her approach and offer Janice an opportunity to compose herself.

Anne signed and spoke a greeting, then added, 'May I join you on the stone?' The signing was probably redundant, since Janice had a natural aptitude for reading lips. But many deaf persons were less fortunate. So Anne habitually signed and spoke simultaneously.

The young woman nodded listlessly, brushing a stray tear from her cheek. Even in her distress, she was extraordinarily attractive: thick black hair, perfect creamy complexion, dark brown eyes, and a slender, shapely body.

'What's the matter?' ventured Anne with a sympathetic smile.

'Mrs Parker scolded me after breakfast. Someone told her that I was at the city market with Captain Howe yesterday.'

Anne pointed to herself and vigorously shook her head.

'No, it wasn't you, I'm sure, but old Grimshaw, my self-

31

appointed watchdog. "You should be more careful with your reputation," Mrs Parker said, "never be alone with the captain. Not in the market or anywhere else." ' The young woman's eyes began to tear again. 'What am I to do? I feel so isolated. No one can really converse with me, except you and the captain. His mother was deaf, so he learned how to sign. He's friendly to me like an older brother, gentle and patient. Anticipates my needs. I can talk to him and he understands, and smiles so kindly. We were planning to attend the coming Sunday festival together, but now Mrs Parker won't let me.'

Janice looked into Anne's eyes for an affirmation. Anne wasn't at all sure about the captain's intentions toward the young woman, but she tried at least to express the affectionate concern that she felt.

'Would you like to go with me to that festival? I'm alone. My husband is away on business for a couple of weeks. To eat and drink, sing and dance on the Sundays during Lent might look strange, too pagan for many of us winter visitors. But let's find out for ourselves. If need be, I'll talk to Mrs Parker.'

The young woman brightened. 'How shall we dress?'

'Like harlequins from the Italian farces, the commedia dell'arte. There should be other such characters at the festivities. And we shall wear masks, so that people will think we come from another village or are travelling entertainers and not rich winter residents. Once the festival gets underway, and people are merry with wine, and are singing and dancing, we can mix among them without calling too much attention to ourselves.' Anne smoothed her dress and rose from the marble slab. 'We have time now to look for costumes at the Maccarani Theatre in the city. My husband and I have gone there often and know the proprietors.'

Janice sprang to her feet. 'Let's go!'

The proprietors welcomed the two English ladies and gave them a guided tour. Late on a midweek morning, the theatre was empty. It was a wooden building erected in New Borough ten years earlier to attract the winter visitors. In that regard, it was unsuccessful. Most visitors avoided the theatre. Its accommodations were below the standard of the London theatres to which the English were accustomed. There were twenty loges, but the furnishings were otherwise plain. Furthermore, the productions were in Italian – which few visitors understood – and consisted mostly of comedies and farces. But Anne and Paul enjoyed hearing Italian on the stage, and Anne found the productions on a par with similar ones at Sadler's Wells outside London, where she used to perform during the summers.

After Anne explained their purpose in coming, they were led to the wardrobe and to costumes that wouldn't be used in forthcoming productions. Could they be rented, Anne asked. Yes, they could be had for the occasion on Sunday.

Anne chose a Harlequin suit. Both the jacket and the tights were composed of bright red and green diagonal patches, generously bespangled. For her head she found a red-visored cap with a fox tail, for her face a black half-mask. A wand completed her costume.

Janice chose to act the part of Pantaloon, a foolish, rich old man. Her costume included spectacles, a loose black cape, and baggy black breeches. Her mask was brown with a large hooked nose, round spectacles, and a white peaked beard. She and Anne tried on the costumes. The fit was close enough. For a little extra money, the proprietors agreed to have minor alterations made by Saturday.

By the time these arrangements were completed, it was early in the afternoon and they were both hungry. Anne proposed a picnic – she had brought along a pair of small wine glasses. Janice loved the idea. They shopped in the market for fruit, bread and cheese, and wine, and found an empty bench overlooking the beach. The sun, even just past its zenith, was gentle. Still, the women wore bonnets to protect their faces from its rays. At the end of their meal, they each enjoyed a piece of chard pie.

Under the influence of the wine, Janice became quite relaxed and signed freely.

Anne felt it was time to probe gently into this young woman's troubled relationships. Up to now, she had not confided in Anne.

'How did you come to be the ward of Mr Parker?' Anne asked.

'My parents died together at sea when I was ten years old, leaving me with a large fortune. Mr Parker, my paternal uncle, became my guardian and the trustee of my inheritance. I have learned over the years that he likes my money more than he does me. He's not permitted to spend it on himself, but he will inherit it if I die before he does. My deafness makes it difficult for us to relate to each other. I'm sure he was happy to place me in Dr Braidwood's care.'

Janice held out her glass. Anne poured a little more wine. 'There seems to be tension between you and Mrs Parker. Would you care to tell me why?'

'She tries to raise me according to her idea of a proper, respectable woman. That's not the kind of person I want to be. It feels like living in silken chains, half dead, able to move only with small, careful steps. Where's the joy and adventure of life?

'Also, communicating with her is difficult. She knows only the most elementary signs and sometimes can't understand my speech. I do my best to read her lips, but often fail. Then she frowns, grimaces, sighs. Frankly, she considers me a burden that Mr Parker has unfairly imposed on her.'

'The issue between you two seems deeper than difficult communication and lack of understanding. You seem to strongly dislike her. Has she hurt you in the past?'

Janice carefully rested her glass on a flat rock, while her mind worked out her response. 'Four years ago, I came down with scarlet fever and nearly died. Mrs Parker feared that she would catch the fever, so she fled to a country house and left me in the care of a hired woman, a careless slut. She didn't follow the doctor's instructions, neglected to cleanse my ears with a syringe. Consequently, I lost my hearing. To this day, I hold Mrs Parker responsible.'

Anne shivered. The young woman spoke in such a slow, deliberate way. No one could change her mind.

Anne assured her, 'I now understand how you feel. Still, be patient with Beverly since you must live together for at least a few more years. And you aren't her only concern.'

'I know,' said Janice, picking up her glass and finishing the wine. 'She and Mr Parker have little to say to each other. He seems to confide more in Mr Grimshaw.'

'And what do you think of that man?'

She fell silent for a moment, the effort of reflection creasing her forehead. 'He's a good teacher and has helped me to read Italian and Latin. But he has become too personal. Do you know what I mean? He stares at me in a strange way and looks for opportunities to touch me. I avoid him whenever I can. I'm a little afraid of him. Still, the servants and Mr and Mrs Parker respect him, so maybe I'm biased or unfair.'

Janice's remarks raised Anne's level of anxiety. She needed to know Grimshaw better. Janice might have good reason to be afraid of him. His interest in her seemed unhealthy.

Late in the afternoon, Anne walked out on to the villa's terrace. Nearby, Grimshaw was overseeing two men excavating a site. He gave her a slight nod, then turned back to his men. Anne sensed an air of heightened interest among them. The tempo of shovelling increased. Grimshaw knelt down and carefully brushed dirt from an object. With a rare smile, he lifted it up and walked toward Anne.

'A bronze hand mirror,' he exclaimed, 'in remarkably good condition.' The size of a large man's hand, it had turned green and was lightly covered with encrustation. Its front was slightly convex to bring the whole image of a face within the reflecting surface. A looped handle was soldered to the back.

'There's probably a design on the back.' With a penknife he started to scrape away a small patch of encrustation, then changed his mind. He put away the knife and handed the mirror to her.

She admired its shape. 'Can it be safely cleaned?' she asked.

'Yes, but the process is slow. The mirror's bronze skin is easily damaged. I'll soak it in olive oil for a month or two and clean it with a soft brush. In a few months you may be able to see your image reflected on its shiny green surface.'

In the course of this conversation Anne noticed for the first time that Grimshaw appeared comfortable with her, smiled easily. He was a tall, sinewy man, his long face browned and creased by the sun, his hair thick and grey. Though near fifty, he was still in the prime of life, strong and vigorous.

'I was going to have a cool drink out here,' she said. 'Would you care to join me and tell me about your project?'

For a second he hesitated. 'Surely, if you wish. Most women would be bored, but you seem interested.'

They sat at a table overlooking the site. A servant brought a cool lemonade and sweet biscuits.

Grimshaw explained that he had uncovered the foundations of a Roman shop that produced fine metalwork. Like much of Cemenelum, it had been looted and destroyed centuries ago. However, he had discovered an undisturbed hiding place beneath the stone floor. 'I had hoped to find a strongbox full of gold coins,' he said with a self-mocking smile. 'But this was the only item of value. When the city was abandoned, the shop owner must have taken his gold with him. Still, this is a pretty piece and makes our effort worthwhile.' He held up the mirror and pretended to study his reflection.

'We see now as in a mirror darkly,' Anne remarked, alluding to Grimshaw's reticence, trying to draw him out.

'But then we shall see face to face.' He looked at her with a steady gaze, studied her closely. She caught a glimpse of the power behind his eyes. An intelligent, strong-minded man. Certainly not a person to trifle with. Captain Howe, beware. And Janice?

'My husband and I happened to be in the market yesterday and witnessed your confrontation with Captain Howe. Would you mind telling me what provoked it? I would not concern myself with the incident, except that the young woman is my pupil.'

The smile vanished from Grimshaw's face. 'Since it happened out in the open for all to observe, it's hardly a private matter. I was surprised to see Miss Parker arm in arm with the captain, a man of notorious reputation. I protested in rather strong terms. He replied in kind. In earlier times we might have arranged a duel. In any case, with no honour to defend he simply walked away with the young woman.'

'I heard him make a parting remark to you. What did he say?'

The question appeared to take Grimshaw by surprise. For an instant he stammered, then replied, 'An insult, I suppose. I was too upset to pay attention.'

That's curious, Anne thought. She recalled that the remark had made him flinch.

An hour before supper Anne was in her room, pacing the floor, searching for a way to discover what Captain Howe had said to Grimshaw. A knock on the door startled her. Janice had come for a speech exercise. Anne recognized an opportunity to get the answer to her question.

They began the exercise by practising the sound *em*. With one of Mr Braidwood's instruments, a slender silver spatula, Anne held the young woman's tongue to the floor of her mouth while she uttered the sound. They repeated the procedure several times until Janice could utter the *em* perfectly.

When they paused for a rest, Anne asked, 'Do you recall what Captain Howe said to Grimshaw as you were leaving the market? It was a word or two that noticeably disturbed him.'

Janice bit on her lower lip, took a moment to reflect. 'The captain spoke while looking over my head. I could read his lips, but he didn't make sense.'

'Can you repeat what he said?'

'It began with *mi* or *my* and ended with *ra*. There was a sound in the middle that I'm not sure of. Possibly a *t*. His mouth opened wide and I could see his tongue flutter between his teeth. He might have spoken one word or two short words.'

Braidwood had worked well with Janice, a perceptive young woman with an inborn talent for lip-reading. She had probably read the captain's lips correctly. Still, *mitre*, *mitra*, or *my tra* didn't seem to make sense or account for Grimshaw's reaction.

At supper, there were only Anne, Janice, Beverly, and Grimshaw at the table. The cook served a fresh vegetable soup and local white wine. To Anne the room seemed empty without Paul. She ate the soup without appetite.

The chief topic of conversation was the forthcoming first Sunday festival in Lent. Familiar with local customs, Grimshaw explained for the benefit of Anne and Janice that the event would take place throughout Cimiez. Hundreds of people would come from Nice itself and from the surrounding villages to enjoy this break in the rigours of the Lenten season.

Grimshaw's voice took on an accusatory tone. 'They'll eat large chunks of greasy roasted meat, drink countless jugs of bad wine, dance until dizzy, and exchange all manner of gossip.'

Anne demurred with an ironic twist. 'Then I believe Janice

37

and I shall thoroughly enjoy ourselves. Is there *anything* uplifting about the festival?'

'Oh, yes,' Grimshaw replied with an apologetic smile, 'particular to the first Sunday in Lent is the Banquet of Reproaches in front of the village church. Following an ancient custom, lovers are free to accuse each other of various infidelities. In the evening, they should reconcile over glasses of wine at neighbouring wine gardens. Or they might wait until the following Sunday for the Festival of Reconciliation.'

Anne noticed that Janice became suddenly alert. This was a festival dedicated to lovers. Might she have thought that she and Captain Howe could rendezvous unnoticed?

'After the festival,' Beverly said, 'you, Janice, and the other winter visitors are invited to a masked ball at the villa. In previous years, Mr Parker made the arrangements. This year the task has fallen to Mr Grimshaw. As usual, I shall serve as hostess.'

'Our doors will be open to any masked person in a proper costume,' Grimshaw added.

'Anyone?' asked Anne with disbelief.

'Yes, I shall hide the silverware.'

After supper, Anne went to Mr Parker's study with Beverly's permission to consult his books. Beverly didn't ask why, nor did Anne tell her. She didn't want to call attention to her new-found interest in Captain Howe's mysterious insult to Mr Grimshaw.

Parker had allowed her to visit the study before, when she had shown interest in ancient Roman culture. The front half of the room was devoted to his collection of Roman tools, weapons, coins, and jewellery, most of it discovered in Cimiez. He enjoyed showing it to her.

In the back of the room was his library, where the walls were covered with bookshelves. A writing table stood by a window. Anne chose a volume of the *Encyclopædia Britannica*, sat at the table, and started to read at the letter *m*. Mitre, she learned, was a bishop's hat and wasn't a word that Captain Howe would have used. Her interest picked up when she found Mitra, a variant form of Mithra or Mithras, a Persian cult that worshipped the sun. Roman soldiers particularly took to it, and spread it throughout the empire. So it was likely,

Anne surmised, that the soldiers stationed at Cemenelum also practised the cult. Grimshaw would have all this information in his head. But it was hard to see how the term could insult or provoke him. Unless perhaps it referred to a dark secret that he shared with the captain.

Anne was in her room undressing for bed when she heard a soft but insistent knocking on her door. Beverly was there, eyes wide with anxiety.

Anne drew her in by the hand. 'What's the matter?'

Beverly was wheezing so badly that she couldn't reply.

Anne sat her in a chair, spoke softly to her, stroked her head until she began to breathe more easily.

'Janice has sneaked out of the villa,' she said in a hoarse whisper. 'I'm frightened. She might be harmed. Mr Parker should never have brought her here. What shall I do?'

Anne understood that *she* was being asked to do something. 'What happened?'

Gasping for breath, Beverly managed to say, 'Ask my maid.'

The young maid was summoned and stood nervously in the middle of the room. Anne motioned her to a chair. The maid explained that Mistress Parker had sent her to check on Janice, who had retired early after supper, claiming to be indisposed. The bed was occupied but not by Janice, who had stuffed it with pillows. The maid reported the subterfuge to Beverly.

'Has Janice slipped out at night before?'

The maid hesitated, then yielded to Anne's insistent gaze. 'This is the first time at night. She used to slip away during the day. Madame Parker ordered us to watch her and follow her if she left the villa without permission.'

'Where does she go?'

'Captain Howe has a small cottage about a mile's distance from the villa, halfway to the city. She took a donkey, and most likely rode there.'

Anne glanced sideways. Beverly was swaying in her chair. Anne and the maid laid her barely conscious on the bed. It was up to Anne to decide what to do. Should she go to the cottage and confront the delinquent young woman in a possibly scandalous act? Or wait in her room until she returned? Anne pondered these alternatives for a long moment. At issue was how best to keep the young woman's trust, while weaning her away from Captain Howe. For he was certainly the man she was running to. Then Anne glanced at the maid. She appeared on the edge of terror. 'What is it?' Anne asked.

'Mr Grimshaw stopped me on the way here, asked me what I was doing. I told him . . . about Miss Janice. I shouldn't, I know. But he insisted. He became very angry, said he'd fix the captain so he'd never bother young women again.' The maid shuddered.

'Show me the way to the cottage,' Anne said. 'We've got to prevent a tragedy.' On the way out of the villa, she checked on Grimshaw. He had indeed left a few minutes earlier. Anne routed the gardener from bed to add muscle to her plan.

The party of three reached the cottage at the precise moment that Grimshaw chose to attack the door.

'Stop, sir, return to the villa,' Anne ordered. 'The young woman is my responsibility.'

The man turned to her, his face contorted with fury. His eyes fixed on Anne, then shifted to her companions. For what seemed like eternity, they all stood frozen before the door. No sound came from the cottage. Finally, Grimshaw breathed a deep sigh. 'I'm not finished with him.' He jerked his head toward the door, then left.

Anne called through the door, 'Captain Howe, send Janice out. I've come to take her home. Mr Grimshaw is gone.'

A minute later, the door opened. Captain Howe stood there, fully dressed, a cocked pistol in his hand. His eyes quickly scanned the scene. Assured that Grimshaw had left, the captain lowered the weapon. 'Odd as it may seem,' he said calmly, 'Janice is still a virgin. She's desperate for friendship. We were going to talk for an hour, then I would take her home.' He beckoned gently to Janice inside. She came hesitantly to the door, confusion and fear etched on her face.

Anne embraced her, took her under the arm, and set out for the villa.

'We didn't do anything wrong,' insisted Janice tearfully. 'We drank tea and ate sweetmeats and told stories. The captain is very amusing. Mrs Parker forbids me to meet him, spies on me all day long. So I had to sneak out at night.' She was sitting up in bed, Anne standing beside her.

'I believe you,' Anne said. 'No one was actually hurt tonight, but you saw Captain Howe's pistol. He might have shot Mr Grimshaw. Would you want murder on your conscience?' That thought seemed to sober the young woman. 'If you continue to meet the captain secretly, someone will surely be badly hurt. I shall suggest to Mrs Parker that she allow occasional chaperoned visits. Would you agree?'

Janice made a grimace, then forced a smile. 'That would be better than nothing.'

'I believe that if you and the captain fail to cooperate, Mrs Parker will go to the commandant, the Comte de Maistre, and lodge a formal complaint against Captain Howe. The count will deport him. And you will be confined to a convent – very much like being put in prison. You wouldn't want that, would you?'

Apparently chastened, the young woman murmured, 'No, I wouldn't like that at all.'

'Sleep on it overnight. I'll ask for your promise in the morning. Then I'll speak to the captain. If all agree, you and I shall enjoy the festival together on Sunday.'

Janice nodded and slid under the covers.

Anne left the room. Out in the hall she signalled the maid. 'I trust her, but keep watch on her room till dawn.'

Six

A Spoiled Pup

Thursday, 7 February

Late the next morning, Anne sat at a table on the terrace reading a book on Roman history from Parker's library. She hoped to understand Jack Grimshaw better. He had studied the ancient Romans so much that he had become like the most noble among them – stoic, grave, upright, stern.

Beverly came out of the villa, shielding her eyes from the sun. Her face was pale and her voice thick, due to last night's stressful incident. She ordered tea and sat across from Anne. 'Thank you for taking charge.'

41

Anne smiled. 'Fortunately, no one was injured.' She set her book on the table and reported on the confrontation at the cottage.

'How dreadful!' Beverly exclaimed, then gave out a sigh of exasperation. 'I simply must ask the commandant to deport Captain Howe and put Janice in a convent.'

Anne lifted a calming hand and related her conversation with Janice. 'I think I may have found a solution. I'll speak with Captain Howe this morning, if I can find him.'

Beverly raised an index finger to her lips. 'Here comes Janice.'

The young woman avoided Beverly's gaze, nodded to Anne, then sat down.

'Have you considered what I said last night?' Anne spoke and signed at the same time.

Janice ordered coffee. 'Yes,' she replied softly, 'I don't want to hurt anyone.'

'Then I'll speak to Captain Howe. He'll have to agree to observe the usual conventions for young women.'

Beverly seemed relieved and gave Janice a cautious, yet warm smile.

The young woman studied her fingernails, ignoring Beverly, then looked up as her coffee arrived.

A forced conversation ensued, Anne translating for Janice when her speech faltered. She appeared fatigued. Her eyes were red from crying, her breathing wheezy. She finished her coffee and left. Beverly's gaze followed her.

A few minutes later, too irritated by Janice to read any more, Anne picked up her book, nodded to Beverly, and rose to leave. At that moment, there was a flurry of activity at the excavation beyond the terrace. Grimshaw had appeared and was staring at her. When he realized that Anne had noticed him, he turned abruptly and furiously attacked the dirt with his shovel.

'He appears to resent my intervention last night,' said Anne to Beverly. 'Passion has twisted his mind. I probably saved his life.'

Early in the afternoon, Anne stood on the road to France, opposite the house that Captain Howe shared with the Comtesse de Joinville. Anne had to speak to him about Janice.

For a couple of hours, it had served as a gambling den. Anne waited outside until the players – almost all of them wealthy Englishmen – left the house on their way to dinner, some pleased, others resigned, a few sad. Then young Mario, the commandant's son, emerged in heated discussion with the captain.

'You're a scoundrel!' the young man shouted, his face red with anger. 'You cheated me out of a hundred pounds!'

Anne was close enough to notice the captain flinch at the insult but quickly recover his usual cool demeanour.

'I lent you that hundred pounds. You had better pay it back by Monday, or I'll go to your father for the money. He's legally responsible for you.'

'You know he'll be angry and won't send me to England. I'll have to stay here and rot.'

'That's your problem, not mine. And by the way, count yourself fortunate that you're still a child. Had you been a man and called me a cheat at cards, I'd have challenged you to a duel. You would soon be either dead or disgraced. Now, good day to you.' He turned his back on Mario and gave Anne a beckoning nod.

'You wish to see me, Madame Cartier?'

'Yes, I do,' she replied, 'in the garden behind the house. I know the way.' As she set off, she caught a glimpse of Mario, paralysed with impotent rage, tears flowing down his cheeks, sputtering obscenities in Italian. Passers-by stopped and stared at the scene.

'Was it wise to humiliate the commandant's son in public, Captain Howe?' Anne asked, when they were seated in the garden's pavilion.

'He's a spoiled pup. If I were to challenge him he'd wet his breeches. Now, what can I do for you?'

'You can help me solve a problem that has arisen at the villa.' Anne went on to describe the new regime that Beverly threatened to impose if the captain and Janice continued to defy her.

'Deportation for me?' he mused sardonically. 'It would merely hasten my departure. I intend to sail to Naples anyway in a month's time. But to confine Janice to a convent would be wrongheaded and cruel. Her lively, tender spirit would wither away. The heart of the problem lies in Beverly herself.'

Anne raised a sceptical eyebrow.

'Yes, she was once as spirited as Janice but without the deafness. A blooming beauty.'

'Did you know her then?'

'We were neighbours, the same age, and lovers. She would rather that I didn't tell you or anyone else. Mr Parker insists that he married a virgin, or nearly one. I've never argued the point with him. Let him believe what he wishes.'

'Does Beverly pay for your discretion?'

The captain put on an injured expression. 'Small amounts from time to time, when the dice roll against me.'

'So why is she the problem?'

'She married Parker for his money and prestige, but has grown disillusioned in the marriage. True, he gives her whatever money can buy, but not love. She suffers from his unconcern, his indifference to her deeper needs. And she's disappointed in herself for the venal choice she made and continues to honour. Her discontent came to a head when he imposed Janice upon her. Beverly dislikes the girl intensely, in part because communication between them is so difficult. Her resentment keeps her from learning how to sign.'

The captain's observations had the ring of truth, Anne thought. His experience with his deaf mother had given him keen perception into hearing people's blind side toward deafness.

'I have persuaded Beverly to allow Janice to have chaperoned visits with you. That is, if you promise not to meet her secretly. Janice has agreed. Do you?'

'For what it's worth, I also promise.' His expression was impossible to read.

Anne realized that she had done as much as she could to bring a measure of peace to the villa. She gathered her skirts, preparing to leave the pavilion. 'By the way, I'll be taking Janice to Sunday's festival. Shall we see you there?'

'Yes, though you might not penetrate my disguise.'

At supper that evening, Anne reported to Beverly and Janice the results of her visit with Captain Howe.

'I find it hard to trust the captain's promise,' Beverly remarked. 'He's a notorious liar and womanizer.'

'You don't know him,' retorted Janice. 'He's an honourable man.'

For a moment the two women glared at each other across the table.

'I'd like to give him the benefit of the doubt,' Anne said with a smile. 'At least he knows the rules now, and the consequence of breaking them.'

The rest of the meal passed in a subdued atmosphere. Neither Beverly nor Janice had much to contribute and they didn't look at each other. Janice soon excused herself and left the table.

Anne had little success making conversation with Beverly, until she came to Mario's violent outburst following the afternoon's gambling.

Beverly waved a dismissive hand. 'Nice is familiar with the young man's tantrums. If provoked, he fills the air with terrible oaths and threatens bloody mayhem. He is said to carry a knife. But he's a coward, easily brought to tears, dangerous only to men weaker than himself. Mr Parker claims that the commandant indulges Mario too much and turns a blind eye to his bad behaviour.'

An unwise parent, Anne thought. He would likely reap a bitter harvest.

After supper Anne retired to her room to reflect on the events of the past two days. Seated at her writing table, she caressed Michou's miniature portrait of Paul and fondly recalled him to mind. He must be told about the growing animosity between Captain Howe and Jack Grimshaw. The captain's reckless courting of Janice had raised the threat of violence to a dangerous level. Last night at the cottage, Howe could have shot Grimshaw. And this afternoon Howe seemed to go out of his way to taunt the commandant's son Mario, an unpredictable, self-indulgent young man.

Paul should be arriving in Toulon at about this time and would remain there for a few days. A letter might reach him before he left for Marseille. She sharpened a pen, dipped it into the inkwell, and began to write.

Seven

Hell on Earth

Shortly after dawn, as Colonel Paul de Saint-Martin lay in bed half-awake, he heard the faint, distant, continuous rattle of chains. It took him a moment to realize that he was in the Hôtel de la Marine, naval headquarters in Toulon, adjacent to the naval prison. From the window of his room he watched with a mixture of revulsion and amazement as convicts assembled into brigades. Guards inspected their chains, pounding on them with hammers to detect flaws. The convicts then shuffled off to work under the watchful eyes of armed guards.

Saint-Martin's voyage to Toulon had taken two days. Favourable winds from Cannes had brought the ship into port late yesterday evening. He had bid farewell to his fellow travellers Parker and Green. They were to sail on to Marseille the next morning.

From the old commercial harbour Saint-Martin had made his way to this naval prison, one of three serving the royal navy. The other two were at Brest in Brittany and Rochefort on the west coast. At the gate he showed letters of recommendation from the Baron de Breteuil and from the Comte d'Albert de Rions, the naval commandant of Toulon. The officer on duty gave Saint-Martin a comfortable room in the prison officers' section of headquarters. It was late. He had a light supper and went to bed.

After breakfast in his room, he met the Comte de Rions in his office. A decade ago, Saint-Martin had been introduced to him in Newport, Rhode Island, during the American War. Rions went on to distinguish himself in naval battles with the British, including the final engagement outside Yorktown that forced Cornwallis to surrender.

The count now sat behind a highly polished mahogany writing table with delicate brass mounts. The cabinets were expertly crafted of exotic woods, and other pieces of office furniture were equally sumptuous. At first, this display of expensive, cultivated taste surprised Saint-Martin, who had expected a more Spartan attitude in the former captain of a great warship and present director of a large prison. But then Saint-Martin recalled that the count received a princely annual salary of nearly fifty thousand livres. With regard to the prison, his position was a sinecure. Junior officers did most of the work.

The count greeted Saint-Martin with official courtesy. But his eyes betrayed a trace of wariness. Lebrun's successful escape had reflected badly on the count's administration of the prison. Saint-Martin, a high-ranking officer from Paris, might have come searching for faults.

'What brings you to Toulon, Colonel?' he asked, gesturing Saint-Martin to a comfortable upholstered chair.

'The Baron de Breteuil and Lieutenant General de Crosne would like my views on the reform of our system of punishing criminals. Since I'm vacationing in the area I thought I should study this naval prison. As you know, many enlightened observers believe that the three naval prisons could serve as models for a national prison system on a rational plan. The convicts would be put to useful work for the state while they were being punished for their crimes.'

'I'm aware of such speculation but don't believe it's practical. Building the prisons would be too expensive. The government doesn't have the money.' He leaned forward, resting his arms on the table. 'Now, how can I help you?'

'To begin, you could tell me what the convicts do here.'

'Most of them are crude, illiterate peasants – savage animals, really – accustomed to heavy labour. We have them do useful tasks in the port – cutting and hauling stone, repairing docks, pulling barges, scraping hulls, and the like. Convicts with skills in carpentry, ironworking, and other crafts build and repair ships. A few literate convicts work in our offices or the hospital. Through extra work, convicts earn money to spend in the prison for food or to save for the day when they are freed. There are more than two thousand convicts here, and many more at Rochefort and Brest. Without them the navy couldn't function.'

Saint-Martin reserved judgement. He didn't expect the count

47

to offer a critical assessment of his own administration. Still, this was a revelation. In five years as a police officer, Saint-Martin had arrested many men and women and he had visited the Conciergerie in Paris, where they were sometimes detained awaiting trial. But he had never been in a prison like Toulon, organized to provide the state with efficient, inexpensive labour.

The count continued, 'My aide can give you more details. He served with me during the American War. I'm sure your paths have crossed.' The aide was summoned and introduced.

'We met in Newport,' said the aide, a congenial officer Saint-Martin's age. They left Rions' office together and renewed their acquaintance.

'I would be pleased to take you on a tour of the prison.'

Saint-Martin agreed, though he wondered if he'd be shown only its best side. He wanted to imagine Lebrun's life in all its horror.

'We call our prisoners *galeriens*, or galley slaves. Originally, they manned the oars of the royal galleys. Forty years ago, the navy decommissioned the galley fleet. The *galeriens* remained the state's slaves but were put to work mainly on shore.'

The aide led Saint-Martin from naval headquarters the short distance to the naval harbour. 'This is where most of the convicts live, at least the healthy ones.' He pointed to a floating prison of hulks and old rotting galleys, stripped of their masts and oars and moored to a quay in the harbour.

The two officers wandered through the prison, almost empty, except for a few guards watching over *galeriens* cleaning or repairing their quarters. Most of their companions were at work on shore. Conditions were grim. Temporary roofs over the galley decks gave shelter from sun and rain, but the decks must often be crowded and difficult to keep clean. Below deck in the hulks the stench was overpowering. It would almost be a relief for the men to spend most of the day outside at heavy work in the port.

This was as close to hell as he would ever care to come, thought Saint-Martin. The rattle of chains disturbed him most. A constant, grating sound, night and day, with varying tempo, volume, and rhythm. For a man whose ears were attuned to the music of Mozart and Haydn, this carceral cacophony was particularly painful.

'Is this where the convict Jean Lebrun lived?' Saint-Martin squinted, looking out over the hulks.

'Oh, no,' his guide replied. 'He was privileged, lived on shore. I'll take you there.'

Compared to life in the floating prison, conditions for invalid or privileged convicts were somewhat better, especially as concerned sanitation. They were housed in former dockside fortifications, recently modified to serve as a prison hospital. The halls were clean and ventilated, from concern to prevent disease. In each hall were long wooden platforms to which the convicts were chained when they weren't working or undergoing treatment. Armed guards kept them under constant surveillance.

As they continued their tour on shore, the aide described in detail the prison system. For security's sake, all convicts slept chained to the decks or the platforms during the night. Those judged to be dangerous or intractable, the vast majority, were chained to each other during the day. They wore distinctively coloured uniforms – red coats and green caps for lifetime convicts, for example. Their heads were shaven.

The majority of the convicts were thieves, poachers, or smugglers with three- to five-year sentences. One in five would serve for life. The prison rules were detailed and inflexible. Punishment for infractions was quick and harsh.

'Suppose Lebrun were recaptured and brought back here,' Saint-Martin asked his guide. 'How would he be punished?'

The officer's lips tightened, his voice lowered. 'He would lose all his privileges and would be moved from the hospital to the hulks for heavy labour.' The officer hesitated, weighing what his master Rions would allow him to say. 'You've noticed that Lebrun has irritated the commandant, made him feel foolish for having treated him so well. I would expect Lebrun to undergo a beating, the *bastonnade*.'

'I've witnessed a similar punishment in the army. How is it done here?'

'In Lebrun's case, all the convicts would be assembled. He would be stripped, placed on his stomach on the floor. Fellow convicts would hold his arms and legs. Another convict would strike him with a tarred cord up to sixty times, depending on the level of the commandant's anger.'

Lebrun could scarcely survive such punishment, thought Saint-Martin. How desperate he must have been to escape, for he surely knew the risks.

In the evening the commandant invited Saint-Martin to supper in his apartment at naval headquarters. The contrast with the squalor in the prisoners' halls could hardly be greater. Turkish rugs lay on the floor, damask drapes were drawn over the windows. Saint-Martin's eye fixed on a cabinet made of exotic woods.

His host remarked, 'That's the work of Jean Lebrun, master cabinetmaker without the title, the only convict to escape from this prison in my tenure.'

This was Saint-Martin's opportunity. 'As Lieutenant General de Crosne has informed you, the Paris police have asked me to look into Lebrun's case. Tell me about him.'

The commandant grimaced, having to revisit an embarrassing episode. 'With few exceptions, convicts are always shackled, usually in pairs. The guards are alert. If they fail, they are severely punished. Still, several months ago, we lost Lebrun. Convicted of strangling his master in Marseille who had accused him of theft, he was sentenced to death on circumstantial evidence. On appeal, the high court in Aix commuted his punishment to life in this prison.

'His health was frail – a weak chest. He wouldn't have survived a year in the hulks. Since he was a skilful cabinetmaker and a literate man, he was too valuable to waste breaking stone or scraping barnacles. We put him in the hospital. For almost twenty years he built fine cabinets for officers' quarters in our battleships and in this building. We also used him in our offices, and he nursed the sick. Then one day last year he slipped away and hasn't been seen since.'

'Would you describe Lebrun for me?'

'He's a thin, wiry man, of small stature, probably wearing a wig to cover his shaven head. Pale blue eyes. Branded on the right shoulder. Still bears the mark of the shackles on his arms and legs. They last almost forever.'

'Where do you think he would go?'

'Most likely to Paris, where he could more easily disappear than in smaller cities and might even practise his craft. His family and friends live there.'

Saint-Martin calculated the dates. The escape occurred at the time Anne and he left Paris for Nice. Shortly afterward, Georges Charpentier must have begun searching for the man.

'The Paris police have probably informed you that they've looked for months and haven't found a trace of him.'

'That's correct. The Royal Highway Patrol, as well as the police in Marseille and other southern French cities, have searched – also without result.'

'Then he may have left the country.'

'We also notified the Sardinian commandant in Nice, the Comte de Maistre. He responded that Lebrun wasn't in Nice but the search for him would continue.'

Saint-Martin made a dismissive gesture. 'De Maistre has a large network of informers but little talent for criminal investigation. With due respect to the count, I'll try to find out if Lebrun is in Nice or has passed through on his way to Italy. To that end, I'll need to look at his prison record and question guards and prisoners who knew him.'

The commandant grimaced. 'We've gone over that ground, Colonel. Still, I'll arrange for you to start tomorrow morning.'

Back in his room, Saint-Martin found the story of Lebrun's escape revisiting his mind. A conviction based on circumstantial evidence meant that Lebrun could conceivably be innocent of the crime, as the high court perhaps sensed when it commuted his sentence. He spent twenty years thinking of how to escape, saving money for the necessary bribes. He succeeded in his attempt and was still free, but he was a fugitive and by this time perhaps desperate and dangerous.

The next morning and afternoon, Saint-Martin read the files on Lebrun and spoke to guards and officers who knew him. The picture that emerged was that of a model prisoner, obedient, hardworking, and dependable. He lived much better than most of the other convicts, since his cabinetwork and his literacy were highly valued.

For a late-afternoon supper Saint-Martin joined the commandant's aide at a table in his apartment. After exchanging anecdotes on their service in the American war, Saint-Martin asked, 'How did Lebrun manage to escape?'

'I think we became complacent,' replied the aide, 'and we didn't watch him as closely as the others. He secretly prepared for his escape over a period of several months, if not longer.' The officer explained that Lebrun gathered civilian clothes and provisions and hid them in a secret cabinet that he built in one of the warships. One early November afternoon, he bribed a guard to remove the shackles from his legs – they impeded his work, he claimed. Once free, he eluded the guard, changed clothes, walked off the ship, and disappeared.

'During your investigation into his escape, did you discover anyone on the outside helping him?'

'No. He must have stolen articles of clothing from shops in the port when he was running an errand or from careless civilians in the brothels.'

Saint-Martin raised an eyebrow.

'Yes, the privileged convicts sometimes visited brothels in the port. For a little money, the guards looked the other way. It was never a problem. But after Lebrun's escape we stopped the practice. We investigated thoroughly and found no one who knowingly helped him.'

'Has anyone subsequently come here to enquire about him and showed an unusual interest in him? Such an enquiry could reveal a hidden confederate, trying to discern the extent of the investigation.'

The officer had to reflect for a moment. 'People in Toulon and the vicinity were understandably curious about Lebrun. They knew I was involved in the search for him and would ask me for news. I received many enquiries from police officers throughout the kingdom. Several cranks wrote to report having sighted Lebrun. All were false leads.'

'Any enquiry from the County of Nice?'

The officer paused again, trying to recall. 'Yes, there was one. In fact, he stopped here and spoke to me. Said he was on his way to Marseille. Come to think of it, he differed from the cranks I've mentioned. Though he began by saying he might have seen him, I noticed that he was really interested in Lebrun's character, his crime, his escape, and so on. He carried on rather like you are doing.'

'Do you remember his name?'

'Spoke French with an English accent. A tall man. I think I have his name here.' The officer opened a large notebook that served as his diary. 'Yes, here he is. Mr Jack Grimshaw.'

The news startled Saint-Martin but he didn't let on. He left the room wondering, why would Grimshaw show so much personal interest in the escaped convict Jean Lebrun?

From the aide's apartment, Saint-Martin went to the prisoners' hall in the hospital. In the evening from six to eight o'clock, after the principal meal, the convicts had leisure, still chained. While most of them played cards, drank, smoked, or worked at crafts, Saint-Martin questioned a few who knew Lebrun. They met him one by one in a small, plain, windowless room used for interrogations and visits. It was furnished with a table and two chairs. A guard stood outside the door, which had a barred opening that he could look through. During the visits, the convicts were shackled to the floor. They agreed that Lebrun was mild-mannered and helpful to other convicts.

The most useful remarks came from the convict who had often been shackled to Lebrun during the day. He was also a privileged artisan, a woodworker. He spoke correct French but in a lifeless monotone. In his rough woollen red suit, his eyes sunken and lustreless, he appeared spiritually, if not physically, beaten to death. His green cap revealed that he was a prisoner for life. The guard said the prisoner had murdered his wife for nagging him.

'Did Lebrun ever speak to you about his crime?'

'As often as he could. He claimed that he was innocent. But why would he say otherwise?'

'How did he say the murder took place?'

'At the end of a day's work in the shop, Lebrun asked for his wages. The master hadn't paid him in weeks, claiming that Lebrun was lazy and incompetent, hadn't even earned his room and board. Lebrun became angry, said the master was cheating him. Their argument grew loud. The mistress came into the shop and ordered Lebrun out or she would call the police. As he left for his room in the garret, he shook his fist and threatened to get his wages "one way or another".'

The convict's eyes grew brighter. 'That threat was Lebrun's undoing. The next morning the master was found strangled, and money stolen from his cash box. The mistress accused Lebrun, the magistrates agreed with her. He was convicted and sent here.' The convict settled back in his chair, his face blank, drained of any emotion.

Saint-Martin could see the picture. The master and his family were prosperous, respected, and prominent in Marseille. Lebrun was a poor journeyman from Paris with no local attachments. He had an ongoing quarrel with the master and had appeared to threaten him. And he had no alibi for the night of the crime. His pregnant wife had returned to her family in Paris.

'According to Lebrun, who killed the master?'

'His stepson, prompted by his mother.'

'And their motive?'

'They inherited the master's shop and his money.'

'Did Lebrun ever indicate where he might go, if he could escape from the prison?'

'He never mentioned escape. Convicts are rewarded if they turn snitch on each other. Lebrun couldn't trust me.'

Early the next morning, Saint-Martin was in his room, preparing to leave Toulon, having satisfied his curiosity about the prison. Notes for a report to the Baron de Breteuil were in his portfolio. There was a knock on his door. It was the commandant's aide.

'I have a letter for you from Nice, just arrived. I'll leave you to read it, then return in a few minutes to see if you wish to send a reply.'

The letter was from Anne, describing Grimshaw's confrontation with Howe at his cottage and the public humiliation that Howe inflicted on Mario de Maistre. As Paul stared at the letter, he got the unsettling impression that the crisis brewing in Nice could touch Anne. Should he return or continue on to Marseille as planned?

After a couple of minutes of anxious reflection, he wrote Anne that he trusted her judgement, she was dealing with events in Nice as well as he could. She should be aware that for whatever reason Grimshaw had shown unusual interest in the escaped convict Jean Lebrun. In conclusion Paul wrote that he would go on to Marseille to learn more about Grimshaw and Lebrun.

When the aide returned, Paul had sealed the note to Anne.

The aide said he'd be happy to dispatch it to Nice. As he was about to leave, he said, 'You mentioned, Colonel, that you were going to visit Marseille and search for traces of

Lebrun. A thought just came to me. In my pursuit of him, a few weeks ago, I went to the cabinet shop where he had worked. He might have gone there to take revenge on his dead master's family who were instrumental in his arrest.

'The stepson who still runs the shop seemed unconcerned but said he'd take a few precautions. His mother, however, reacted strangely. A bedridden invalid, she became visibly frightened and glanced anxiously toward her son. He remained stone-faced. She seemed afraid of him and said nothing.

'I searched the neighbourhood, then returned to the shop to report that they were safe, Lebrun was nowhere to be found. The son was busy, so I took the opportunity to slip into the mother's room, as if to bid her goodbye. She gave me a polite but cool welcome. I was, after all, a stranger and a policeman. I asked what frightened her.

' "I fear for my life," she whispered. "He will kill me one day." I tried to reassure her that the police would keep watch for Lebrun in the neighbourhood, should he return seeking revenge. She listened to me, but didn't react when I mentioned the convict's name. I gained the impression that she was afraid of someone else. I asked but she wouldn't tell me. At the time, I suspected she might be demented. Now I'm not so sure.

'As I was leaving, a priest arrived, the Abbé Gombert, her confessor. She received him with a welcoming smile. He should know the old lady's secrets, though he might not disclose them. Afterward, from neighbours I learned that he also knew Lebrun. You might want to talk to him.'

Eight

Gathering Clouds

Nice, Saturday, 9 February

In the Temple of Apollo a cock proclaimed the beginning of a new day. Anne left her bed and padded to the open window. The hour or two after dawn was her favourite time of the day.

The air was fresh, cool, and fragrant with the scent of flowers. Birds chirped, warbled, and sang with abandon. Human voices were muted or silent.

With longing, Anne thought of Paul in Toulon, probably also leaning out a window, taking in the dreadful sights and sounds of the prison. These were moments when he might regret being a police officer.

Yesterday, the fragile peace she had arranged after the incident at Howe's cottage had persisted. Janice and Beverly had spoken politely to each other. Janice had come to Anne's room for instruction. Afterward, they had taken a long walk through the estate, stopping at the orchard to pick lemons for tarts that the cook had promised to make. Anne had also spent hours in Parker's library reading about the Mithras cult, its bloody rituals and its spread throughout the ancient Roman Empire.

She had not seen Captain Howe yesterday, and Janice never mentioned him. But she must have had him on her mind. During the day, she often seemed distracted. Her eyes had a dreamy, faraway look. Her nemesis, Grimshaw, had discussed estate business with Beverly, then had retreated into his study to restore the Roman mirror he had discovered a few days ago.

Leaning on the windowsill, a light breeze caressing her face, Anne reflected on these two men. Grimshaw in particular intrigued her. Strong, intelligent, and well educated, he was also awkward in polite conversation and too earnest to be either witty or charming. He spoke little of himself and evaded searching questions. Was he hiding something in his past, either shameful or too painful?

In contrast, Captain Howe readily revealed his venal, philandering nature with wit and charm. He enjoyed talking about his past, whether true or fancied, and was frank about his taste for gambling and other sordid pleasures.

The conflict between him and Grimshaw baffled Anne. She could understand them quarrelling over an attractive young woman. But what did Mithras have to do with it? Yesterday, while working with Janice's problems in pronunciation, Anne had probed for any connection the young woman might have to the ancient cult. There didn't seem to be any.

Anne left the window, dressed, and ordered coffee out on the terrace. She had nearly finished breakfast when Grimshaw began to work at his excavation among the ruins. Determined to speak to him, Anne waited almost an hour, pretending to read a book. Finally, when he stopped for a rest, she approached him with a smile.

He looked up, squinting in the low eastern sun. As he recognized her, a guarded, puzzled expression came over his face, followed by a frown.

Anne excused herself for intruding. 'I find it so interesting to live near this site. Last night, while trying to learn more about the Romans, I browsed in Mr Parker's books and came upon Mithras, a fascinating cult. Roman soldiers took to it and spread it across the empire. Has anyone found signs of Mithras here in the County of Nice?'

He studied her for a long moment. She must have appeared sincere, for he gave her a cautious smile. 'There were soldiers here, of course, to defend the city from barbarian tribes in the mountains to the north. Merchants also carried the cult from the eastern to the western provinces. Some merchants passed through our Cemenelum on the Via Julia or settled in the city. Nonetheless, the cult doesn't appear to have established itself here. I've searched but found no evidence of it.' He looked at her with a hint of impatience, as if to ask whether she had any more questions, then he picked up the shovel and returned to work.

Anne sensed that he didn't care to discuss the topic. That piqued her curiosity. Yesterday, Grimshaw's assistant told her that he had earlier been ordered to keep his eyes open for signs of the cult. Then, recently, he was told to stop looking. What could that mean? she wondered.

Later in the morning, Anne and Janice walked to the city to pick up their festive costumes at the Maccarani Theatre. The fit was good. The wardrobe lady neatly packaged the costumes for them. They had just left the theatre when they met a surge of traffic on the road to France. A person asking directions momentarily distracted Anne. Meanwhile, Janice stepped out on to the street in front of a fast-moving cart. The driver called out a warning, but she couldn't hear it. At the last moment, a gentleman grabbed the young woman and pulled her out of danger.

Anne witnessed the scene with horror, then relief, and finally

57

concern. For the gentleman who saved Janice was Captain Howe. For a moment he held the young woman in his arms, gazing at her with tender affection. She responded with glistening eyes, then pressed her head against his chest.

A few steps away, staring aghast at this scene, was the Comtesse de Joinville, who had been on a promenade with the captain. Her lips tightened, her eyes narrowed in anger. While the captain was still holding the young woman, Louise turned abruptly on her heels and stalked away.

'What was that all about?' Captain Howe had released Janice and was watching Louise as she disappeared into the street crowd.

The question was addressed to the world in general, but Anne answered it. 'She apparently hadn't noticed Janice's predicament. So she took offence at seeing her in your arms. You had better explain to her what had happened.'

'A waste of time,' he growled. 'Her moods govern her and they're fickle. Loves me one day, hates me the next. I think I need a game of cards.' He tipped his hat to Janice and Anne and walked off.

Janice stared after him with a longing look.

The Comte de Maistre stood at the window of his office in the royal palace, gazing out at the sea. Fishing boats trolled its turquoise blue surface like lazy waterbugs. The view often calmed his spirit, but not this morning.

'Sir, your son is here to see you. Shall I show him in?' The clerk had stepped inside the office and closed the door, in case the commandant would not wish his reply to be heard outside.

'Show him in,' said de Maistre sternly, trying hard to control his temper. His anger was prompted by reports of Mario's gambling and especially his public disgrace Thursday afternoon at the hands of Captain Howe. The commandant had summoned his son for an explanation, though aware that he would offer only a litany of excuses. He was incorrigible.

Mario entered the office dressed in a well-tailored pink silk suit embroidered with delicate goldwork in an intricate pattern. His black wavy hair was lightly powdered, adding a touch of gravity to his youthful, handsome features.

'Going to dinner, are you?' asked his father, certain that his son would not be paying for the meal. 'This is Saturday. Is it not Lent? The festival in Cimiez is tomorrow.'

'Gabriella believes that the Lenten fast ceases at sundown. She has invited me and a few other admirers to her home. It will be a select, festive company.'

'She serves an excellent meal, I'm told. But I've called you on a much less pleasant matter. Word has come to me that two days ago you were at the centre of a public dispute over a gambling debt. You accused Captain Howe of cheating. He ignored your charge as unworthy of a gentleman to consider. Then you wept! What a scene! I had to ask my informant twice. I couldn't believe that my son could be such a craven coward. You disgraced me as well as yourself. This is not just a matter of money but of honour.'

Mario averted his eyes, remained silent.

'I've also been informed that Captain Howe demands that you pay him by Monday or he will come to me for the money. Well, you may save him the trip. If he comes, I shall state publicly that I am no longer legally responsible for your debts. Thereafter, you will be unable to borrow any more money, not from him or from anyone else. Nor will I give you any. So you had better make whatever arrangements you can with the good captain. Polish his boots, brush his clothes, pour his bath. Do whatever he demands in order to pay what you owe. Otherwise, you will be a thoroughly disgraced young man, unable to hold up your head in Nice. You might as well move to Corsica and tend sheep. Needless to say, until you mend your ways, I shall not send you to England.'

The commandant paused, awaiting his son's usual string of excuses. But there were none. The young man studied the floor, chewed on his lower lip. Finally, de Maistre said coldly, 'You shall remain in your room tomorrow and forgo the festivities. That will be all. Enjoy your dinner.'

Mario left Gabriella's house as early as he decently could. It was dark on the road, and few persons met him as he walked toward the city. That suited his mood. He had felt ill at ease at dinner. Gabriella and her admirers must have heard of his disgrace. Nothing was said, of course, at least not within his hearing. But he noticed questions in Gabriella's eyes when she looked at him. Her admirers, always envious of his privileged place in her affections, boldly smirked and exchanged glances when he spoke.

His father's speech about honour had cut him to the quick, spoiled the evening's pleasure for him. There was truth in what he said, but he said it with such contempt. Polish Howe's boots indeed. No, he would never stoop to curry the captain's favour, or beg for relief.

By the time he reached his room in the palace, he had begun to think of other ways of settling scores with the captain. In an hour or so he had narrowed them down to one. But it would be dangerous and risky. In a candid moment he realized that he didn't have the courage. Then he thought of the contempt etched in the captain's face, the contempt in his father's parting words. Mario slumped into a chair and wept.

Nine

Festival in Cimiez: Reproaches

First Sunday in Lent, 10 February

In the morning, Anne and Janice dressed in their costumes and went to the Cimiez church square. A crowd was gathering after the last parish mass. In the centre of the square the rattle of drums and the blast of horns mixed with a rising babble of excited voices. Country dances began spontaneously. Many in the crowd had donned masks and wore fantastic costumes, admired by onlookers of all ages. At the edges of the square food stalls did a lively business. Wine flowed freely. The pungent odour of roasting lamb, garlic and onions and other spices wafted over the crowd.

After first surveying the crowd, Anne nodded Janice forward and the two women edged in among the revellers almost without notice. Masked men and women were coming from all parts of the county and couldn't be expected to know each other. Gradually, the revellers sought out relatives, acquaintances, and friends by voice and manner. Small groups formed at tables, couples paired off.

Revellers, both men and women, approached Anne and Janice like the others, tentatively, with cryptic questions, to which Anne replied in kind. They quickly disengaged, moved on. The square in front of the church came to resemble a field of moths flitting about, lightly touching each other. In this setting, it was convenient for Janice to hear nothing and say very little. She felt comfortable – she wasn't expected to make sense.

Then a tall man in a Harlequin costume approached. 'May I dare to guess who you are?' he asked in English. A full face mask muffled his voice.

'You may try,' Anne replied, certain of his identity.

'Madame Cartier and Miss Parker,' he signed.

'And you must be Captain Jeremy Howe,' Janice signed with noticeable agitation.

'At your service.' He lifted his mask and gave the women a brilliant smile, then slipped back into the crowd. Anne noticed a masked man dressed as Scaramouche attempting to eavesdrop. When Howe left, Scaramouche followed. Anne beckoned Janice and they trailed him in turn.

A minute later, an olive-skinned woman in a bright yellow silk gown and a black half-mask intercepted the mysterious stranger and held him in a playful embrace. They both lifted their masks.

'Who are they?' Janice asked.

'The handsome young man is Mario, the commandant's son. The woman is Gabriella Rossi, the young widow who manages rental properties for winter visitors. Mario is one of her favourites.'

'So he's the one who called Jeremy a cheat! Silly Mario is lucky to be still alive.' Her brow furrowed as she struggled with a concern. Apprehension crept into her signing. 'Why is he following Jeremy?'

Anne shrugged. 'I can only guess that he's looking for an opportunity to confront Captain Howe and negotiate a way to pay his gambling debt.' To herself Anne murmured, 'At least, that's what I hope.'

Meanwhile, locked in Gabriella's embrace, Mario had lost sight of Captain Howe and was now craning his neck, apparently searching for him.

* * *

61

Early in the afternoon, when the festive crowd had sorted itself out and individuals had come to know who were behind the masks, the traditional custom of reproaches began. Seated at long banquet tables, masked revellers accused each other of various wrongs and infidelities. What Anne could overhear ranged from the frivolous and light-hearted to the serious and troubling. The accused sometimes defended themselves, or replied with a counter-accusation, or received a reproach in silence. In no case did she notice any bad temper or threat of violence.

Throughout the afternoon, she looked for Captain Howe, who stood a head above the average local men. When he finally reappeared, he moved about easily, seeking out the few local people who spoke English or French. From out of the crowd Mario approached him. Howe stiffened. Anne moved in as close as possible but couldn't hear them or read their lips. To judge from their gestures, the two men exchanged heated words. In the end they nodded, apparently in agreement.

Grimshaw also arrived, masked and disguised as Pierrot. He introduced himself to Anne and Janice. The young woman acknowledged him with a cool smile. Then he also followed the captain.

Janice signed, 'Jeremy seems to be the centre of attention. I wonder why?'

As Anne began to reply, she was interrupted by a shriek.

A masked woman, dressed as Columbine in a white silk gown, had confronted Howe. He backed up a step, alarmed. Anne moved quickly to within earshot of the pair.

'You liar!' The Comtesse de Joinville's shrill voice rose above the babble. People nearby took notice. The noise from the crowd diminished. 'I accuse you of taking my money again, after you promised not to. And last night you slept with a harlot instead of with me. I've had enough, I'll make you suffer.' She didn't give him an opportunity to defend himself, but quickly slipped back into the crowd. A buzz of astonished voices followed her. Shaken by the incident, Anne had difficulty translating for Janice but managed to convey the substance of the countess's reproach.

Her face pale, the young woman signed, 'Has the countess lost her senses?'

62

'No, I think she means what she says,' Anne replied. 'After past quarrels she always pardoned Captain Howe. This time, she appears unforgiving. If I were him, I would take great care this evening.'

Early in the evening the crowd in the church square scattered. Many families went home to supper. Anne and Janice followed a lively group, costumed and masked, in the direction of a wine garden. Anne overheard them say that they were going to work out a friendly reconciliation with those whom they had earlier reproached. They didn't want to wait until next Sunday's festival, which would be dedicated especially to reconciliations.

Anne and Janice sat at the table next to the group, as close as they dared, in order that Anne could overhear what a young couple seated side by side had to say. The young man forgave his girlfriend for flirting with other men and promised to pay her more attention. She in turn regretted having deliberately provoked him. They embraced tenderly, then drank to their undying love.

Throughout this scene Anne signed for Janice, who appeared rapt, her lips parted, her eyes fixed on the pair of lovers. She must have imagined herself and Captain Howe in their place.

Public confession followed by forgiveness and absolution seemed to make sense. Anne wondered if that might partly explain the generally positive attitude that she, and other winter visitors, observed in the local people. Despite their poverty there were few signs of depression; there was little violence, virtually no public drunkenness. The beautiful weather couldn't entirely account for their happiness.

On the other hand, she believed that certain human passions, even in Nice, were beyond the reach of this custom. True, it quieted many of the small, petty disputes that sour relations within families and between friends. But it could not cope with seriously aggrieved persons who were resolutely unwilling to forgive. Such a person was the Comtesse de Joinville.

'May I join you?' The captain's voice jolted Anne out of her reflections. He had come from behind her. He asked, 'Could this be considered a chaperoned visit?' Janice looked up at him with a radiant expression.

'Yes, I suppose it could,' replied Anne. 'Please sit down.' She moved her chair so that he could sit next to her and opposite Janice. 'You were the centre of attention at the "Reproaches" this afternoon.'

'I had told Louise that our relationship wasn't good for either of us and should end. I was going to move to the cottage that I lease near here. She became very angry.'

'She claimed you stole her money and slept with a harlot.'

He shifted uneasily in his chair. 'I took a little to pay my debts. She banished me from her bed so I went to a more willing woman.' He spoke frankly, his embarrassment quickly overcome.

Anne and the captain signed for Janice as they conversed with each other. He seemed to captivate the young woman, even though his sanguine remarks revealed a character that no woman in her right mind should trust.

For several minutes Captain Howe entertained Janice with tales of adventures, perhaps more fictional than real. While serving with British forces in India, he claimed to have ridden elephants, had held diamonds as large as a man's fist, had known many dark-eyed exotic women, and so on. Anne slipped into the role of an observer, fascinated by the scene before her. At his charming best, Howe signed rapidly, gestured elegantly, his face as expressive as any actor Anne had ever seen. Janice gazed at him, eyes wide, lips parted.

Finally, Anne said they must return to the villa for the masked ball. Howe leaned across the table, kissed Janice's hand, then looked into her eyes and mouthed a few words which Anne couldn't see. Janice blushed, lowered her gaze. He left.

'May I ask what were his parting words?' Anne asked as they left the wine garden.

'I love you,' Janice replied, looking straight ahead.

Was the man sincere or still acting? Anne wondered. In either case, he had bewitched the young woman. She walked with a light step as if on air.

Anne and Janice were among the first to arrive at the villa's festival ball, still masked and dressed in their theatre costumes. As hostess, Beverly met them in the foyer, where she was welcoming guests. She was stunning in a pale green silk gown, her beautiful face partly concealed by a narrow silver half-mask. Grimshaw, who directed the ball, stood behind her in his Pierrot costume.

All the principal winter visitors were invited, excluding servants and children. The intendant, the commandant and his son, as well as a few other local people with links to the foreigners were also invited. The commandant excused himself. He had to attend a ball in the palace for the local nobility. His son, Mario, said he would represent his father. In all, about a hundred men and women were expected to come to the villa, and they would wear masks and festive dress.

Anne heard some visitors murmur that Mr Parker should have been here. However, the ball had been planned before he learned that he needed to suddenly depart. The villa was also by far the largest and the most appropriate place for the winter visitors to gather.

Grimshaw had provided a buffet of British and French, as well as local, delicacies, and a bar serving excellent wines. There were rooms set aside for games of chance and for cards. A band of musicians assembled on the terrace to play for English country dancing, since the evening weather was mild.

'What would you like to do?' Anne asked Janice.

'Dance,' she replied. 'I remember the melodies from before my illness. As a child, I often danced. Now, I can usually feel the music vibrate in my chest or figure it out from the movements of other dancers.'

They made their way through the crowd to the terrace. A dozen others had gathered. The band began a country dance. Anne and Janice paired off. The young woman moved to the music's beat with skill and grace.

For the following dance Anne found herself paired with Mario, Janice with Captain Howe. The young Italian cut a very fine figure, darkly handsome but for a weak pouting mouth.

He gestured toward Janice. 'Captain Howe has won her heart, wouldn't you agree?'

Without reflecting, Anne nodded. It was obvious. Janice and the captain danced in perfect harmony, seemingly unaware of everyone else.

At the next dance Grimshaw placed himself opposite the

young woman. Her eyes followed Captain Howe as he left the terrace and walked out among the ruins. She danced stiffly with Grimshaw, as if under orders to be civil. For his part, the archaeologist seemed clumsy and awkward, more at ease moving ancient earth than young women.

When Anne went inside the villa again, she saw the Comtesse de Joinville in conversation with Beverly. The countess had a glass of wine in her hand and seemed unsteady on her feet. She hurried away as Anne approached.

Anne remarked to Beverly, 'I'm surprised to see her here, after her display of bad temper at the festival this afternoon.'

Beverly seemed worried. 'Several glasses of wine haven't cooled her anger. She told me that she had more to say to Captain Howe and asked where she could find him. I told her that he's most likely on the terrace.'

A moment later, Janice appeared, her mask in her hand. 'It's been a long and tiring day. I'm going to my room to retire.' As she walked away, Anne and Beverly exchanged sceptical glances. A maid would keep watch at the young woman's door.

Beverly suppressed a yawn. 'It's twelve o'clock. I'll also retire.' She patted Anne's hand. 'Good night.'

Anne moved to a quiet corner, mulling over in her mind whether or not to go back to the terrace and see what mischief Louise might be up to.

'Madame Cartier, may I have a word with you?' A masked man in a black silk suit came up to her. She didn't recognize his voice. A hint of displeased surprise must have appeared on her face, for he quickly removed his mask, revealing the intendant for the County of Nice, Marco de Spinola.

'Yes, of course, sir.' Anne quickly recovered her composure. 'Shall we use Mr Parker's study? The festival ball has taken all the other rooms.'

The door to the study was ajar. She pushed it open; the room was empty. She stepped in first, scanned Parker's collection of Roman artefacts and books. Everything seemed in order. Odd, she thought, she had expected Grimshaw to lock up the villa's valuables. Well, perhaps he deemed Parker's collection somewhat less than precious.

Spinola arranged two chairs so they faced each other, then began to speak rather formally. 'As the intendant I am responsible for the county's financial well-being. That depends in great measure on the winter visitors. If they are pleased, they will come back and bring others with them. If conflict or scandal were to frighten or annoy them, they would go elsewhere.'

He paused, cleared his throat nervously. She encouraged him with a smile.

'Would you tell me,' he continued, 'if I am correct in thinking that a worrisome conflict has recently emerged between certain visitors? I ask you the question because you and your husband know the Comtesse de Joinville and he is related to her. The countess and Captain Howe have quarrelled violently – she has attacked him with a knife and he has beaten her. Her shrill reproach to him this afternoon went far beyond what we are accustomed to hear during this festival. I feel I must act to prevent a serious injury or death and to avoid a scandal that would turn visitors away from Nice.'

'I believe your concern is well founded,' Anne replied. 'The problem also involves others besides those to whom you refer.'

'Please tell me about the countess. Ever since she arrived in Nice, she has behaved irrationally. Has she always been so?'

Anne took a moment to reflect. 'I've known her for almost two years. In that time, she has been unhappy – drunk too much brandy, acted promiscuously, maligned others. But I haven't known her to be violent. That's happened since she came here. I don't know why. For months she and the captain lived peaceably together in Paris. Perhaps she feels less constraint on her passions here where she's a stranger and far away from the Baron de Breteuil's guiding influence.'

'Another question, if you please. What is the baron's interest in the countess? I've learned that he sends her money.'

'She's the baron's daughter by his first mistress. He has never acknowledged paternity. But he has always supported her with money and protection, as well as a noble title and social advancement. Thanks to him, she has become a wealthy, prominent woman.'

The intendant frowned. 'The baron complicates the picture for me. Frankly, I hesitate to resolve this problem in a way that offends him. Nor, for that matter, do I wish to appear arbitrary or harsh in the eyes of the winter visitors. I would need very strong reasons to have the countess deported to France. It would be much easier to banish Captain Howe.'

He clapped his hands on his thighs to indicate that the conversation was nearly over. 'You have been most helpful, Madame Cartier. And I look forward to your husband's return, as I'm sure you do. I'll challenge him to a match of court tennis. He's a diplomat, you know, as well as a sportsman – he often lets me win.'

They donned their masks and said good night. She left the door ajar as she had found it and went to her room. Though fatigued, she sat at the writing table and began a letter to Paul, for delivery in Marseille. He would want to know that the Comtesse de Joinville's increasingly erratic behaviour had caught the attention of the Sardinian intendant. She wrote a page and went to bed. For nearly an hour, her mind churned the day's events into a vague feeling of dread. Finally, weariness overcame her and she fell asleep.

Ten

An Old Case Revisited

Marseille, Sunday, 10 February

As he left Toulon for Marseille on a rented horse, Saint-Martin felt exhilarated like a hunter on the chase. The leisurely study mission into Provence the Baron de Breteuil had asked him to undertake had suddenly grown into a full-blown criminal investigation. What he had learned in Toulon about the convict Jean Lebrun, and the mysterious link between him and Jack Grimshaw, had engaged his mind and awakened his deeply rooted instinct to correct injustice. He sensed that something might have gone badly wrong for Lebrun in Marseille twenty years ago.

Halfway to Marseille, Saint-Martin's thoughts turned to Anne – her letter was in his pocket. He recalled her description of Grimshaw's nearly fatal confrontation with Howe at the captain's cottage. Her wise, brave intervention had prevented bloodshed and restored at least a makeshift truce. He felt a surge of pride in her.

Church bells in the distance reminded him that this was the first Sunday in Lent. Anne would take part in the festival at Cimiez. He imagined her in costume and mask in the midst of the festivities, an actress once again on stage. For a moment he yearned to be there and share her pleasure.

At noon, he arrived in Marseille, stiff and sore from a thirty-mile ride. He went directly to the Hôtel de Provence, next door to police headquarters. Georges was waiting for him, having arrived that morning, greatly fatigued after a ten-day trip from Paris. From early dawn to late at night his carriage had stopped only to change horses and drivers. He had largely recovered, though his eyes were still red from lack of sleep.

Over a light lunch in Saint-Martin's room, he and Georges exchanged news, then turned to the business at hand. Georges began, 'I think that Lebrun's strategy might be to hide out in coastal Provence, or Nice, where the winters are mild. When the search for him wanes and the weather improves, he might attempt to reach Paris after all. His wife almost convinced me that he's dead. But she might be trying to trick us into calling off the search.' He handed a packet across the table. 'Here are copies of his letters to her.'

Saint-Martin read the letters with a sceptical eye. 'They are perhaps self-serving. Still, the court might have wrongly convicted him of the master's murder. The victim's wife and stepson look suspicious. Their motives for murder were as strong as Lebrun's and they had as much opportunity.'

'We should visit the cabinet shop, then try to find the police agent in charge of Lebrun's case twenty years ago,' said Georges.

'Yes, but first I need to speak to the head of the local police and get him on our side.'

Lieutenant General Augustin Clary received the two visiting policemen in his office. His greeting was courteous, but his eyes were cautious, even wary. A reasonable man, thought Saint-Martin. At the least, these strangers from Paris would upset his routine. They might also stir up sleeping controversies and expose past judicial failures to no useful purpose.

Saint-Martin took the lead, describing the progress Georges had made in his search for the escaped convict. The royal government in Paris had given him a broad mandate to continue the investigation in Marseille in cooperation with local authorities.

While Saint-Martin spoke, Clary appeared to sink into serious reflection, his brow furrowed with the effort. He addressed Georges. 'Do I understand your mission correctly, Monsieur Charpentier? You have come here to see if Jean Lebrun's conviction was flawed. If another person were found guilty of the crime, Lebrun would presumably surrender himself in order to clear his name. That is, if he's still alive.'

'That's an avenue I want to pursue,' Georges replied. 'My mind is also open to the possibility that he's guilty as charged and convicted.'

'Then you must also know how difficult it will be to persuade our magistrates to change their decision. You will need strong proof.' Clary paused for a moment. 'On the other hand, you will find allies here who have always doubted Lebrun's guilt. Foremost among them is my own Captain Barras, who conducted the original investigation. He's out of the office today on a case, but in the evening he will dine at his favourite quayside fish restaurant in the harbour.'

Clary turned to Saint-Martin. 'What role do you play in this mission, Colonel?'

'I shall assist my adjutant,' Saint-Martin replied with a self-deprecating smile in his voice. 'I'm officially on vacation, spending the winter months in Nice to recover my health. During the past few days, however, while visiting the naval prison in Toulon, I learned that an English winter visitor of my acquaintance, Jack Grimshaw, had stopped at the prison to enquire about Jean Lebrun. According to the commandant's aide, Mr Grimshaw betrayed a suspicious curiosity.'

The lieutenant general leaned forward, interest growing in his eyes.

'If I were to describe Grimshaw,' Saint-Martin continued, 'would you instruct an agent to uncover his tracks in Marseille?'

'Surely. There's an agent in the building who could do it.'

In a few minutes, the agent arrived and Saint-Martin gave him a physical description. 'Grimshaw's tall, lean, tanned by the sun, and speaks fluent French with a strong English accent. An archaeologist by profession, he discovers ancient Roman artefacts, buys and sells them. I would expect him to contact dealers, collectors, bankers.'

'Give me a few days, Colonel,' said the agent. 'I'll tell you what I've found.'

Outside the office, Saint-Martin turned to Georges. 'Let's find Lebrun's trail. We'll start with the cabinet shop where he worked.' Georges smiled inwardly. His 'ailing' superior on vacation had taken charge.

They found the shop quickly enough. For a couple of hours they studied the building, a well-built three-storey stone structure in the old town. From neighbours, they learned that the victim's stepson, Henri Duclos, had married a much younger woman, Francine, and had prospered. His mother, Cécile, had become infirm and was seldom seen outside the house.

'In Toulon,' Saint-Martin explained, 'the commandant's aide described not only the stepson but also the maid, Amélie, who took care of his mother and was the only servant in the house who was with the family at the time of the murder. She would then have been about fifteen years old.' He pointed to a woman leaving the building. 'There she is, Georges. Follow her. I'll keep an eye on the shop.'

After a ten-minute walk through the city, Amélie led Georges into a large, busy wine tavern serving a mixed clientele, mostly men. She bought a glass of wine, took it to a table, and began to drink alone. She was a comely woman, plainly dressed, who glanced about the room as if expecting someone. When no one came, Georges also bought a glass of wine and sat across from her at the table. She looked up, startled at first, then gave him an inviting smile.

'I've engaged a room,' he said. 'Will you come with me?' He discreetly pushed a coin across the table. For a long moment she studied him, then took the coin and nodded.

Once the door closed behind them, she began to loosen her bodice. Georges wasn't surprised. He had guessed correctly

71

that she added money from occasional prostitution to her scant income in the stepson's household.

'That's not what I want,' Georges said with a gentle smile. 'Be calm, I'm an officer of the Royal Highway Patrol and mean you no harm.' He showed her his identification. 'I need to speak to you privately.' He directed her to a table and sat facing her. She appeared baffled, a little apprehensive.

He took another coin out of his purse. 'I'll make it worth your while to tell me about your household, and especially your mistress.'

She reared back in her chair. 'Why do you want to know?'

He put the coin on the table, stared sternly at her. 'Police business.'

The maid hesitantly nodded, took the coin, then explained that she had served in the household for twenty years, beginning at age fifteen in the kitchen, and later as the mistress's personal maid. With a mixture of coaxing and threats, Georges learned that the stepson Henri was a wealthy domestic tyrant. His wife, Francine, sharp-eyed and mean-spirited, was almost as bad. As his mother Cécile aged, they regarded her as a troublesome nuisance, neglected her, even sometimes abused her.

'Have you heard about Jean Lebrun?'

The maid's eyes widened, her lips parted in alarm. 'Why do you ask?'

'As you know, he has escaped from prison. Who is the person he's most likely to visit to settle an old account?'

'Henri Duclos,' she replied. 'Months ago, the police searched the neighbourhood and warned the master and his wife. There's been no sign of Lebrun.'

'He's not stupid,' Georges said. 'Do you really think the first thing he'd do after his escape would be to rush to Marseille and to the cabinet shop? No, he knew the police would be waiting for him. We believe that he has been lying low until everyone thinks he's left the country.'

'Then he might come back any time now,' the maid said, anxiety rising in her voice.

'Do you have any reason to be afraid of him?'

'Not really. Twenty years ago, I was just a young scullery maid. He used to eat in the kitchen with me and the cook. I liked him. He was kind to me – made a little wooden box for my trinkets. I still have it.'

'Do you think he killed old Jacques Duclos?'

'They all said he did. He was angry at the master for cheating him.'

'What do you say?'

She was silent for a minute, staring into her clasped hands resting on the table. 'He didn't kill the master.' She hesitated, as if paralysed.

'Yes? Go on.'

'Henri did it. He killed his stepfather.' Her voice had dropped to a whisper. 'He'll kill me if he finds out that I've spoken to you.' She began to cry.

Georges patted her hands. 'He won't find out. We'll keep this secret until I'm ready to arrest him. If you cooperate, you will receive protection and a reward. Now tell me what happened.' His heart was pounding. This looked like a break-through in Lebrun's case. He might be innocent after all.

She glanced up at Georges, biting her lower lip, gaining courage. 'It was like this.' She explained that on the night of the murder, Henri came to her little room off the kitchen in the basement. He often slept with her.

'On that night, however, while I was sleeping, he left the bed. I woke up as he stomped up the stairs to the shop – he's a heavy man. Then I heard his footsteps on the creaky wooden floor above me. The master was in his room behind the shop. He never slept with his wife. They didn't like each other. I could faintly hear angry voices, then the sound of a chair falling over. A few minutes later, Henri returned to my room. I pretended to wake up. He was shaking. Sweat dripped from his face. He asked, "Did you hear anything?" From his voice I knew what I should answer. I replied that I had just woken up. He said, "If anyone asks, tell them I was with you all night." '

'Did the police question you?'

She shrugged. 'They asked, had I heard or seen anything that night. I replied that I had slept soundly. They seemed satisfied and didn't ask me any more.'

'How did the son treat you afterward?'

'A few months later, after Monsieur Lebrun was convicted and put in prison, Henri came to me. "I see you're an intel-ligent, trustworthy servant. From now on, you'll be my mother's personal maid." As a scullery maid, I had only room

73

and board and the rags on my back. He ordered decent clothes for me and gave me a small salary.'

'Tell me about your mistress. Was she involved with her son in the master's murder?'

'I didn't hear her voice – it's shrill, easy to recognize. Didn't hear her footsteps, either. For a while, she pretended to grieve – wore black, of course. She was quick to accuse Monsieur Lebrun, claimed he stole money, threatened the master. Said she saw him sneaking downstairs that night. I wouldn't know if that was true or false.'

The maid seemed to fall into a reflective mood. 'After the murder, she and her son ran the business together for several years and made a lot of money. Then Henri decided to marry and brought his wife, Francine, into the business. She and her mother-in-law didn't get along. Cécile's health failed. Eventually, the son sided with his wife and forced his mother to retire to a room in the garret. She hates both of them, lives like a prisoner in the house.'

'Has she ever mentioned Monsieur Lebrun?'

'While she was busy in the shop and making money, I doubt that she even thought of him. After she retired, she seemed to change. I would mention his name from time to time. She nodded as if she too were thinking about him. When I told her that he had escaped, she became agitated, complained that her son wasn't taking steps to protect her. I asked her why she worried. "Lebrun thinks I once gave false testimony against him." She must have seen the surprise on my face and immediately defended herself. "It wasn't false, it was the truth," she said. But she didn't sound convincing.'

Georges leaned forward, met the woman's eye, and asked gently, 'How does Henri treat you?'

'Badly, as you can guess from the fact that I'm here, looking for men, and not for the first time.' Her mouth settled into an ironic smile. 'I shared in his mother's disgrace. He cut my salary in half. I can't leave his service because he refuses to give me a recommendation. So I have to sell myself in wine taverns.'

'I think I can improve your lot, Amélie. But first we must find a way to persuade bitter old Cécile to help us bring her son to justice. If we succeed, then our escaped convict Monsieur Lebrun will no longer need to hide and might cease

74

to frighten the shopkeepers and the magistrates who condemned him.'

Meanwhile, after waiting until there were no customers, Saint-Martin entered Henri Duclos's shop to gain an impression of the man and his establishment. The showroom testified persuasively to the beauty of wood. Several mahogany cabinets with mixed exotic inlays were displayed on a polished hardwood floor, and many designs for cabinets hung on the oak-panelled walls. The ceiling was panelled as well.

Husband and wife stood behind a counter, engaged in conversation. He was a huge figure of a man, with a closely trimmed beard on his porcine face. His small, black, beady eyes were fixed on his petite wife. To judge from the bits that Saint-Martin could hear, the man was complaining about the growing scarcity of fine wood. His wife must have heard his complaint before. She was struggling to appear interested.

They turned to face Saint-Martin, who had dressed in a well-tailored buff silk suit and carried himself as the elegant gentleman that he was. Their faces brightened as they recognized a potential rich customer.

After browsing among the cabinets, he opened a conversation with the husband about their prices. They were high – only a very wealthy man could afford them. Saint-Martin pretended to be seriously interested. 'I think I might rather commission a cabinet. Could I visit your workshop?'

'By all means.' Henri instructed his wife to mind the showroom. Saint-Martin followed him through a room that served as a parlour and an office. He noticed that the floor was an unusually fine parquet of walnut and fir. It creaked underfoot. On the far wall to the left behind a curtain was a bedded alcove. To the right a wooden stairway descended to the kitchen in the basement. Saint-Martin could smell dinner cooking.

The workshop was at the rear of the building. A journeyman and an apprentice stood around a half-finished cabinet. As he entered, Saint-Martin breathed an air thick with fumes from glue and lacquer. In a few minutes, his eyes were smarting. He stayed no longer than necessary to survey the shop and its contents, pronounced himself favourably impressed with what he saw, and promised to return.

Out on the street, he drew in deep breaths of cool, less

toxic city air. In the shaded terrace of a cafe across the street he continued to observe the Duclos shop. Fresh impressions of the husband and wife came to his mind. Henri was a rough-hewn, oaken block of a man, of short stature, dark complexion, thick chest, powerful arms, and ham-sized hands. His hair was wiry and grey. His jaw jutted out pugnaciously. His nose was flat, his nostrils flared. He moved about with quick, determined steps. A man with such a strong, intimidating presence was likely to insist on having his own way and ride roughshod over anyone who disagreed with him. He must have many enemies in the city and a problematic relationship with his household.

His wife was a small, slender, attractive woman, energetic and a dozen years younger than he, with a sly, self-interested look. She managed the showroom for her husband and seemed familiar with the rest of the business. Could he have intentionally or perhaps inadvertently confided to her that he had killed the master? Would she have desires at odds with his and be willing to betray him? Saint-Martin mulled over these questions, recalling her shrewd face. Yes, if it were to her advantage, she probably would betray him.

Early in the afternoon Georges joined Saint-Martin at the cafe. They ordered cool lemonade, exchanged information, and observed the shop. Within a few minutes, Henri hurried away in an expensive red silk suit, its silver embroidery glittering in the sunlight.

The maid Amélie had given Georges the household routine. 'He dines regularly with other shop owners – or so he says – from two to four in the afternoon, Monday through Friday.'

Saint-Martin studied his lemonade. 'Those hours offer us an opportunity to persuade Cécile to cooperate with the investigation. But we would have to get past his wife.'

'Francine might also cooperate if we promised her the shop after hanging her husband.' Georges was half-serious.

'Before we hang Duclos, we must see to his arrest and conviction.'

While sipping the lemonade, Saint-Martin pondered the obstacles facing the investigation. Henri had become a major figure among the city's master artisans. It would be difficult to charge him, even more difficult to convict him of a twenty-year-old murder. The case against him was circumstantial. True, his mother, together with her maid, might be persuaded to testify against him. But he would claim that they were merely two disgruntled females and their accusations should be regarded as baseless.

A slim elderly man in a black hat and soutane approached the shop.

'Here comes the old priest,' Georges remarked. 'Amélie told me that he regularly visits the mother for tea. Henri can't stand the sight of priests, but he tolerates this one's visits while he's away. Amélie says the priest is kind, cheers the old woman with amusing stories and news of the town. After an hour he says a few prayers, gives her a blessing, and leaves. She protests that she's not religious but she enjoys his visits.'

'Gombert is his name,' Saint-Martin added. 'I heard of him when I was in Toulon.' He raised his glass in a salute to the priest. 'He just might serve as our Trojan horse into Duclos's house.'

Saint-Martin sent Georges off in search of the police agent in Lebrun's original trial. When the priest left Duclos's shop, Saint-Martin followed him home. At the door, he showed his official papers, and said he had to ask a few questions. Taken by surprise, Gombert held him in a probing gaze for a moment, then invited him into his study.

It was a scholar's den. Shelves of books covered the walls. Piles of books and paper stood on the floor. Gombert sat behind a large old writing table, its scarred surface spotted with ink. He gestured Saint-Martin to a worn but comfortable upholstered chair facing him. A servant arrived with brandy, poured, then retired. Saint-Martin explained his errand.

'Yes, I knew Jean Lebrun well,' said Gombert, his eyes gazing into the past. His mouth broke easily into a smile at the memory. He had a thoughtful, welcoming face and spoke the soft, melodic French of the Midi. His manner was gracious, cultivated. He was about seventy years old but carried his age well. In the cafe Saint-Martin had learned that the priest was generally liked and respected. Henri Duclos's negative attitude was an exception.

'Do you believe that Lebrun murdered Jacques Duclos?' asked Saint-Martin.

'Given severe provocation,' Gombert replied, 'even decent men and women will do evil deeds. Monsieur Duclos, cabinetmaker, was a harsh and greedy master. His journeyman, Jean Lebrun, was young, impulsive, and aware of his worth. Their quarrel could have grown into lethal violence.'

'Did anyone else in the household have a strong motive to kill the master?'

'My friend, I see where your questions are leading. Do you have reason to believe that someone other than Jean Lebrun is guilty?'

'Yes, I do. My adjutant, Monsieur Georges Charpentier, has just received a detailed, credible testimony from the maid Amélie who heard, though didn't see, Henri Duclos commit the crime. Circumstantial evidence points in the same direction. Unfortunately, I still lack sufficient evidence to bring the murderer to account before a magistrate.'

'Why has this information come to light now after twenty years, rather than during the original investigation?' The priest took a sip of the brandy, studied Saint-Martin over the edge of the glass.

'Because the circumstances are different. Magistrates and other judicial officers are more enlightened today. The persons involved in this crime have changed. Our principal witness Amélie was then young, immature, and intimidated by the killer. She is now a mature adult, better equipped to surmount her fears. A second witness, Cécile Duclos, has also changed and now could reveal the truth, if she would. Need I remind you, sir, that even back then certain magistrates contested the original verdict against Lebrun. For that reason the sentence was reduced from death to imprisonment.'

The priest nodded. 'I am aware that several persons, close to the facts, doubted that justice was done.' He paused, inclined his head sceptically. 'You have come here to ask something significant of me. Would you mind if I ask why you are pursuing this investigation?'

Saint-Martin replied, 'When Lebrun escaped from the prison at Toulon, the Lieutenant General of Police in Paris, Thiroux de Crosne, ordered my adjutant Georges Charpentier to search for him in the Paris area, where he was likely to flee. After several weeks, Charpentier ended the fruitless search. In the meantime, he had learned a great deal about Lebrun from family, friends, and his wife. His trial and conviction raised questions of fairness in Charpentier's mind. The lieutenant general agreed and sent him here.

'Meanwhile,' Saint-Martin continued, 'the Baron de Breteuil asked me to visit the naval prison at Toulon while I was vacationing in Nice. At Toulon, I found officers who also expressed reservations about Lebrun's conviction. So I've joined my adjutant in thoroughly questioning the original investigation.'

'Well spoken, Colonel. Now I'll share my doubts with you. Lebrun was probably a scapegoat. At the time, the master artisans were angry at the journeymen for seeking better wages and working conditions, and fearful of strikes and malicious destruction of their shops. Many magistrates were of the same mind, and therefore inclined to suspect Lebrun. I cannot with certainty tell you who killed the master. But the police investigation too quickly focused on Lebrun. The victim and his stepson had also quarrelled over who should control the shop. And Henri had equal opportunity to kill his stepfather during the night. The key witness in the original investigation was Madame Duclos, the victim's wife. Her testimony incriminated Lebrun. She exaggerated his threats and claimed to have seen him on the stairway at the time of the killing.

'Since she retired from the shop and shortly afterward became invalid, I've been visiting her in the hope of easing her mind of its bitterness and anger over her situation. She is quite feeble and may not live much longer. As death draws near, she also seems to feel a burden on her conscience. Lebrun's escape has surely reminded her of the central, shameful role she played in his unjust conviction.'

'Could you persuade her to confess, not only to you but also to a magistrate and thus clear Lebrun's name?'

'I can try, but I'm not confident of success. The mere suggestion of speaking to a magistrate would make her very anxious.'

'I'm not surprised,' Saint-Martin admitted. 'She could rightly wonder what might become of her, should her son be arrested. Would she lose her room and what little else she has? Where would she live? Who would take care of her? Would the police imprison her for the lies she told and the harm she caused?'

'I think we could lessen her fears,' Gombert replied. 'I

know Marseille. Perhaps I could find a convent that would offer her decent accommodation and humane care.'

'My adjutant and I will consult with police and magistrates for a solution to the legal problems.'

'Speed and secrecy are of the essence, Colonel. If Henri Duclos learns of our plan, he may find a way to propel his mother into eternity, and her maid along with her.'

Early in the evening, Georges found René Barras in a small restaurant in the port district. He was the police lieutenant who had conducted the original investigation. Now a captain, Barras was still in service, though approaching retirement. A short, thick-bodied, swarthy man, he wore a scar across the left side of his face from ear to mouth.

He was sitting alone at a small table and eating bouillabaisse, a local fish stew. A variety of boiled fish lay on a large plate in front of him, a tureen of steaming spiced soup to one side, a pitcher of white wine to the other.

Georges stared at the scar and hesitated to approach the man. Then he recalled that, despite this sinister appearance, Barras was known as a simple, good-natured man, fierce only to lawbreakers.

Georges presented his identification papers. 'May I join you, Captain?'

Barras glanced at the papers. 'Pull up a chair, Charpentier. You've come a long way for a plate of fish.' He ladled soup from the tureen onto the fish, ate a mouthful, bit off a piece of bread, and drank half a glass of wine. He wiped his mouth while Georges signalled the waiter.

'I'll have the same,' Georges said, pointing to his colleague's plate, then addressed Barras. 'I've looked for Jean Lebrun in the Paris area and concluded he's here on the coast waiting for us to give up and take on a different case.'

Barras gave Georges a doubtful glance. 'We've searched the coast from here to Italy. What more can you do?'

The waiter came with another plate of fish and replenished the soup tureen and the pitcher of wine. Georges recognized pieces of eel. The rest was a delicious mystery. The white wine was to his taste, dry and strong. Barras finished his wine and poured another glass from the pitcher.

'It's a waste of time to look for him,' Georges remarked.

'My commander, Colonel Saint-Martin, and I want to investigate again the murder of Master Jacques Duclos twenty years ago. We doubt that Jean Lebrun killed him. When we find the true killer, Lebrun will come out of hiding – if he's alive.'

'Really! Is it that simple?' Barras pushed his plate aside and leaned forward. 'You must know that I'm familiar with the case, as I'm sure that you are, too. Lebrun's escape made me think about it again, though it's never been far from my mind.' He paused, recalling events from the past. 'When I first examined the crime scene, I thought a burglar had strangled old Duclos. Money was missing from the cash box. But there were no signs of a break-in. Circumstantial evidence pointed to the journeyman Jean Lebrun and the stepson Henri Duclos. Both men had grievances against the master. The widow's testimony implicated the journeyman.

'I knew of her bad feeling toward her husband and suspected that she had wrongly accused Lebrun in order to divert attention from her own son. The magistrate in charge of the case nonetheless ordered Lebrun's arrest and a divided court convicted him.' He stared at Georges with hardened, sceptical eyes. 'You must know that our magistrates don't like to admit a mistake and rarely correct one.'

Georges ate a piece of eel, poured more wine for himself and for Barras. 'Much has changed since they put Jean Lebrun in the naval prison. Duclos's widow Cécile and her maid Amélie seem prepared to incriminate the real killer, Henri Duclos.' Georges realized that his claim for Cécile rested more on hope than on evidence.

'That's encouraging,' Barras admitted, saluting Georges with his wine, then drinking half of it. 'And today, the case might receive a more open-minded hearing. The worst of the original magistrates are dead. More enlightened men have taken their places.'

'Still,' Georges pointed out, 'we need a local officer to lead the new investigation, someone committed to getting the verdict right this time.'

'That sounds like me, doesn't it? But I'm planning to retire in two months. Why should I take on such a difficult task?' He fingered his scar, stared into his wine. 'On the other hand, why not leave the job in a blaze of glory?'

Eleven

Death in the Arena

Nice, Monday, 11 February

Anne awoke early; she hadn't slept well. Too much on her mind. Beneath the surface of yesterday's festivities, intense personal conflicts had flared up. At the centre of each of them was the charming, heedless Captain Howe. Of his three principal enemies, the Comtesse de Joinville had openly reproached him in the church square and had not reconciled with him. Jack Grimshaw and Mario de Maistre expressed their grievances less openly, but Anne could sense their antipathy when they encountered Howe at the festival ball.

She would have liked to discuss these issues with Paul. But he was a hundred miles away in Marseille. How she missed him! She threw on a housecoat and hurried downstairs. In the kitchen, Janice and the cook were drinking coffee together. Anne poured a cup for herself and joined them.

'The party went on till dawn,' the cook complained. 'Such a racket. I hardly got a wink of sleep.'

Janice signed, 'So there's some good in being deaf.' Anne translated for Philippa.

The cook laughed kindly and patted the young woman on the shoulder.

In return she gave Philippa a faint, grateful smile. 'But I didn't sleep well either. Bad dreams.'

The young woman's expression grew bleak. Nonetheless, Anne asked cautiously, 'Would you care to share a dream with us?'

She replied reluctantly, 'I was standing on the bank of a deep, rapid river. Jeremy was on the opposite side. I waved to him, but he didn't see me. I tried several times without success. Finally he disappeared.' She sighed. 'The other dreams were worse. I don't want to talk about them.'

'It looks like the beginning of another beautiful sunny day,'

Anne declared, hoping to distract the young woman into a sunnier frame of mind. 'Let's take a walk.'

Janice shrugged. But since she couldn't think of anything better to do, she agreed.

After dressing, they walked to the Roman amphitheatre, an oval stone structure built around an arena about the year 250 after Christ. According to Grimshaw, a crowd of five thousand could comfortably watch gladiators fight each other to the death. A canvas cover shielded the spectators from the sun.

The two women stopped at the southern entrance and surveyed the structure. Even in its ruined state, it was impressive. The low, early morning sun threw a golden light on the western half, the best-preserved part, revealing a bank of several rows of seats that rested on great stone vaults. In the centre of the arena, a man lay on his side, his back turned toward them.

'Perhaps he's a reveller from last night's ball at the villa,' Anne remarked, 'had too much wine and spent the night here.'

As she advanced toward the man, she recognized the Harlequin costume. A shiver ran through her body. Something was dreadfully wrong.

Janice broke away from Anne and dashed up to the man. For a long moment, mouth agape, she stared at him, then threw her head back, shook her fists at the sky, and screamed. And screamed again. Finally, she cast herself on the dead man's body, weeping, choking in her tears.

As gently as possible, yet firmly, Anne pulled the young woman to her feet and sat her down at a good distance against an olive tree. Then she walked around the body to inspect it from all sides. As she had suspected, it was Captain Howe.

He had been stabbed in the neck. A great quantity of blood, now dried, had soaked his shirt and pooled around his head. He had removed his mask and still held it in his hand. The instrument of his death was a bloody dagger lying nearby. Anne recognized it, the ancient Roman weapon that she had seen last night hanging on the wall in Mr Parker's study.

Less than an hour later, the Comte de Maistre rode up to the villa with several of his men. Madame Cartier had summoned him. On his way, he had thought of the challenge ahead. A crime this serious required prompt, personal attention. With a frisson of anxiety, he readily admitted to himself that this was his first investigation of murder, and he wasn't sure of his footing. Unfortunately, his men were as inexperienced as he. Their talent lay in chasing bandits in the mountains and detecting smugglers. Moreover, he was new to Nice, ignorant of English, and barely acquainted with most of the winter visitors.

This crime had extraordinary significance. During the past few years, these rich, influential, and numerous foreigners had become an important source of revenue for the County of Nice. The investigation of the British captain's murder must be discreet and expeditious, lest it frighten the visitors away and discourage others from coming. The Intendant of Nice, Marco de Spinola, would closely watch the case and report to the royal government in Turin. The count's enemies would rejoice at his every false move.

Madame Cartier met de Maistre at the door and greeted him in French. He felt reassured. She spoke his language and understood his culture. As the French colonel's wife and partner, she had gained some experience in criminal investigation and could be helpful in this case. Nearly thirty, she was tall, intelligent, and attractive. Her direct, self-assured gaze could disconcert men. But the count, who fancied himself a good judge of women, preferred her to the addle-brained, simpering court ladies he knew. Time would tell how well he and she would get along.

'Sir,' she began, 'Mademoiselle Parker would join us, but she is ill, suffering from shock. Could you meet with her later in the day? I would be happy to translate for you.'

The count expressed his regrets, agreed to see Mademoiselle Parker when she had recovered, then said, 'Tell me, Madame, what you and she discovered this morning in the amphitheatre.'

She gave him a succinct account and finished with the remark, 'I hoped you would come quickly, so I left the body as I found it. I'll take you there.'

Anne had thrown a blanket over the body, but had otherwise not disturbed it. Her cool, almost numb reaction distressed her. The shock would come later. Now, still devoid of feeling, she stood next to the Comte de Maistre, while his adjutant removed the blanket. The count studied the body and examined the ground nearby. When he noticed the Roman dagger, Anne told him that it came from Mr Parker's collection.

The count stepped back, stroking his chin, and remarked to his adjutant, 'There are no signs of a struggle. A single blow to the neck severed an artery, and the victim died almost instantly. He must have been taken by surprise, though he probably knew his assailant.'

The count turned to Anne, 'When did you last see him alive?'

'About midnight, on the terrace, then he walked down among the ruins.'

'He died an hour or two later,' offered the adjutant. 'His blood has thickened and dried. Rigor has begun.'

'Madame Cartier,' asked the count, 'has anyone seen the body, besides you and Mademoiselle Parker?'

'As far as I know, sir, no one but us has seen it. I haven't even told anyone yet that he's dead. And I put Janice to sleep. I realize that certain details of the crime scene are best kept secret.'

'Correct. Tell me, madame, did the captain have any enemies who could have wanted to kill him?'

'Captain Howe's behaviour was often reckless, heedless of the feelings of others. Some were angered. I can't say that they would have killed him.'

The count's eyes narrowed. 'The Comtesse de Joinville is surely among them. Her quarrels with the captain are notorious in Nice. Can you name any others?'

'I believe Mr Grimshaw's differences with Captain Howe are also public knowledge.' Anne hesitated at the name of the count's own son. 'I regret to mention your son, Mario, who exchanged harsh words with the captain a few days ago on a public road for all the world to hear.'

'I've heard about that incident. My son must learn to better govern his tongue.'

And give up gambling, Anne thought.

'I'll begin by questioning Madame Parker,' de Maistre continued, as they walked back to the villa. 'Would you inform her and arrange for a meeting place?'

'Yes, of course,' Anne replied. 'She doesn't speak either French or Italian. Do you want me to assist her?'

The count agreed, then gave orders to his men to move the body to a cool room in the villa's basement. Anne went off to make arrangements, her spirit heavy. For she knew from experience how easily a criminal investigation could reveal closely held, damaging secrets, or even turn a household into a cage of snarling beasts.

They met in a parlour, the count and Beverly facing each other, Anne sitting to one side as a translator. Pale and drawn, Beverly appeared near collapse. Her presentiment of horrors had come true. Anne had just given her a brief, general account of Howe's murder. A servant brought tea, poured for them, and withdrew.

Recognizing Beverly's fragile state of mind, de Maistre addressed her gently with a sympathetic tilt of his head. 'You must pardon me, Madame Parker, but I should ask you a few questions.'

She forced a thin smile. 'Please do your duty.'

'How well did you know Captain Howe?'

'He was frequently a guest in this house. My husband enjoyed his company.'

'Were you acquainted with him before arriving in Nice?'

She shot Anne a quick, apprehensive, involuntary glance. Too late she realized that she had given a secret away. 'Yes,' she admitted, 'he was a neighbour and acquaintance many years ago, before I married Mr Parker.'

'Does your husband know of that early relationship?'

'Why should he?' she asked sharply.

'Has the relationship continued until the present time?'

'Sir! What kind of woman do you think I am?'

'I regret that my questions appear indelicate, even offensive. Still I must ask them. The captain was reputed to extort money from women whom he had compromised. Did he receive money from you?'

The direction of the count's questions surprised and stunned Anne. He seemed far better informed than she had expected. Suddenly it occurred to her – the servants. They were local people, who probably understood more English than they let on. Some of them must be in the count's pay, serving as his eyes and ears in the villa of the most wealthy and influential of the winter visitors.

'For old friendship's sake, I gave him small sums of money from time to time to help cover his gambling debts.'

'With your husband's knowledge?'

'No,' she stammered. Her expression had become desperate. She had begun to wheeze.

'I see.' The count paused to let her recover. They all drank some tea. When her breathing had sufficiently improved, he asked her, 'Please describe for me your movements late last night and early this morning.'

'Am I being accused of killing Captain Howe?'

'Simply answer my question, madame.'

She raised her head, swallowed, then said, 'At about midnight, I felt exhausted. Though the ball was still going on, I excused myself to the guests and went to my room. There I remained until Madame Cartier called me a short while ago.'

A soldier entered the room and whispered in the count's ear, then left.

'That will be all for now, Madame Parker. You may leave. My men have searched your rooms, checked your gowns and shoes for blood, but didn't discover any incriminating evidence. You will find your things in a state of disorder. I apologize.'

She struggled from her chair, wild-eyed, speechless. The search of her clothes had profoundly distressed her. Her husband would find out about her early affair with Howe and accuse her of duplicity. And, worse yet, she had lost her illusion of self-respect and felt soiled. Anne pitied her.

When Beverly had left the room, de Maistre remarked to Anne, 'Madame Parker remains a possible though unlikely suspect. Would you please write down the main points of my conversation with Madame Parker and also fetch Grimshaw for me? I would like you to assist in my investigation.'

It was early afternoon before Mr Grimshaw returned from the city, where he had been on the villa's business. Anne met him at the door and walked with him to the parlour.

'The Comte de Maistre is waiting for you,' she said.

'Why? What has happened?'

87

'Captain Howe has been murdered.' Anne glanced sideways to study Grimshaw's reaction.

'Well, that *is* a surprise!' He raised an eyebrow, pursed his lips, nodded thoughtfully. 'Captain Howe was a reckless, selfish, proud man, who taunted Fate. He was destined to come to a bad end. I can't say that I'm sorry.'

Indeed, Anne observed that he appeared profoundly satisfied.

The count was waiting in the parlour, having questioned the servants. The two men shook hands and sat opposite each other. Anne found a chair off to one side. The count had asked her to take notes. Grimshaw gave Anne a slightly nervous glance, then turned respectfully to de Maistre. 'How can I help you, sir? Madame Cartier has just told me that Captain Howe has died.'

'That's true. And I'm searching for the person who killed him.' The count met Grimshaw's eye. 'Your differences with the captain have come to my attention. They seem to revolve around his friendship with Mademoiselle Janice Parker. Is that correct?'

'Yes, his pursuit of the young woman was inappropriate. He was taking advantage of her youth and her deafness.'

'Was that not the concern of her guardian, Mr Parker, and his wife? What was your interest in the matter?'

The count's question appeared to momentarily disconcert Grimshaw. 'Why, I acted as any gentleman would to protect the young woman. Madame Parker also objected to the captain's behaviour and never cautioned me to stand aside.'

'Was there no other contentious issue between you and the captain?' The count's voice had a distinctly sceptical tone.

'No, sir. What can you mean?'

'Never mind,' the count replied, then went on, 'The animosity between the two of you reached a dangerous level several nights ago, when you attempted to break down the door to the captain's cottage while he stood on the other side with a pistol drawn and cocked. So I must ask you to describe your movements between midnight and two o'clock this morning.'

'During most of that period I was looking after the guests at the ball, providing refreshments and the like. I also withdrew to my rooms for short periods to rest. The party became quite noisy.'

'Then you didn't leave the villa or its terrace?' The sceptical note again appeared.

'Yes, I did take a walk into the estate.'

'And did you meet the captain?'

'No, I did not.'

'That will be all, Mr Grimshaw.'

When Grimshaw left the room, the count turned to Anne. 'Do you have the feeling that Mr Grimshaw is holding something back?'

The question surprised Anne. She hadn't expected the count to seek her opinion. Except for her husband and his adjutant, Georges Charpentier, the male policemen she knew often had low regard for a woman's intelligence. But she was growing aware that in the count's eyes she represented the winter visitors as an unofficial observer. Through her, he hoped to reassure them that the investigation would be fair and judicious.

Up to a point Anne was willing to cooperate. 'I can tell you,' she replied, 'that he and the captain may have had another difference, apart from their conflict over Janice Parker.' Anne described her investigation into Howe's curious reference to Mithras during the confrontation in the market. 'It seems to make no sense,' she concluded.

'I shall keep it in mind,' the count said thoughtfully.

Janice sat at a tea table, pale and lethargic. By late afternoon, she had recovered from shock sufficiently for a conversation with the count. Anne and a maid had dressed and groomed her. The maid brought her a pot of herbal tea and biscuits. Janice hadn't eaten since a small breakfast early in the morning.

Anne and the count sat side by side facing her. Anne translated when the young woman's speech became incomprehensible, and she turned to signing. Her articulation had suffered from the shock.

'I'll be brief,' said the count. 'I realize how dreadful you must feel.'

She gave him a weak smile, sipped from her cup.

'When did you last see the captain alive?'

'About midnight on the terrace. He said he was going into the ruins to meet someone. Didn't say who.'

'Did you notice anyone follow him?'

She paused to think. 'I didn't stay on the terrace long enough to notice.'

Anne added an aside, 'Persons went among the ruins frequently during the party to relieve themselves.'

'As I should have guessed,' the count remarked with a smile, then addressed Janice again, 'How would you describe your relationship with Captain Howe?'

Janice signed defiantly to Anne. 'We were in love. Jeremy intended to ask Mr Parker for my hand in marriage. He said he could persuade Mr Parker to agree.'

Anne was astounded, and her face must have betrayed her. Janice smiled ruefully. The teacup in her hands trembled so much she had to put it down. The count paused, reflecting. He seemed about to speak, then reconsidered.

'That will be all, mademoiselle. You should rest. We'll continue this conversation at another time.'

Anne felt that the conversation could have continued, so when she and the count were alone, she asked why he had broken it off.

'The young woman is in an unhealthy state of mind, still feeling the effects of shock. Her Jeremy Howe has also duped her. One of my informants, a waiter in a wine tavern, overheard the captain boast that to secure a fortune he had won the heart of a rich young deaf woman. It would be difficult to arrange a marriage, but he thought he could gain the approval of her guardian.' The count paused. 'This isn't the time to give Mademoiselle Parker a dose of bitter truth. We may find a more appropriate occasion.'

Or, Anne thought, let Janice live on in ignorance. What harm could come of it? Besides, she wasn't likely to believe him capable of such duplicity and would hate anyone who tried to tell her otherwise. Howe's boast in that tavern might not have reflected his deepest feeling. A part of him might have honestly cared for the young woman.

The Comte de Maistre, his adjutant, and several soldiers made their way to the Comtesse de Joinville's house on the road to France. The count had asked Madame Cartier if she wished to join them. Her note-taking was far superior to his adjutant's. But she had declined on this occasion, pointing out that her assistance wasn't really essential. The countess spoke excellent French. Moreover, Madame Cartier and she were at odds. Their personal enmity might complicate the conversation to no purpose.

At the door the count sighed. From what he already knew, the countess would be the most challenging of the persons he would interview, but also the most likely suspect. She had actually once attacked the captain with a knife.

She made them wait for half an hour before coming to the parlour, wearing a thin pink silk housedress. And little else, as the count noticed. Her speech was slurred from drinking.

'I suppose you've come to talk about the death of my former friend Captain Howe. You will have noticed that I'm not in mourning garb.' She flounced her pink dress. 'He and I had just come to a parting of the ways. His things are outside, waiting to be moved to his cottage.'

'My men will load them into our wagon and take them to my office in the city, Comtesse.' He took a seat, she sat facing him. The adjutant sat off to one side with pad and pencil. The count remained silent, gazing at the countess.

'Well, what do you need to know?' she asked, annoyed.

'I already know that you often quarrelled and that you recently attacked him with a knife. You also publicly reproached him yesterday afternoon. What I must know now is where were you between midnight and two o'clock this morning?'

'I was drinking wine, playing cards, and dancing in the villa.'

'All the time?'

'I stepped out on the terrace for air occasionally.'

'Did you venture out any further?'

'If you must know, sir, I went out into the ruins to relieve myself.'

'That's all I need to know at present, Madame la Comtesse. You will remain in this room in the custody of my adjutant, while my men and I search your house and question your servants.' He left the room under a hail of protest and with a sympathetic thought for his adjutant.

The countess had gone to the ball as Columbine, wearing a fancy white silk gown and black mask. With help from a servant, the count found the gown hidden in a trunk. In her befuddled condition the countess had not had an opportunity or the wits to clean the bloodstains on the sleeves.

Back in the parlour, the count held the gown for her to see. 'How do you account for this, madame?'

Her hands flew to her mouth. She rose from the chair and took a step forward, staring at the blood-soaked garment. 'He was dying when I got there. Pity overcame me. I embraced him, told him I loved him after all, and wanted him to live. He died in my arms. I laid him on his side, as if he were asleep, and left.'

'Why didn't you raise an alarm?'

She pointed to the gown. 'Everyone would think I did it – especially after our many quarrels. So I slipped away from the villa and came directly home.'

The count handed the gown to one of his men. 'Take this to my office, together with the rest of the material we have gathered.'

'You do believe me, don't you, Monsieur le Comte?'

He read desperation in her eyes. 'I consider you the chief suspect in the death of Captain Howe. While I continue the investigation, I shall hold you here under guard. You shall not leave this house. The French border is too close to leave you at liberty. Out of respect for your rank, I'll spare you the discomfort of our prison.'

'Oh, my God!' She sank unconscious to the floor.

The Comte de Maistre paced the floor of his apartment in the royal palace, preparing himself for the visit of his son. The count stopped at the window. The sun had set, turning the evening sea into dark ink. It was calm, but he was not.

He thought of himself as a patient man, a virtue he had learned over many years of difficult service in the royal government. The provocations to lash out at foolish courtiers and bureaucrats were as nothing compared to the aggravations he experienced raising his son Mario. The Comtesse de Maistre had died when the boy was very young, leaving her husband unprepared, as well as temperamentally unsuited, to the role of sole parent. He could not bring himself to marry again. So he satisfied his emotional and sexual needs with a series of congenial mistresses, all of whom disliked or detested the boy. His care fell to a parallel series of inept, indifferent governesses.

Mario was now a twenty-year-old young man, hopelessly spoiled. From his mother he inherited his thick black wavy hair and long black eyelashes, his clear complexion and fine-featured face, his supple, well-formed body. To this excellent natural endowment, he added a certain grace and charm. Silly young women swooned when he approached them.

Unfortunately, he had also become sly and treacherous, vain, obstinate, and rebellious – traits that seemed to become more and more pronounced as he grew older.

His most recent vice was gambling. The modest allowance that his father gave him was usually spent in a few hours at cards or dice. His companions lent large sums to him in the expectation that his father would pay. And he did pay for a while. Then, last week, after repeated warnings, he declared he would no longer honour his son's debts. Mario nonetheless continued stubbornly to gamble for high stakes and lost more than he won.

In the public confrontation with Captain Howe, Mario was reduced to a blubbering, petulant child. De Maistre refused to pay the debt to Howe and ordered Mario confined to home over the festival weekend. On Sunday, the young man slipped out, joined the Banquet of Reproaches, moved on to the ball at the villa, and hadn't been seen since. Finally, de Maistre sent his adjutant to find Mario and bring him home – by force if necessary. An hour ago, the adjutant reported having discovered Mario together with a woman in the city and asked for additional men – Mario would not come willingly. De Maistre sent soldiers in civilian dress. They should return with Mario at any minute.

Loud voices out in the hall broke the late evening quiet. De Maistre's heart began to pound. He dreaded facing his son. The door opened and Mario was literally thrown into the room. Their faces red with exertion, the adjutant and two soldiers stood guard at the door. Dishevelled, his face slightly bruised, Mario struggled to his feet, avoiding his father's eyes.

'Sit down, son, I must put serious questions to you.'

Mario glared at his father but said nothing and took a seat.

'Where were you in the early hours of this morning?'

'At the ball in the villa until shortly after midnight.'

'Contrary to my orders, but I have a more serious matter on my mind. Do you know what happened there?'

'I suppose you're referring to the death of Captain Howe. I didn't kill him, if that's what you think.'

'Did you go into the old Roman ruins?'

'No, I left Cimiez and returned to the city.'

'Any witnesses?'

'Why? Do I need any?'

De Maistre didn't answer.

'Gabriella will vouch for me.'

'Do you mean the young widow Gabriella Rossi, your fair lady?' His voice had a touch of sarcasm.

'Yes, my friend Gabriella. I went to her house on the road to France.'

'Where is the costume that you wore at the ball?'

'At her house.'

'I will check it tomorrow. For the time being, you will remain under guard in your rooms in the palace. I dearly hope you have told me the truth.'

Twelve

The Chief Suspects

Tuesday, 12 February

Anne rose at dawn, shuffled barefooted to the open window. Breathing deeply, she stared out at a hazy blue sky. In her mind's eye she saw the Roman arena and the fallen figure of Captain Howe. The gaping wound in his throat drew her attention. She couldn't imagine why. Then it slowly dawned on her. The knife had entered by the right side. Therefore, Howe's assailant struck with his left hand.

Anne tried to recall who among the guests at the ball were left-handed, but when she reflected further, she realized that some right-handed people use their left hand for certain tasks, so she gave up that line of speculation as unpromising. The count might shed light on the question. Yesterday afternoon, his men had moved the victim's body from the villa to the city morgue for examination. He would return to the villa today with a report.

She went to her table and read again the letter to Paul that she had begun on Sunday and finished last night, informing him of Howe's murder and the count's investigation. Unable to think of any more news, she added a loving greeting, sealed the letter, and carried it downstairs. In the kitchen she entrusted the letter to Angelo, the cook's sixteen-year-old son, to take it to Monsieur Seurre, the French Consul, for dispatch to Marseille this morning.

While Anne was in the kitchen, she learned from a maid that Janice was up, moving around in her room. Anne saw an opportunity. She prepared a breakfast tray and took it to the young woman. She seemed alert, but her face was wan, and her eyes red from weeping. She still needed more time to grieve.

Anne tried a gentle approach. 'Can you remember if the captain indicated during the ball that he would meet someone in the arena in the early hours of the morning?'

Janice stared into her cup as if she hadn't heard the question. Finally, her hand began to tremble. She carefully put the cup down and wept. The effort to recall Captain Howe on that fateful night was still too painful.

When she grew calmer, she said, 'I had asked him if we could take a walk together among the ruins. I wanted to embrace him, kiss him good night. He said he had to meet someone out there. He waved in the direction of the arena, said he'd come back to me in the villa. I waited but he never came. I didn't know what to do. It hurt terribly to imagine that he had just forgotten me. I thought of going to the arena alone in the dark. But what if I were to find him with another woman. Maybe the countess. Finally, I just went to bed.'

She looked up at Anne, tears pouring from her eyes. Anne rose, put her arms around the young woman, and comforted her. 'We'll talk again another time.'

Anne joined Beverly at the breakfast table in her room. She appeared to have recovered from the count's distressing intrusion into her life. But Anne feared that there would be more such revelations to come. 'I'll just sit with you,' Anne said. 'Janice and I ate together earlier.'

95

'How is she?'

'Grieving.'

'How *could* she get involved with that man!'

Anne was sorely tempted to remind Beverly that she had made the same mistake years ago. Instead, she asked about Grimshaw.

'He came to us shortly after Mr Parker leased the villa three years ago. Before hiring him, we spoke to persons who knew him, both in England and abroad. They spoke highly of him. Previous employers gave him good references. He had worked many years in southern France and Italy as a guide and an archaeologist, knows the languages and cultures very well. When we met him, he made a favourable impression.'

'His character?'

'He's diligent, efficient, reserved. Mr Parker trusts him with the affairs of the villa – supervising the servants, maintaining the property, keeping accounts, and so forth.' She tilted her head quizzically. 'Are you wondering about his interest in Janice?'

Anne nodded. 'He is so much older than she. In contrast to Captain Howe, Grimshaw doesn't sign and can hardly communicate with her.'

'Words aren't always necessary between men and women,' Beverly remarked drily. 'Janice's beauty and innocence may attract him, as they would any normal man. But his interest in her is paternal and chivalric. He disliked, perhaps hated, Captain Howe for exploiting her youthful naivety and deafness. I've often seen Jack take the side of the poor, the unfortunate, the helpless. Have you noticed the concern he shows for the men he hires? Pays them well, praises their work when he can, never berates or demeans them.'

'I'll grant that you know him better than I.' Anne noticed that Beverly called him by his familiar name. 'I could be wrong, but the fierce passion in his defence of Janice disturbs me. It seems unhealthy, even dangerous.'

'Oh, really?' Beverly frowned. 'You might have a different opinion, were you to know his personal history as I do.' She took a few moments to finish her coffee and pat her lips dry. 'You see, Jack is a widower. His wife died giving birth to a baby girl. She grew up to be a beautiful young woman. When she was a little older than Janice, a soldier of easy virtue and

96

charming manner won her heart, made her pregnant. Then he left with his regiment and disappeared.'

Beverly's voice had wavered. She looked away.

Anne inclined her head in an encouraging gesture.

Finally, Beverly shook off the emotion and spoke in measured words, 'Jack's daughter hung herself from a rafter in the stable.'

'The poor woman, how ghastly!' Anne recalled her young friend Sylvie's similar experience, though Paul and Georges had saved her in the last moment. 'And how did Grimshaw react?'

'He was the one who found her. You can imagine the shock. I doubt that he has ever fully recovered. He surely sees his daughter in Janice and feels he must protect her. He's convinced that Captain Howe didn't really love Janice and would have exploited her.'

'Then could Grimshaw have killed the captain?'

Beverly slowly took the napkin from her lap and carefully folded it. 'No,' she said emphatically. 'I don't think he could.'

Anne didn't challenge her friend's statement. But in the light of Grimshaw's personal tragedy, she was inclined to suspect otherwise. As she was leaving, she had an afterthought. 'Do you know the name of the man who betrayed Grimshaw's daughter?'

'No, I don't. I've asked. But he won't say. Too painful. Perhaps he's not sure. His daughter had met the villain secretly. The note she left didn't identify him.'

Anne took Beverly's breakfast tray downstairs to the kitchen and lingered there awhile. She felt comfortable in kitchens, especially if the cooks were good-natured. That was the case with Philippa, a short, stout Niçoise, married to the gardener. She and Anne often had tea together. Occasionally Anne would bring along a pair of hand puppets for a quarter-hour of Punch and Judy. Philippa's bright black eyes would dance with pleasure.

'Have they found out who killed Captain Howe?' the cook asked.

'No, it's too early,' Anne replied.

'I hope they don't blame Mr Grimshaw, there having been hard feelings between them.'

'I'm sure that the Comte de Maistre will think very carefully before he blames anyone.' Anne pretended to be puzzled. 'By the way, why did Mr Grimshaw resent the captain so much?'

Philippa lowered her voice to speak in confidence. 'It had to do with Miss Janice, of course. But there was also a quarrel about one of Mr Grimshaw's excavations. The captain looked like he'd been insulted. I asked Mr Grimshaw what he had said. He replied that he told the captain to mind his own business.'

Later that morning, the Comte de Maistre came to the villa with his adjutant to question the servants again, a routine procedure, he told Anne. Afterward he met with her in Parker's study and they discussed Howe's murder. The weapon was still a secret. By noon yesterday it had been cleaned and replaced on the wall of the study. Grimshaw was the only person who might have noticed its absence during the morning. But he had no reason to enter the study, and he hadn't said anything. No one else seemed to have noticed either.

Prompted by her conversation with Janice, Anne wondered aloud, 'Why did Howe and his killer meet in the arena? They could have found privacy elsewhere outside the villa.'

'Olive groves shield the arena from the villa. Whatever happened couldn't be seen or heard. It's also an appropriate place for an attack with a knife, as it was in ancient times.'

'That has crossed my mind. A duel could have appealed to both Howe and Grimshaw.'

De Maistre shook his head. 'There was no duel. The killer clearly took Howe by surprise. He was a soldier, strong and skilled in the use of weapons. A duel with him would have left evidence of a violent struggle. No, someone he knew assassinated him with a single blow of the knife.'

'Can you say whether the blow was delivered by the killer's right or left hand?'

'The surgeon who examined the wound is certain that the killer faced the victim and struck with the left hand. However, all of the possible suspects are right-handed. One of them must be nimble with the left hand as well.'

'Have you narrowed your search for suspects?' asked Anne.

'Yes,' the count replied. 'The strongest evidence points to the Comtesse de Joinville. She had threatened Howe and had attacked him before with a knife. Blood was found on her gown. Grimshaw is also suspect. He and Howe quarrelled violently over Miss Parker and nearly came to blows at the door to Howe's cottage.' The count paused. 'Then there's my prodigal son.'

With a pained expression the count described his encounter the previous night with Mario. 'My men have already searched the house of his friend Gabriella Rossi, a young widow. His costume had been freshly laundered, with no traces of blood. They questioned Rossi, who supported Mario's story. He had come to her at about twelve thirty in the morning. His costume wasn't bloody, she claimed. She had it laundered because on the way to her house he had slipped and fallen into a pile of mule dung.'

A likely tale, Anne thought, but it would serve as an alibi.

The count seemed relieved but still apprehensive. 'Because of the countess's rank and the Baron de Breteuil's concern for her welfare, I wish to accommodate her needs as much as possible. Would you visit her to ensure that she is well cared for? If you discover a problem, please suggest a remedy. As I'm sure you realize, the countess is devoted to Bacchus and sometimes fails to look after herself. You could ask if she would like assistance from the French Consul, Monsieur Seurre.'

Well! Anne thought. De Maistre fears that were Louise to appear ill-treated or suffer from neglect the winter visitors would think badly of Nice. And the royal government in Turin would blame him.

What would Paul advise her to do? She conjured him up in her imagination. He would say, 'Don't join de Maistre's band of informers. But be independent and helpful to Louise where you can.'

'Sir,' Anne said evenly, 'the countess and I are less than good friends, but I'll visit her this afternoon and recommend the services of the French Consul.'

In the early afternoon, Anne went to the Comtesse de Joinville's house with a feeling of trepidation. She wasn't sure how she would be received. A pair of bored uniformed guards stood at the door. They read her permit from de Maistre and admitted her.

Louise met Anne with a cool, distant expression. Momentarily at least, she seemed calm and rational, probably mindful of her precarious situation. In a simple housecoat and without makeup, she looked years older than her age. Still she carried herself erect, unbowed.

After a cup of tea and a few minutes of polite conversation, Anne felt that Louise was not displeased with the visit and was willing to discuss more serious matters. She had had several hours to realize that she was in serious danger of being charged and convicted of murder. And this was happening in a foreign country where her noble rank and social connections might mitigate her confinement but could not save her from imprisonment.

'Is there anyway I can help you?' Anne asked. 'I could contact the French Consul.'

'There's nothing he can do for me. His job is to help bankrupt wine merchants, wayward sailors, and the like.'

'But if you wished to write a message, I could send it to Paul at Marseille and he could pass it on to the Baron de Breteuil.'

'That might be helpful. I'll write something before you leave.' Louise gazed at Anne with an expression akin to gratitude. For the first time that Anne could remember, Louise appeared to drop the hauteur so typical of her and think of Anne as an equal. She felt emboldened to probe.

'What can you tell me about Captain Howe's relationship with Grimshaw?' Anne watched Louise carefully for any sign of displeasure.

Louise didn't balk. Her expression became reflective. 'They met at Grimshaw's excavation in the ruins and quarrelled. The captain wanted to look for ancient coins and trinkets, hoping to keep what he found. Grimshaw ordered him out of the site, claimed that the captain was interfering with his work. And furthermore, he said, everything of value discovered on the estate belonged to Mr Parker.'

'Did the captain ever show an interest in Mithras?' Anne realized that Louise was an educated woman and had probably taught Howe a thing or two.

Louise raised an eyebrow at the question but replied, 'Yes,

he knew who Mithras was. Though Howe wasn't a cultured man, he was intelligent. As soon as he became curious about Mithras, he spent hours in Mr Parker's study reading Plutarch and other ancient writers, as well as the Comte de Caylus.' For Anne's benefit, she quickly added, 'Caylus is a fairly recent expert on Roman remains in this part of the world. We also visited Arles, Nîmes, and other Roman sites in Provence.'

'How do you account for the captain's interest in Mithras?'

She smiled through thin, pressed lips. Regret shone in her eyes. 'Howe was a charming, often lovable man. But with him it was always money that came first. He never had enough, thanks to bad luck in gambling. Somehow he learned that Grimshaw had secretly sold a third-century gold Mithras medallion to a British collector. Howe guessed that it had come from a treasure that Grimshaw must have discovered in the ruins near the villa and was concealing from Mr Parker. Howe tried but couldn't find the site. So he threatened to go to Parker with his suspicion. Grimshaw paid Howe more than once – I don't know how much – to keep him quiet.'

Anne thought, now there's a motive that could tempt Jack Grimshaw to murder.

Late in the afternoon a letter came from Paul, dated Marseille, Sunday evening, 10 February. Anne took it to her room, sat at her table, and began reading. He had received with great interest her account on the seventh concerning the mounting controversy around Captain Howe. Paul could not know that it had culminated in Howe's violent death.

Georges Charpentier had joined Paul. Together they were working on the case of the escaped convict Jean Lebrun. He could be dead or hiding in southern France or the County of Nice. Grimshaw had stopped at the Toulon naval prison en route to Marseille and had shown unusual interest in Lebrun. Paul didn't know what that might mean, but he was investigating Grimshaw's movements in Marseille.

Paul closed with an affectionate adieu.

Anne laid the letter on her table and allowed her mind to wander. It stopped at Grimshaw: a man of shadows, reticent, intense, emotionally scarred by the tragic death of his daughter. His relationship to the escaped convict appeared to go beyond mere curiosity. Anne recalled the commandant's fruitless search of the villa almost three weeks ago, confident in the credibility of his informant. Who could better have hid Lebrun then warned him of de Maistre's search, than Grimshaw? But why would he take such a risk? Beverly praised his concern for the poor and unfortunate. Could that concern have also embraced an escaped convict?

Thirteen

A Dubious Alibi

Wednesday, 13 February

Anne stood at the window in Janice's room. They had just finished breakfast and a brief conversation. With the resilience of youth, Janice was recovering well from the shock of the captain's death. At least on the surface. Deeper, Anne couldn't see. Part of the young woman's spirit would heal slowly, if ever. Now, anger had begun to appear.

'Whoever killed Jeremy is a beast,' she signed vehemently. 'I hope you find him soon. He must pay dearly. If he hangs, I shall be there.'

Anne took note of her assumption that the killer was a man, almost certainly Grimshaw. This wasn't the time to argue with her. 'I'll leave you now, Janice, pleased to notice that your health is mending.'

On an impulse Anne glanced out the window. The figure of a man in the courtyard below caught her eye. His manner seemed furtive. She studied him. It was Grimshaw walking northward into a large grove of olive trees, carrying a full sack over his shoulder. She wondered why he went there rather than to the excavation south of the villa.

'Is anything the matter?' Janice asked.

'No, just Grimshaw looking after the estate. I was surprised to see him just as we were talking about him.'

But Paul's reference to Grimshaw's suspicious behaviour in Toulon was still fresh in Anne's mind. She hurried downstairs into Parker's study, sat by a window facing the olive grove, and pretended to read a book. A half-hour later Grimshaw reappeared in the same furtive manner. The sack was still on his shoulder, but it appeared empty. He disappeared around the villa on his way to the excavation.

Her curiosity aroused, Anne dressed for a walk and entered the grove following Grimshaw's likely trail. In five minutes she came to a small clearing at the end of the grove. Beyond the clearing, a desolate slope rose slowly, scarred by rocky outcroppings among dense patches of bramble and stunted trees. Several olive trees had been cut down to make the clearing and lay in pieces off to one side near large piles of dirt. Someone had dug out of the beginning of the slope an area about ten feet long and three feet wide and built a low shed at the far end. Its door was locked.

'Can I help you, madame?'

Anne nearly jumped out of her skin.

Behind her stood a man with an axe, Grimshaw's assistant. 'Sorry to startle you. I've come for wood for the kitchen.'

'I didn't hear you. Next time whistle. I was taking a walk and stumbled upon this excavation. Perhaps you can explain it to me.'

'Surely.' He rested the axe on the ground. 'A few months ago, we searched here for signs of Mithras. Mr Grimshaw had earlier found a monument to Mercury, who is sometimes associated with Mithras. So we cleared this area and explored in different directions. Found a chamber with a few Mercury medallions but nothing we could connect directly to Mithras. We built this shed over the chamber to protect it.'

Anne examined the lock.

'Mr Grimshaw keeps the key, madame.'

'Is he planning to resume work soon? He was here less than an hour ago.'

The man appeared puzzled, shrugged. 'He hasn't told me.'

Then, Anne wondered, what was he doing in this place? She surveyed the hillside beyond. Perhaps he went up there. To explore the hillside, however, was a task for another day. Now she had business in the city.

At midmorning Anne went to de Maistre's office, a large, tastefully furnished room located in the King of Sardinia's palace in the old town. On an upper floor above the neighbouring red-tile roofs, his office commanded a spectacular view of the sea.

With a courtly bow, he made her feel welcome.

She in turn reassured him that Louise, at least for the present, was taking proper care of herself and didn't need help from the French Consul. 'Between Grimshaw and Howe,' Anne continued, 'there were more than competing claims over Miss Parker. Grimshaw may have had a treasure that Howe coveted.' Anne reported on the gold Mithraic medallion and Howe's extortion of money from Grimshaw. It was premature, she thought, to mention Grimshaw's interest in the olive grove and the hillside beyond.

'Before you came, madame, I was about to arrest and imprison the Comtesse de Joinville in preparation for a trial before the Senate of Nice. But I had better wait. In view of what you've said, I need to look more closely at Mr Grimshaw's possible additional motive to kill the captain, extortion. I shall check on Mr Grimshaw's selling of antiquities in Nice, Turin, and other places in northern Italy that he sometimes visits.

'And, would you, madame, enlist your husband in a similar investigation of Grimshaw in Marseille? He might sell gold under cover of sales of much less valuable antiquities. We must check with financial houses to see if he is building up unusually large savings or investing in property.'

Anne agreed to pass his request on to Paul. As she left the count's office, she reflected on the count's eagerness to pursue another potential suspect, Grimshaw, as if a welcome distraction from his own son's possible complicity in Howe's murder. To Anne's mind, Mario was a serious suspect with the means, motive, and opportunity to kill Captain Howe. She was concerned that the count appeared too much inclined to accept his son's alibi and look elsewhere for the killer, especially in Louise's direction.

Anne spent the afternoon with Dr McKenzie at his home, discussing Mario's friend Gabriella Rossi. The alibi she had given him was too convenient and needed to be tested. As a semi-permanent resident of Nice, McKenzie knew Madame Rossi well and rented his house from her.

'Let's walk to the city and promenade on the seaside terrace,'

McKenzie suggested, offering Anne his arm. 'The widow Rossi will be there now.' The early afternoon was often the most pleasant time of the day in the month of February. The temperature was mild, the wind light. The people of Nice flocked to the terrace to regard each other and to gossip.

'There she is,' he said, nodding toward a shapely olive-skinned strong-featured woman of Anne's age. She wore a colourful silk gown in the local style and her thick black hair was tied back in a chignon. She walked arm in arm with Mario, proud as a peacock in a buff silk suit.

'A handsome pair,' Anne observed.

'But she's in no hurry to marry again,' the doctor added, 'she enjoys being her own mistress.' When Gabriella and her partner were out of earshot, McKenzie explained that she was a wealthy merchant's daughter, an educated woman, spoke French and Italian, understood English but spoke it with a heavy accent. From her house on the road to France, she managed her deceased husband's business. Aided by a handyman and his wife, a young maid, and a few servants, she maintained and rented or leased dozens of rooms and houses to the winter visitors.

'What do you know about her relations with Mario?' Anne asked.

'Gabriella regards me as a friend,' McKenzie replied, 'and speaks openly to me about Mario. When she first met him, she thought he could help her. He talked as if he could, and he was well connected and personable. But she quickly learned that he couldn't be trusted with any important responsibility. She never lent money to him and kept him out of her business, but gave him small coins for running errands.'

'Doesn't he resent being treated like a child?'

'In a sense, he still is a child. She's gentle with him, gives him the mothering he's never had. And he enjoys being her favourite escort, or *cicisbeo*, as they say here. You will see him with her on the terrace, at the Maccarani Theatre, or in the markets.'

'She's several years older than him. Is that a problem?'

'Not that I can see. They appear suited to each other.'

Anne and the doctor had followed Gabriella and Mario into the market, where she caressed him fondly on the cheek. Anne realized that Gabriella would take Mario's side in his quarrel with Howe, who had probably cheated the young man at cards.

'Putting sentiment aside,' McKenzie continued, 'their relationship also has a practical aspect. Gabriella believes correctly that the Comte de Maistre values her stabilizing influence over the young man. She's the only person who can reason with him.'

'Then if Mario had killed Howe, he would have fled to Gabriella, told her what had happened, and asked for help. Gabriella would have concluded that the count wanted her to give his son an alibi if at all possible. So she would vouch for him and put the count in her debt. There might come a time when she would need the count's favour.'

'Exactly. Would you like to meet her?' McKenzie asked.

'Yes, indeed,' Anne replied. 'I want to look at that alibi more closely.'

They approached Gabriella and Mario. The doctor made the introductions.

'Pleased to meet you, Madame Cartier. Mario has told me about you. How unusual! A woman who investigates crime.'

'My husband is responsible for law and order in the area around Paris. On occasion, I've been helpful to him. By the way, I understand that you arrange housing for the winter visitors, not an easy task. You must be a shrewd, tactful, and accomplished diplomat. I would imagine that few women in Nice have the skill or the opportunity to conduct such a business.'

Gabriella smiled, her black eyes sparkled with amusement. 'I think I would enjoy doing business with you, Madame Cartier.'

'Then may I call upon you, Madame Rossi?'

'By all means, any time.'

As the team of horses plodded up the steep hill to Cimiez, the doctor remarked, 'A few years ago I'd have chosen to walk this road. Now I must conserve my energy.'

Anne studied McKenzie. For his age, about seventy, he looked trim and fit, but even moderate exertion brought a flush of bright pink to his face and a shortness of breath. So Anne had proposed that they ride in a carriage to the villa. She wanted the doctor to examine Beverly and Janice.

In the course of conversation McKenzie turned to Anne

with a puzzled expression. 'While you and Gabriella were chatting, I observed Mario. He appeared remarkably anxious, for good reason I'd say.' Anne had given the doctor a brief account of events at the villa.

'He's an excitable young man,' Anne remarked. 'My presence reminded him of Howe's murder and the ongoing investigation. He's a suspect with a dubious alibi.'

While the carriage rattled on, Anne pondered Mario's alibi and recognized its potential weakness. She asked the doctor, 'Can you tell me anything about Gabriella's maid?'

'Why does she interest you?'

'Howe's death was bloody. Some blood must have soiled the killer's clothes. I believe the maid cleaned Mario's costume almost as soon as he arrived at Gabriella's house.'

'I see what you are getting at. Catherine's her name and she's a local girl, uneducated but intelligent. To make her more useful, Gabriella has taught her to read a little, to sign her name, and to understand simple English. She cleans, cooks, shops, and helps look after the rental houses. She seems to get along with Gabriella, but I've noticed that she doesn't like Mario. Sneers at him behind his back. I don't know why.'

'And the handyman?'

'Carlo. He and his wife also watch the gate to the courtyard. At least one of them should have seen Mario return from the villa.'

'That's odd,' Anne remarked. 'Why hasn't the Comte de Maistre mentioned them? He has questioned everyone else who could have a connection to Howe's murder.'

A light supper was about to be served as Anne and the doctor arrived at the villa.

'Please join us,' Beverly said eagerly and seated the doctor facing her at a small round dining table. The prospect of dining alone with Janice must have seemed unappetizing, thought Anne.

Doctor McKenzie readily accepted the invitation. He and Beverly were friends. Janice gave him a polite smile but otherwise seemed indifferent.

Anne took a seat facing her. 'How are you feeling this evening, Janice?'

'Much better, thank you,' she replied with fair articulation.

'I followed a normal routine today and felt no ill effects.' Her face had recovered its lovely creamy colour. She had overcome the lassitude that followed Howe's murder and had regained her previous energy and grace.

Conversation circled around the captain's death and the subsequent investigation. Janice's questions were particularly insistent and she reacted sceptically to Anne's cautious replies. There was no solid evidence, no significant development to report. It seemed unwise to engage in speculation.

But Janice was not to be deterred. 'Neither Mario nor the Comtesse de Joinville could have killed Jeremy. She's not strong enough and he's not clever enough to have taken him by surprise and stabbed him. Only one man could have done it and he is . . .'

Anne reproached her. 'The Comte de Maistre insists that we keep the manner of his death a secret. It's a way to trap the killer.'

Janice made a dismissive gesture. 'Why bother with secrets? I know who killed Jeremy.' She glanced from person to person. 'His name is Grimshaw, and he shall be punished.' Janice's throat tightened, and her words became nearly inaudible. But Anne heard her add, 'I'll see to that.'

Neither McKenzie nor Beverly could hear the last few words and looked to Anne for their meaning. She hesitated, then repeated them.

Beverly seemed taken aback, then shrugged her shoulders and led the conversation elsewhere.

Anne and McKenzie exchanged quick glances: Janice meant what she said.

That evening Anne wrote to Paul in Marseille. She had earlier sent him a note, informing him of Howe's murder. Now she described Louise's precarious situation as the prime suspect, and the need to check on Grimshaw's financial dealings. They might reveal a motive for killing the captain. If Grimshaw were to become a prime suspect, he would draw the count's attention away from Louise.

At the end she added:

Janice's mental condition is taking a worrisome turn.
She has recovered from the initial shock, but anger has

*set in and grows rapidly stronger. She blames Grimshaw
and seeks revenge. I'll watch her closely.*

Anne concluded with a wish for his speedy return, closed the
letter with a kiss and a prayer, and sealed it. A courier would
set off with it early tomorrow morning.

For almost an hour, she lay sleepless in bed, her mind busy
with the complex threads of the investigation. Her feeling
grew that she and the count were beginning to work at cross-
purposes. She aimed at a fair hearing for the Comtesse de
Joinville; he wanted to divert attention from his son Mario.
A conflict seemed inevitable. Finally, she tired and fell asleep.

Fourteen

A Countess in Chains

Thursday, 14 February

An hour after dawn, Anne went for a long walk through the
estate. Fresh air and brisk exercise would help bring order to
her thoughts. They came into focus on Grimshaw and his role
at the villa. She was struck by how quickly he had replaced
Mr Parker as master of the place. And as Beverly's partner
as well, judging from the signs of familiarity between them,
such as the use of their Christian names.

Anne followed a path into the orchard, where she picked
an orange. The fruit was fully ripe, sweet, and juicy – unlike
the pale, sour specimens that pedlars sold outside London
theatres. She recalled with fondness her stepfather, Antoine
Dubois, at the Vauxhall, gleefully dodging oranges thrown
by a disgruntled audience. Ardently French, Antoine had
deliberately insulted their witless patriotic British sentiments.

She was returning to the terrace, plotting the course of her
day, when she noticed Grimshaw among the ancient ruins,
together with an assistant, the man who had come upon her
yesterday in the olive grove.

The two men exchanged a few words, then Grimshaw

walked up to the terrace, an inscrutable expression on his weathered face.

'My man tells me that you've been to our Mithras excavation. If you wish, I'll show it to you, let's say, an hour from now.'

'Agreed, Mr Grimshaw, gladly. In an hour.' This excursion had not been in her plans, but she felt that she should seize the opportunity to know Grimshaw better.

An hour later, they were walking into the olive grove. 'Allow me to say, Madame Cartier, that you amaze me. None of the other female visitors, and only a few of the males, such as Mr Parker and Dr McKenzie, show any interest in the antiquity of this place.'

'I confess, Mr Grimshaw, that I find no pleasure in playing at cards or gambling, and I dislike gossip and idle conversation. But I do enjoy solving a mystery. That's what you do here, uncover the truth about this ancient Roman city and its people.'

When they reached the shed on the edge of the clearing, Grimshaw opened the door with his key. The shed covered a low, narrow dark passage that inclined into the slope. Grimshaw lit a lantern. 'I'll go first and lead you. Are you willing?'

Anne was beginning to wonder whether she had been wise. Although Grimshaw and she had lived under the same roof for almost three months, he was still a largely unknown character. She screwed up her courage and said, 'Yes, thank you. I believe I can manage.' She had at least dressed properly for the occasion in a plain brown light woollen dress and sturdy shoes.

She hitched up her skirt and walked through the passage into a small rectangular chamber. Its walls were constructed of evenly cut and fitted stones. Its ceiling was a low stone barrel vault. Two slender columns at the far end were the only decoration.

'I believe this was once a shrine to Mercury,' Grimshaw explained. 'A friendly hand closed it at the time the Roman Empire became Christian. We found a few coins from the fourth century. Any precious objects had been removed, including the slabs of polychrome marble that hung on these walls. When Cemenelum was abandoned, the chapel was simply forgotten.'

110

Anne walked to the far end of the room. 'Did you look behind this wall?'

'No, I believe there's nothing but rock and dirt on the other side. The wall is solid, as you can see. I have more promising work in the ruins south of the villa to keep me occupied for years. But if I were to run out of projects, I could return here. The shed over the passage protects the site.'

It was an eerie experience to be with Grimshaw in this room, so much like a burial chamber. His lantern flickered, casting weird shadows on the walls. The air was still and clammy. His manner was courteous, scarcely threatening. But Anne sensed a constraint in the way he talked and moved about. He wasn't entirely comfortable with her. That was understandable, given conventional attitudes concerning women being alone with men. Or was he anxious that she might discover a secret?

'Are you pleased with what you've learned?' he asked casually, when they returned to the surface.

'Yes, I am, and I'd like to know more.' What was behind that far wall? she wondered. Only dirt? Really?

A hint of apprehension flit across his face. He had read her mind.

At midmorning Anne rode a mule down the hill to Dr McKenzie's house on the road to France. 'I have a question,' she said when he opened the door. 'Could you throw light on a Roman building that I've just seen?'

McKenzie smiled broadly. 'Please come in, Madame Cartier. I'll do my best.' He led her to a parlour and seated her. 'Tell me about the building.'

She described her visit with Grimshaw to Mercury's chapel north of the villa. 'Could the chapel be related to the cult of Mithras?'

He warmed to the topic. 'On my trips to Italy, I visited several sanctuaries dedicated to Mithras. The chamber that Grimshaw showed you resembles a typical entrance hall. I can't account for the solid wall at the far end. Later in the day, I'll consult my books and travel journals. In the meantime, let's have tea.'

While waiting for the tea, Anne asked, 'By the way, does your house need any repair?'

He smiled, his forehead creased in good-natured puzzlement. 'Of course, there are little things that I save for a day when I haven't anything else to do, which is never. Why do you ask?'

'I'd like you to entice Gabriella's handyman, called Carlo, to this house. I need to question him in a place free from de Maistre's spies. He should be willing to come. This is, after all, one of Gabriella's houses and he should keep it in good condition. If necessary, offer him a little extra money.'

'Who is going to pay Carlo?' asked the canny Scottish doctor, as he poured tea for Anne.

'The Comtesse de Joinville. She should bear the cost of her own defence. Since Captain Howe no longer steals from her purse, she can afford to pay.'

'I fear that you will have to struggle to get the money from her. Meanwhile, I'll keep the handyman busy, and treat him well.'

'Good. He may tell us the truth about Mario's return to the city on the night of Howe's murder. Then we'll find it easier to question Gabriella's maid.'

'How shall we know that we've reached the truth?'

'If the maid's testimony agrees with Carlo's. At least that's enough for most magistrates. Or, so my husband tells me.'

The creases in McKenzie's forehead grew deeper. 'Do you really think Carlo would say anything to incriminate Mario?'

'My friend and mentor, Georges Charpentier, claims that every man has a weak side. I must find Carlo's.'

McKenzie finished his tea and laid down his cup with a flourish. 'Then, by all means, I'll have a word with him.'

'And I'll run an errand in the city and return in a couple of hours.'

With a heightened sense of adventure, Dr McKenzie set out for Gabriella's house, only a few steps away in the direction of the older part of the city. At noon, the road was full of carts, sedan chairs, donkeys, and foot traffic. Dressed in a plain brown woollen suit, McKenzie took up a position in the shade of a building across the street from Madame Rossi's house. The handyman's wife, a thin, sharp-eyed shrew, was at the gate, opening and closing it for a steady stream of visitors.

When the woman was free, McKenzie approached her. 'They tell me that your husband can fix almost anything. I know he's busy, but if he can find the time, would he do some extra work on a house that I rent from your mistress? I'll pay good money for him.' Madame Cartier had mentioned a figure above the going rate.

The woman hesitated, pondering the offer. Her husband might prefer to rest in his free time, or Gabriella might not approve of him working on the side for extra money. But the prospect of money from one of the rich winter visitors outweighed every other consideration.

'Yes,' the woman replied, 'I'll send him this evening.'

McKenzie gave her his address and left, after pressing a small coin into the palm of her hand.

When Anne returned to McKenzie's house from her errand in the city, she found the doctor at a table in his study. He explained the arrangements he had made with Carlo the handyman.

'Good,' she said. 'Now what have you found for me about the cult of Mithras?'

'I've done some research.' He pointed to a sheet of paper before him. 'From my Roman travel journals, I've drawn the plan of a typical Mithraeum or sanctuary. It would fit into the site by the olive grove.' He laid the plan before her.

'The entrance hall, similar to the Mercury chapel, is at the foot of a gradual rise of land.' He pointed to the plan. 'Between the two columns at the far end there's an opening to a couple of stairs going down to a vestibule. Straight ahead, another short stairway descends to the hall where worshippers gathered. Stone benches line the side walls. At the end of the sanctuary in the apse, there's a raised platform for the display of sacred images, especially the young man Mithras killing a bull.'

Anne leaned over the plan for a closer look. 'So the entrance hall was once partially above ground. The rest of the sanctuary would have been dug into the hillside.'

'That's right. Now, I wonder if there once was a second entrance.' He pointed again to the plan. 'There's one here off to one side of the apse. A narrow circular stairway comes down from the ground above.'

'I can hardly see it,' Anne remarked. 'Tomorrow, with the help of your plan, I'll explore the hillside beyond the present excavation. Would you care to join me?'

'You would attract less attention if you went alone. I'll go to the villa and visit with Mr Grimshaw. Do you perceive my meaning?'

Anne nodded with a smile.

She had one more stop to make in the neighbourhood, at Louise's house. The guards recognized Anne and let her pass without ceremony. Louise was seated in a parlour, wearing a plain rose housecoat. Her hair was brushed and hung loose to her shoulders. She had applied a little rouge to her pale cheeks but no powder.

She noticed Anne studying her. 'I didn't feel I had to groom myself for the two guards outside. A pair of dolts. Nor for the Comte de Maistre, a pretentious fellow from a family of country gentry. His father bought the title. At the royal palace in Versailles the count would be a doorman.'

'Did he call on you today?'

'Indeed! He had been questioning everyone who knew me. Came with a long list of things I was supposed to have said. For example, "Captain Howe, if you are seen again with that brainless deaf girl, I'll flay you alive," and the like. Many of the words on the count's list I didn't remember saying. I wasn't always sober when we quarrelled. And the servants may have invented a phrase or two. He pays them to spy on me. So they earn more by telling him what he wants to hear.' She gestured toward the door and whispered, 'I'm sure that one of them is listening to us.'

Anne made a mental note to be careful. 'It's beautiful outside – as usual in Nice. I propose that we walk in your garden.' Anne gave the countess a knowing look.

She replied with a sardonic smile, 'Yes, I need the air.'

The garden was enclosed on both sides by vine-covered walls. At the far end was a gate with low buildings to left and right for storage and servants' quarters. A broad gravelled path ran beneath a pergola from the house to the back gate. On either side grew orange and lemon trees heavy with fruit. Beneath them were beds of flowers and vegetables.

The two women walked up and down on the broad path.

114

'I believe we can speak safely here,' Louise whispered in a mocking tone.

Anne glanced about. No one in sight. She began to speak, keeping her voice low. 'The count's visit today was intended to build a case against you. Still, he's concerned about possible protests from the French government. Out of prudence, he's also investigating Mr Grimshaw, whom he might prefer to arrest. But he has no evidence against him. For now, you are his chief suspect.'

'Chief suspect, to be sure,' Louise remarked. 'I sense his personal antipathy toward me. He's jealous of my birth into one of the greatest noble families of France, and I told him so. You should have seen his face. He flushed and spluttered. Didn't know what to say. Finally, he threatened to consult the intendant and the French Consul.'

Anne was too annoyed to pretend otherwise. 'It's probably true that he resents your high birth. Unfortunately, he has the power and perhaps the inclination to put you in prison for the rest of your life. The Baron de Breteuil, I'm sure, would expect Paul to defend you, were he here. So the task falls to me. The only way I know is to find the person who killed Captain Howe. That will require money and information from you.'

Louise looked displeased, as if she had smelled rotten eggs. 'I can defend myself, thank you.' She stared coldly at Anne, reproaching her impertinence. 'I've had enough air,' she said and returned abruptly to the house.

A powerful flash of anger kept Anne rooted to the path. When her feelings cooled, she entered the house – she had to pass through it to reach the street. Suddenly, there was a loud knocking. The front door burst open. The Comte de Maistre strode in, several soldiers at his heels. Startled, Louise tried in vain to protest. In less than a minute, she was chained and shackled and lifted rudely into a donkey cart. Off she went with the soldiers surrounding her.

Anne approached the count, who stood stiffly just inside the door waiting for her. 'What's going on, sir?' she asked.

'In view of the countess's uncooperative attitude, as well as the evidence against her, it seemed unwise to leave her in this lightly guarded house. She could too easily slip over the border into France. I've ordered her confined in a secure room of the royal palace. I'll begin arrangements for a trial. Thus far, our investigation has failed to uncover evidence against any other suspect, including Mr Grimshaw.' He tipped his hat to Anne and stalked out of the house.

Anne stood in the doorway and watched him march off, back rigid. She thought, he's angry enough to teach Louise to regret her hurtful tongue.

In the evening, when Anne returned to the villa, Beverly and Janice were about to sit down to supper. Anne joined them, and a place was quickly set for her. Beverly gave her a friendly smile. Janice nodded, then stared at her plate, an unhappy expression on her face.

'Do you have any news for us?' Beverly asked.

'Yes, the Comte de Maistre has made an arrest.'

'Really!' exclaimed Beverly.

Janice looked up sharply. 'Who is it?'

'The Comtesse de Joinville,' Anne replied. 'She might indeed be guilty, the only suspect with physical evidence against her, the blood on her clothes.'

'In that case,' Janice said, 'the count should also arrest Mr Grimshaw. Today, I learned from the maid who does the villa's laundry that he too had blood on his clothes.'

'Why didn't she tell the count's men when they questioned her?'

'At the time, she liked Mr Grimshaw. Up to a few weeks ago, they used to sometimes sleep together. Last night, she wanted him. He refused and broke off their relationship.'

'Janice!' sputtered Beverly plainly irritated. 'Respectable young women don't spy into another person's private affairs.'

Anne was also troubled. She had studied Janice carefully as the young woman was speaking. A trace of malicious satisfaction appeared on her face. She might have misunderstood the maid. Or for whatever reason the maid's accusation might not be fully credible. Anne would have to check before bringing this to the count's attention.

After supper Anne found the maid in her little room off the kitchen. She was a full-figured young woman with gold-tinted black eyes and a swarthy, sensual face. Anne could imagine only one reason why Grimshaw might be attracted to her. Her

116

French was better than Anne expected, making the interrogation easier. The maid continued to insist that she had at first covered up for Grimshaw. His costume had been bloody. Anne decided to confront him.

He had eaten earlier and was in his rooms on the villa's second storey overlooking the ruins. He seemed surprised by Anne's visit, but invited her in. The proper thing to have done was to ask him to meet her in a downstairs parlour. But she also wanted to get a glimpse of his quarters.

The room that she entered was his study or office. Papers were spread out on his writing table. Books and file boxes occupied a wall of shelves. Another wall was covered with engravings of ancient sites.

He followed Anne's gaze. 'You are looking at a plan of this villa and its property, indicating the excavated areas.'

Anne studied the plan. 'I see the arena where Captain Howe died. I was told that traces of his blood are still visible there.'

'I don't follow you, Madame Cartier. What are you getting at?'

'The captain's blood is also on the clothes of whoever killed him. Unless of course they've been carefully washed. The maid who washed your costume now claims it was bloody when she received it. I thought I should ask you to explain before going to the Comte de Maistre.'

Grimshaw's jaw grew rigid. 'We are dealing with a simple misunderstanding, Madame Cartier. The maid had not washed my costume, but a pair of gloves and the apron that I had soiled while butchering a lamb last Saturday, the day before the festival in Cimiez. There are several reliable witnesses.' He smiled thinly. 'The maid apparently seeks revenge for a recent difference between us. I am pleased that you came to me before going to the count.' He walked to a cabinet and pulled out a pair of long-cuffed work gloves. 'These are the ones she washed.'

'There seems to be no reason for me to speak to the count about this matter. I'm grateful for your explanation and sorry if I offended or disturbed you. Good night.'

As she left, she regretted that Janice, in her eagerness to punish Grimshaw, had uncritically accepted the maid's slander.

* * *

117

In her room before going to bed, Anne sat at her table, composing a letter to Paul. She had just finished describing Louise's arrest and was about to add a few lines about the misunderstanding concerning Grimshaw's gloves and apron. She felt compelled to reflect more on the matter. Finally, she wrote:

> *If Grimshaw set out with the knife to kill the captain, he would have gone prepared to shed blood and would have taken steps to avoid being soiled. Wouldn't he have worn the work gloves and the apron that were already bloody from the previous day?*

She closed, sealed, and addressed the sheet, then held it in her hands, staring at it. Paul's image came to her mind, reassuring her. Yes, Grimshaw remained a serious suspect.

Fifteen

A Measure of Justice

Marseille, Monday to Thursday, 11 to 14 February

Meanwhile, in Marseille, Colonel Saint-Martin, Georges Charpentier, Captain Barras, and the Abbé Gombert were pursuing the man who killed the master cabinetmaker Jacques Duclos twenty years ago. If successful, the judicial error that put Jean Lebrun in prison could be corrected. Then, if he were still alive, he would come out of hiding.

Georges's role in the scheme was to investigate Francine Duclos. As Henri's wife, she could have gained useful information about his character and his past. But this approach involved delicate negotiations, since she could balk at incriminating her husband and might alert him to the investigation.

That danger diminished on Monday, 11 February, as neighbours told Georges that Francine and the journeyman in the workshop had recently become lovers. She had also confided to a neighbour that Henri was a beast and beat her. Moreover, he kept a mistress and 'dined' with her almost every after-noon, when he was supposed to be with fellow artisans.

That information encouraged Georges. Francine most likely hated her husband and would defend him only when it was in her own interest to do so. Her infidelity also opened a way for Georges to urge her cooperation. Francine certainly under-stood the dire consequences for her, if someone were to reveal her affair to Henri. He had a notoriously violent temper. And it would not matter that he was unfaithful to her.

The next day, Georges won the confidence of the young apprentice in Duclos's workshop. Assured that the journeyman wouldn't find out, the boy confirmed what neighbours had told Georges.

The following day, armed with this compromising infor-mation, Georges waited with two police agents in an alleyway near the shop until Henri was at 'dinner' and Gombert had ended his visit with the old lady. Francine then customarily locked up the shop. Minutes later, she and the journeyman went upstairs to her bed. The apprentice unlocked the back door and gave Georges a signal. He had paid the boy rather than attract attention by picking the lock in broad daylight.

In full blue uniform with a sabre at his side and a pistol in its holster, Georges led one of the agents quietly up to the lady's bedroom. The other agent remained with the appren-tice downstairs. Georges listened carefully, his ear to the door. At a critical juncture in the affair, Georges and his agent entered the bedroom.

'Don't panic,' Georges said to the lovers, 'this may work out better than you think. Get dressed. We're going down-stairs to talk.'

After several minutes of desperate weeping and futile outrage, the two culprits went with Georges to the shop's office. The agent followed them. Georges pulled a chair up to a writing table and sat facing them. The agent sat to one side taking notes.

Sullen but attentive, they listened to Georges point out their folly. 'In little more than a day, I figured out what you were doing.' He turned to Francine. 'Even your thick-headed husband will eventually find out. Can you imagine his reac-tion?' Georges glowered at the pair, his expression suggesting the horror that would befall them.

'He will probably kill us,' replied Francine barely above a whisper.

'And *this* time he needn't bother to shift the blame to someone else, would he? The magistrates would forgive him.'

To support that insinuation Georges had calculated that Henri, a braggart, had less control over his tongue than most men, especially when he was drinking. He had probably incriminated himself.

'What do you mean?' asked Francine, alarmed.

Georges ignored her question and asked, 'Has Henri ever told you that it was he rather than Jean Lebrun who killed the old master Jacques Duclos?'

The question stunned her. She glanced helplessly at her lover. He shrugged his ignorance.

Georges met her eye, pressed her silently for a response.

'Yes,' she finally replied with a weak voice. 'When Lebrun escaped from the naval prison a few months ago, Henri became terribly agitated and began to drink heavily. One evening, while drunk, he told me that Lebrun would try to kill him. "Why," I asked, "what harm have you ever done to him?"

'He answered, "I killed the old man and put the blame on Lebrun. He spent twenty years in prison because of me." '

Georges encouraged her with a smile to go on.

Her voice gained strength. 'Later Henri didn't remember what he had said, and I didn't remind him, much less go to the police. Too risky. If I accused him, he would deny everything. It would be my word against his. He would punish me.'

'I understand,' said Georges. 'At that time you couldn't do anything, but now you have a choice. We're building a strong case against Henri. Either he'll go to prison for life or he'll hang. If you refuse to cooperate, the crown will confiscate Henri's property and leave you with nothing. If you cooperate, I'll arrange for you to take over the cabinet business in partnership with your lover here. He could then afford to buy a master's licence.'

The journeyman threw Francine a hopeful glance. She wavered, nodded tentatively.

Georges raised a cautionary hand. 'To make our plan work, you will have to pay a pension to Cécile for her care in a convent – a light burden, since she isn't expected to live long. Amélie will also receive a pension in return for her testimony implicating Henri.'

A cunning look came over Francine's face. 'Can we think about it?' Her sly nature had begun to reassert itself.

'Certainly.' Georges drew an official document from his portfolio and placed it in her hands. 'You and your lover have five minutes to study this agreement concerning the cabinet shop and the pensions. Meanwhile my agent will write out a deposition of Henri's drunken confession. That's for you, Francine, to sign.'

Francine opened her mouth, about to protest.

Georges cut her off with a baleful glance. 'I didn't come all the way from Paris to play games here. Henri Duclos is going to pay for his crime. You need to decide if you wish to suffer with him.'

As Georges checked his watch, Francine began to read the agreement, explaining passages to the journeyman. The document trembled in her hands. Five minutes later, she said, 'The terms are what you described. Fair enough. I accept them. Henri can go to hell.' The journeyman gave his agreement as well.

In a few more minutes, all the papers were signed and safely in Georges's portfolio. He cautioned Francine and her lover to say nothing to Henri. 'If aroused, he would probably kill both of you.' On that note, and with a similar warning to the apprentice, Georges and the agents slipped out the back door.

Early Thursday morning on 14 February, Saint-Martin, Georges Charpentier, Captain Barras, and the Abbé Gombert met in the priest's study. The atmosphere in the room was tense, as in a council of war. Their chief enemy was the powerful inertia of the French judicial system.

Saint-Martin knew from experience the mind of magistrates. He had recently struggled successfully to save a young deaf servant at the palace of Versailles from the palace provost's stubborn, self-serving insistence on her guilt. Magistrates generally resented and strongly resisted outside pressures, even the King's. Left to itself, their system would never change or correct its own abuses. That inertia was fully present in Lebrun's case.

The reopening of his case presented the magistrates with the prospect of being officially proven to have erred in their judgement. But they still had the power to do nothing and let their decision stand.

Encouraged by Georges's success, the four men discussed their plan to expose the injustice of twenty years ago. Saint-Martin studied the faces of his colleagues. The one who most needed convincing was Captain Barras. He would have to arrest Henri Duclos. It was also Barras who knew the local magistrates best and would be responsible for preparing the case for them. At the moment, his expression was sceptical, arms crossed over his chest, the knife scar livid on his cheek.

'Two parts of our plan are now in place,' Saint-Martin pointed out to encourage the others. 'The maid Amélie and Henri's wife Francine have committed themselves to testify that Henri Duclos murdered his stepfather.' He added in an urgent tone, 'We must complete the third and most problematic part of our plan today.'

Georges agreed. 'Our investigation can't be kept secret from Henri indefinitely. His temperament is mercurial. If he were alerted, he might flee Marseille or lash out at the persons arrayed against him.'

'Yes, we must act today,' said Gombert, with a nod to Barras. 'I've met Cécile every afternoon since Sunday, gradually insinuating in her mind the idea that it was time to put her soul right with man as well as with God. I've told her, "Think of any harm that you may have done to others in thought, word, or deed, and now do what you can to repair the damage."

'Yesterday, I could see in her eyes that she has become anxious and troubled. So I told her not to worry, that I had a way to protect her from harm and enable her to live out the rest of her life in comfort and dignity. But she had to tell the truth about whatever troubled her soul. And she would also have to say that she was sorry for the wrong she had done. I told her that I would come back today and we would decide what to do. I believe that she'll do the right thing.'

'To make it easier for her,' Saint-Martin added, 'I've persuaded the royal procurator that Cécile should not be held responsible for her false testimony twenty years ago – if she were to cooperate now.'

'And I've found a convent,' the Abbé Gombert said, 'that would give her care for a reasonable sum.'

Captain Barras had listened carefully to his companions,

but had said little. He showed signs of discomfort – the creases in his brow, the sceptical tilt of his head. Now he spoke up. 'Let's remember that twenty years ago, this old lady eagerly conspired to murder her husband, encouraged her son to do the deed, gave him an alibi that incriminated Lebrun. She was truly a villain. I should arrest her as well as her son. Granted, there's no way to send her to the naval prison at Toulon, but she should at least be publicly shamed for what she did.'

Saint-Martin privately agreed with Barras but saw the need for compromise. 'I share your feelings, Captain. But I fear that if we tried to force her to admit her evil deeds in court, she would refuse to cooperate with us. We would lose her testimony and our case would be weakened.'

Gombert added, 'Cécile has come to think of herself as a victim of her son's brutality. In her imagination he forced her to incriminate Lebrun. We could perhaps destroy this delusion, make her confront the whole truth about herself and the heinous things she did to Lebrun and her husband. But I agree with Colonel Saint-Martin that such a forceful measure would work against our goal. I hope that she will see the truth for herself and in some measure regret what she's done. In any case, her delusion inclines her to testify against her son and contributes to our plan's main purpose, which is justice for Jean Lebrun.'

Captain Barras had continued to listen attentively, his fingers nervously rubbing his scar. But eventually he began to nod, and the sceptical lines left his face. Finally, he clapped his thighs and spoke again. 'I think we are ready to take on the old lady. If she signs a deposition pinning blame on Henri, I shall arrest him this afternoon. There will be enough evidence to convince the magistrates to convict him and to exonerate Lebrun.'

As the meeting ended, Gombert served brandy to his colleagues. He raised his glass to salute Captain Barras. 'Be patient, sir, our Cécile Duclos will soon face a more perfect justice than the magistrates of Provence can offer.'

Having agreed on the plan, the four men gathered several hours later at the cafe near the Duclos shop. Captain Barras was in uniform, Saint-Martin and Charpentier in civilian dress, and Gombert in his long black soutane. When Henri left for his 'dinner' engagement in his customary red silk suit, the priest entered the shop as he usually did and greeted Francine. She summoned the maid Amélie, who led him up the stairs to Cécile's room. Amélie served tea and biscuits, then withdrew into the next room, where she was supposed to overhear what was said.

After enquiring about her health and telling her the latest news from the neighbourhood, Gombert asked, 'Have you considered what I said yesterday about putting your soul in good standing with God and man?'

'I'm sorry for many things I've done, but I don't know what to do.'

'What troubles you most? Perhaps I can help you figure out a way.'

'Many years ago, I told a lie that hurt a man.'

'How was he hurt?'

'He went to prison.'

'Then you should tell the truth and help him get out of prison. Otherwise, you run the risk of suffering in this life as well as in the next.'

'How so?' she asked.

'We both know who was hurt,' he replied, 'Jean Lebrun. His escape has opened up again the question of his guilt. High-ranking police officers and magistrates in Marseille have doubts about the justice of the original verdict. If they vindicate Lebrun, he will come out of hiding. Henri and you will be arrested and put on trial for conspiring to kill your husband, Jacques Duclos, and to put the blame on an innocent man.'

'I'm afraid.'

'I understand.' He met her eye. 'Lebrun didn't kill your husband, did he?'

'No, he remained in his garret room. He would have had to pass by my door to go downstairs. I was awake all night, the door was open. I would have seen him. It was Henri who killed his stepfather. He told me he was going to do it. I didn't dare tell anyone, or he would have killed me, too. He has a vicious temper.'

'So he made you tell the lie that you saw Jean Lebrun go downstairs to your husband's bedroom.' As Gombert expected, Cécile would mitigate her own guilt by insinuating that Henri alone conceived the idea of the murder.

'Yes, he said I had to help.' Her eyes grew wide as she imagined the scene: the overbearing son, the small, timid mother. 'But what will happen to me if he goes to prison?'

'The nuns will care for you, and I will visit regularly to see that you are satisfied.'

'And the shop? Who will manage it?'

'Henri's journeyman will buy a master's licence and go into partnership with Francine.'

Cécile frowned at the mention of her son's wife.

Gombert quickly added, 'They've signed an agreement to pay you a decent pension for your share of the shop. It's to your benefit that the shop continue to show a profit. Francine may not be your friend, but she knows how to manage the business.'

The old lady nodded grudgingly. 'I understand what I must do. Have you something for me to sign? I want to put this dreadful thing behind me.' She was beginning to look weary.

'The police officers are across the street. I'll call them. They will write down what you say and ask you to sign it. Then your conscience will be free.'

She gave him a wan smile.

In a few minutes Captain Barras took down her words in legal form. Colonel Saint-Martin and the Abbé Gombert witnessed her signature. She sighed with relief, and Amélie returned to tend her.

Afterward, downstairs, Amélie also signed a deposition that placed Henri at the scene of the crime.

'I have as much evidence as I need,' said Captain Barras, sweeping Saint-Martin, Charpentier, and Gombert with a glance. 'You will want to see what happens next. Let's go.'

An hour later, Barras, Charpentier, and Saint-Martin gathered in front of a house on a side street in the area north of the port. Gombert had excused himself. This was going to be police business, he said, and he wasn't needed.

The house was recently built of stone and expressed a taste for comfort rather than luxury. At ground level there was a millinery shop, with a sign saying closed for dinner. Above the shop were two residential levels and a garret.

'We'll wait until he leaves,' said Barras. 'Then we won't have to cope with his mistress. She could be a handful.'

'Tell me about her,' Saint-Martin asked, concerned about the wider effects of this arrest.

'She's a young seaman's widow, vigorous and strong, a vixen when crossed. Henri has established her with a small business in the shop and living quarters in the floors above. She will regret losing Henri's money and will protest, perhaps violently.'

Barras appeared tense. He had taken the precaution of bringing along two agents, hard-looking, muscular men equipped with clubs and shackles. 'Since Lebrun's escape, Henri has been carrying a cane with a small hidden pistol. We must disarm him.'

'Here he comes,' said Georges, as the door opened and Henri emerged. 'At the naval prison in Toulon he'll change from fine silk to rough wool. But at least it will be red, the colour he likes. He'll be there for life.'

Duclos stood still for a moment, his huge frame filling the portal. Then he embraced his mistress and stepped into the street.

The captain waited until the door closed, then signalled his men, who blocked Barras's path. While Barras read the arrest warrant to him, the agents knocked the cane from his hand and seized his arms. Before they could shackle him, he roared, 'Never!' He threw them off and picked up the cane.

Georges had placed himself near the scene. As Henri pulled the pistol from the cane, Georges delivered a powerful kick to the stomach that lifted the man off his feet. He fell to the pavement, bent double, groaning piteously. The agents shackled him. Georges seized the pistol. Barras brought up a mule cart. The agents heaved Duclos in and drove off.

The commotion had brought Henri's mistress into the street. She began to run after the cart, cursing at the top of her voice. Putting aside chivalry, Barras tackled the vixen. She fell hard on the pavement, knocking her head. Barras and Georges carried her into her shop and left her dazed on the floor.

Saint-Martin observed the incident with a mixture of awe and satisfaction. Georges and Barras worked together as if they had been partners for years. He congratulated them. The captain wiped perspiration from his brow and remarked, 'The wheels of justice turn slowly. It has taken me twenty years to catch that man!'

* * *

After Henri Duclos was securely locked in prison, Saint-Martin and Georges returned to police headquarters. The agent who had investigated Grimshaw's movements in Marseille was waiting for them.

'I have a report,' he said, handing a sheaf of papers to Saint-Martin. 'Mr Grimshaw has many ties to Marseille.'

They all sat around a table and Saint-Martin began to read. The agent had begun his investigation with antiquarians and collectors, with whom Grimshaw had done business over the years, usually as a broker in ancient Roman artefacts for wealthy British clients. The transactions appeared legal and paid him well.

'Here's something we should look into, Georges.' Saint-Martin handed a sheet to his adjutant. 'Twenty-one years ago, Grimshaw worked for the British banking house Barrett and Sons, and helped establish their office in Marseille. He still has an account with them. The record of that account could offer clues to the treasure that he is supposed to have hidden.'

Georges palmed his bald pate. 'Let's go there tonight. I'll tell them to expect us after business hours.'

They returned to their hotel for a light meal. As they entered, the concierge waved to catch their attention. A courier had just arrived from Nice with a letter for the colonel.

'It's from Anne,' Saint-Martin explained, while reading. 'Captain Howe has been murdered. Anne discovered his body Monday morning. Among the possible suspects are the Comtesse de Joinville and Jack Grimshaw. Here, you can read the details.' He handed the letter to Georges.

While his adjutant read, Saint-Martin reflected on the captain's death. It was shocking but not entirely a surprise, given the captain's reckless behaviour. In any case, it added new interest to their investigation of Grimshaw.

That evening, Saint-Martin and Georges went as planned to Barrett's. The bank's manager met them in his office with a sour face.

'We must protect our clients' privacy. How can they trust us if we open our records to every official claiming authority to investigate them?'

Saint-Martin took the seat offered to him and replied calmly. 'I realize that customs agents, tax farmers, and certain other financial officials might abuse their powers, harass you or your clients. My adjutant and I, however, are not concerned with financial crime but with the escape of a *galerien* from the naval prison at Toulon. One of your clients, Mr Jack Grimshaw, may have assisted him with money. A few hours ago, we learned that he's also a possible suspect in a murder in Nice. We need to search his records.'

The mention of murder widened the manager's eyes. With trembling hands and deep sighs he examined their papers from Lieutenant General de Crosne and the Baron de Breteuil. 'This is most irregular, gentlemen. Nonetheless, I shall admit you and assist your research.' They sat around the manager's writing table, discussing Grimshaw, while a clerk fetched the files.

While skimming files for 1766, Saint-Martin stopped at an entry. 'Look at this. As the bank's assistant manager, Grimshaw was in charge of outfitting the new office with furniture. Can you guess where he purchased the cabinets?' Saint-Martin handed the file to Georges.

'From the shop of Jacques Duclos,' his adjutant replied. 'So it's likely that he met Jean Lebrun.'

'He did indeed,' the manager spoke up from the far end of the table. 'They became good friends. Grimshaw visited the workshop to discuss the design, Lebrun came to our office to take measurements and install the cabinets.' He pointed to the wall behind him. 'There they are.'

Saint-Martin walked up to the cabinets and inspected them. Even his untutored eye could recognize the work of a master craftsman.

The manager went on, 'I recall clearly how much Lebrun's arrest upset Grimshaw. But nothing could be done. Soon afterward he left Marseille, lived in Paris for a while.'

Georges broke in, 'And met Lebrun's wife, I'll bet.'

'Correct.' Saint-Martin began to see a connection. 'Show us your record of Grimshaw's transactions for November 1787.'

A few minutes later the manager returned with an account book and handed it to Saint-Martin.

He went immediately to the entry for 7 November. 'Grimshaw withdrew one hundred livres. That's the day before Lebrun escaped from the naval prison.' Saint-Martin turned to his adjutant. 'What does that suggest to you, Georges?'

'That Grimshaw may have helped Lebrun bribe a guard, buy clothes and food, and walk away from the prison.'

Saint-Martin grimaced. 'How could the police fail to notice a possible connection between Lebrun and Grimshaw?'

'I would guess,' replied Georges, 'that their friendship was initially hidden in a business relationship. Then for twenty years, Grimshaw only occasionally visited the area and didn't do anything that would call attention to himself. For weeks the police focused on Lebrun's connection to Paris.'

'When we return to Nice, we shall have much to discuss with Mr Grimshaw.' Saint-Martin turned to the manager. 'By the way, how large is Grimshaw's current balance?'

'It's more than thirty thousand livres, a modest fortune. I checked when I knew why you were coming.'

'Has he entrusted any treasure to you?'

'A small locked chest. I don't know what's in it, and I don't have the key.'

'Shall I open it, sir?' Georges asked.

'Yes,' Saint-Martin ordered the manager to fetch it.

He put it on the table and Georges went to work with the tools he always carried. In a few minutes he had opened the lock. 'Will you do the honours, sir?' Georges asked.

Saint-Martin slowly, carefully lifted the lid. He paused, dipped into the chest, then handed a pair of coin pouches to the manager. 'Would you examine these?'

For a few minutes he studied their contents. 'Third- and fourth-century Roman gold and silver coins. They might fetch a thousand livres, a year's income for a man in Grimshaw's position.'

'A serious amount but hardly a treasure trove,' remarked Saint-Martin, 'but there may be one hidden elsewhere.'

The rest of the chest was full of personal treasures. Saint-Martin and Georges sorted out diaries, miniature paintings of Grimshaw's deceased wife and daughter, a lock of hair, small packets of letters. A quick study revealed the man's tragic private life. His wife's death in childbirth deeply distressed him. Devoted to his daughter, he was nearly destroyed by her suicide nine years ago.

'Look at this, sir.' Georges handed his superior a diary and pointed to a page.

'I see what caught your attention, Georges.' The lengthy

entry recorded Grimshaw's attempt to kill a Captain H., who had seduced his daughter in England, then abandoned her, prompting her suicide. Grimshaw had loaded a pistol and ridden twenty miles to the town where the officer's regiment was stationed.

Grimshaw arrived, his anger at white heat, to find that the regiment had left for America the previous day. Frustrated, enraged, Grimshaw put the pistol to his temple. But a priest dissuaded him from pulling the trigger. Over the next few days, the priest guiding him, Grimshaw regained his senses and abandoned his murderous project.

Saint-Martin laid the diary on the table. 'Georges, there's little doubt who that Captain H. was. A few months ago, they met by chance in Nice.' Saint-Martin examined the daughter's portrait. A lovely dark-haired young woman with large, soulful brown eyes. Her similarity to Janice Parker was remarkable. Saint-Martin wondered aloud. 'By courting Miss Parker, Captain Howe may have reawakened the rage that had simmered in the dark part of Grimshaw's mind. Perhaps, this time, he got the date right, chose a different weapon, and avenged his daughter's honour.'

'That's a likely scenario, sir.'

'When we are back in Nice, we shall try it on Grimshaw.'

Sixteen

A Discovery

Nice, Friday, 15 February

The cock crowed at dawn, awakening Anne. Her attitude toward the bird depended on how well she had slept. This morning she felt refreshed and lay in bed for several minutes listening to him trumpet in another beautiful day. Her mind sought out Paul in Marseille. She wished she could share this moment with him.

When he returned in a few days, he could help her deal with Janice. Anne had grown fond of this lovely, talented, spirited girl in need of parental love. Unfortunately, the Parkers could be neither mother nor father to her. Anne understood that she could not become the girl's parent. But while they were together in Nice, she could at least help her through her grief for Captain Howe.

After breakfast, Anne sought out Janice. When she wasn't in her room, Anne could guess where to find her. She had taken to sitting in the amphitheatre and staring at the arena, an understandable but unhealthy obsession with the captain's death.

'Janice,' Anne signed, as she approached, 'may I join you? I have information that you should know.'

The young woman nodded though her eyes seemed confused, as if her mind was returning from a distant place and had not yet fully arrived.

'It's best that you have the truth.' Anne signed vigorously, trying to catch Janice's attention. 'In her anger the kitchen maid misled you. She had washed blood from Mr Grimshaw's work gloves and apron but it came from a lamb he had slaughtered on the previous day. His costume from the night of the ball was never stained. So, we still don't know whether he murdered the captain or not. We must keep an open mind while we search for the killer.'

'The captain is gone,' Janice signed, her eyes dry. 'And I feel lost, beyond caring anymore about Mr Grimshaw, or Beverly, or anyone else.' She checked herself. 'I don't mean to be rude – I appreciate what you are doing for me.' She drew a deep breath. 'I can't just sit here feeling sorry for myself. I'll go to the kitchen and help the cook.'

The two women returned to the villa, arm in arm.

At midmorning, Anne sneaked out of the villa and into the olive grove, intending to search the hillside. Dr McKenzie's drawing of a typical Mithraeum gave her a vague idea of the size and shape of the sanctuary that might lie hidden in the rock beneath her. For the rough terrain she had dressed in riding breeches and cap, a light woollen shirt, gloves, and sturdy shoes. She had also armed herself with a small shovel and a lantern. Minutes earlier, Dr McKenzie had come to the villa to visit with Grimshaw at his excavation near the terrace and to keep him engaged during her search.

131

She climbed the hillside behind Grimshaw's shed. A narrow path wound between rocks and low dense vegetation. After about a hundred paces, she came to a tall rocky outcropping, where the hill rose sharply. This was a likely place for an exit, about the distance McKenzie had calculated.

She began to search more carefully. On the ground near the path the charred contents of a pipe caught her eye. She smelled the tobacco. Rather fresh. A man had come this way recently. Grimshaw? Most likely. A frisson of fear ran through her body. She prayed that McKenzie could hold Grimshaw at the villa.

She edged across the band of loose stones at the base of the outcropping. Several paces from the path, she came to a deep cleft in the rock. A bush blocked the way. She crawled under its branches. Her heart nearly jumped. A cave opened before her.

She lit her lamp and crawled down into a chamber barely high enough for her to stand. There were probably hundreds like it in the rocky hinterland of Nice. The floor was an uneven mixture of dirt and stones. The air was cool and musty. She imagined wild animals slipping into the cave for shelter, but she could find no signs of man . . . until she caught the faint smell of excrement, then saw it near the back wall.

Her heart was racing now. This cave held a deep secret. In the dim light of her lantern she studied the walls and the ceiling. Nature alone had shaped their surface. She knelt on the floor, donned gloves, and with her shovel dug through the stones and dirt, beginning in the centre of the cave. The loose material was about six to ten inches deep, covering a hard rock surface. Soon she had cleared a sufficient area to see that someone had carefully laid out large flat odd-shaped rocks, fitted neatly together as in a puzzle. In the centre of the cave, one rock was larger than the others and nearly square, with a grip carved into each of its four sides. Anne tried to lift it. Too much for her. It needed the strength of two women or a strong man like Grimshaw.

To avoid being seen, she returned to the villa by a back way. Tantalized by what she had discovered, she gave her mind free rein to imagine what lay beneath the cave's stone floor – a mysterious chamber, a treasure trove of gold coins, a grave?

* * *

At noon, Anne engaged one of Beverly's maids to load a donkey cart with supplies for Louise in prison. When it was ready, Anne climbed in and they drove the short distance to the city.

The two women entered the royal palace without difficulty and made their way to the Comte de Maistre's office. He received Anne coolly but gave her permission to visit Louise and assurance that she was being properly fed and cared for.

She had a small plain room to herself on the ground floor with a bed, a table, and a couple of chairs. A crucifix hung on one wall; the others were bare. The plaster walls and ceiling were painted a dull yellow. The tiled floor was clean. A single barred unglazed window overlooking the courtyard admitted sunlight and fresh, cool air. She had probably never been in such a simple room before.

Still, Anne thought, Louise should consider herself fortunate. Anne had personally experienced more typical prison conditions in the course of her confrontation with the bully Jack Roach, in Islington, near London. She had slept on mouldy straw in a small dank and dirty cell that she shared with three pitiful women. It was the worst night of her life.

As she surveyed Louise's room, she judged the accommodations favourably and gave the credit to the Comte de Maistre's basic decency. And his prudence – he would avoid aggravating the French government as much as possible. The room might seem like hell to the Comtesse de Joinville, but it was heaven compared to what a common prisoner had to endure.

To lift Louise's spirits, Anne and the maid had come with baskets containing a shawl, a change of underwear, toilette articles, a few books, writing materials, an oil lamp, fruit, and a bag of sweetmeats. Louise was shivering and near tears, sitting numbly at the table. Anne threw the shawl over her shoulders, while instructing the maid to empty the baskets.

'I miss him,' said Louise in a low voice, without prompting.

Anne wasn't sure what to make of the remark. She smiled sympathetically, inviting Louise to say more. But she lapsed into silence, staring at the table.

After depositing their gifts as neatly as possible, the two visitors stood by the door for a few moments. When Louise didn't react, Anne signalled the guard. The door opened. Anne threw a last glance toward Louise. She raised her head, met Anne's eye, and murmured, 'Thank you.'

On the way home in the late afternoon Anne stopped at Dr McKenzie's house and sent the maid on to the villa with the cart. In the garden under a blossoming fruit tree, Anne and the doctor enjoyed cool lemonade while she reported on her discovery in the hillside beyond the olive grove.

During her report McKenzie began to look distressed.

'Is something the matter?' Anne asked.

'Forgive me, Anne,' he replied. 'Your description of the cave sent my thoughts back to my agile youth, tramping through the wild Scottish highlands, climbing Mount Vesuvius near Naples, and the like.' He sighed. 'I would dearly like to remove that large stone. It almost certainly covers the stairway down to the sanctuary. What a thrill it would be to go down there. But I've become too old and weak for the task.'

Anne felt sorry for the doctor. The loss of strength and energy in old age had depressed him. 'Should we bring this discovery to the Comte de Maistre?'

'Not yet. My confidence in him has weakened since I've sensed his desire to divert suspicion away from his son. And I can't think of anyone else whom we can trust.'

'Then we must wait until my Paul returns in three or four days.'

As the sun set, they went into McKenzie's house for supper. Carlo the handyman had come the evening before and started repairing a leaky roof in advance of the rainy season. He would return in the evenings until done with this and other projects.

A stout, little man of quick movements, he arrived just as Anne and McKenzie were about to sit down to eat. A savoury lamb stew was on the table. Carlo smelled the aroma and for a moment stood transfixed in the doorway.

'Would you join us at the table?' Anne asked, sensing an opportunity to win his goodwill. 'There's more than enough stew for us all. The roof can wait.'

Carlo acknowledged that he hadn't eaten since breakfast. Madame Gabriella and his wife had kept him busy all day. McKenzie's maid set a place for him, a blessing was quickly said, and the stew was served. From his collection of fine

Provençal wines, the doctor had selected a robust red and poured for his guests.

At first the handyman was shy in the company of strange, rich foreigners. But since the doctor spoke the dialect quite well and Anne could make herself understood, the chief obstacle was overcome. After a helping of the stew and a glass of wine, Carlo felt at ease. A talkative man, as well as a sharp observer of human behaviour, he was easily led to tell anecdotes about the odd ways of winter visitors he worked for. From there, he was brought to talk about his own household, especially his formidable wife. 'Hawkeye, I call her, though not to her face.'

After another helping of the stew and a second glass of red wine, he began to speak of Gabriella. She was reasonable to work for and generally kind to him and his wife. But he had nothing good to say about her *cicisbeo* or acknowledged gallant, Mario de Maistre, who was rude to him and to other servants.

'He is reputed to be hot-tempered, is that true?' asked McKenzie.

'Yes, indeed. He has laid his stick on my back when I was too slow opening the gate.'

'Oh!' said McKenzie. 'You ran the risk of sharper prodding. It's said that he carries a knife and has threatened to use it on men who cross him. It's even rumoured that he's one of those suspected of killing the British captain up at the villa.'

Anne objected, tongue in cheek, 'But that can't be true, Doctor. After all, he's the commandant's son and wouldn't do such a thing.' She turned to Carlo. 'And what do you say?'

Carlo allowed the doctor to refill his glass, took a sip, and smacked his lips with approval. Then he leaned forward and lowered his voice, as if the commandant's spies were in the next room. 'Well, I can tell you that when he came to my gate after that festival ball, I could smell the filth on his costume. And when I brought the lantern up close to him, I saw blood spattered all over his sleeves. I asked, "Are you cut, sir?" But I could see no wound.

'He became very angry. "Damn you, dog. Don't sniff at me or I'll slit your liver." ' Carlo's eyes were wide, now, with full-blown fear.

'Your secret is safe with us, Carlo.' McKenzie reached into his pocket and pulled out a coin for a day's wages. Pressing it into the man's hand, he said, 'The roof can wait until tomorrow. You've worked hard all day. Go home and get some rest.'

The handyman squeezed the coin, thanked the doctor, and bowed to Anne. He started for the door, wobbling dangerously. Anne rose to steady him, but he managed on his own. She opened the door and watched him march away on unsteady legs.

McKenzie said to Anne, 'Bloody sleeves! How shall Mario explain that to a magistrate?'

'Rather easily, I should think. For he will face no ordinary magistrate but his indulgent father, the Comte de Maistre, the King's law in the County of Nice.' Anne paused for a moment, as another thought came to her mind. 'Seriously, I think Mario will claim that Carlo couldn't have seen blood that night. When Mario came to the gate, it was dark, the hour was late, and the lantern's light was feeble. Too much wine had also fogged Carlo's eyes.'

'If I were the count,' McKenzie remarked, 'I might agree with Mario's version.'

Anne added grudgingly, 'In fact, Carlo might have invented the more lurid parts of the tale he just told us. We need to hear from an independent, second witness, the maid Catherine.'

Seventeen

A Desperate Maid

Saturday, 16 February

After breakfast, disguised in a servant's plain woollen gown and a bonnet, Anne anxiously waited opposite Gabriella Rossi's house on the road to France. The task ahead was daunting. Though she couldn't fully trust the handyman's story from last night, she still assumed that Mario had arrived at the house with blood on his sleeves. Gabriella had surely warned the maid Catherine who washed the costume to say nothing about the blood.

Anne asked herself how could she persuade Catherine to tell the truth. The young maid would have to undermine the testimony of her mistress Madame Rossi, ruin Mario's alibi, and thereby also anger the Commandant de Maistre. In such a situation even much stronger women than the maid would balk. Nonetheless, Anne did not lose hope. Catherine still was largely uncharted territory and might offer hidden access to the levers of her mind.

At Anne's side was the cook's son, Angelo, a clever boy. He knew the city well and spoke the dialect. A few days ago, Anne had hired him to spy on the maid Catherine. His observations had agreed with Anne's own impression that the maid had a good character and was loyal to her mistress. However, the boy had also noticed an odd pattern in the maid's movements that needed to be checked.

Anne and the boy blended into a bustling crowd. Alongside the road, pedlars were offering their wares and peasants were selling flowers and vegetables. At midmorning, Catherine emerged from the house with a large shopping basket on her arm. Carlo's wife let her through the gate and out on to the street.

'Let's go,' said Anne. She and Angelo followed the maid to the markets in the city, where she bought fish, vegetables, and herbs. Next, she went to a cafe near the flower market for a lemonade, then to the Chapel of Saint-Gaetan on the Cours Saleya. Anne and the boy slipped in behind her and hid in a shadowed side chapel where they had a clear view of the unusual elliptical interior. Its curved walls were brightly painted and framed by tall polychrome marble pilasters. For a moment, Anne let her eyes delight in this lively, joyous expression of popular piety.

Meanwhile, Catherine knelt at a prayer desk in a chapel on the other side of the nave. After several minutes, she rose to leave.

'Now watch carefully,' the boy whispered.

Anne took a spyglass from her pocket and trained it on Catherine. On the way out of the church, she glanced furtively over her shoulder, drew a small package and some food from her basket, and handed them to an old woman standing in the shadows just inside the front entrance to the church.

'Follow the old woman,' Anne whispered to the boy. 'Find out her name and where she lives. I'll keep track of Catherine and meet you in front of Gabriella's house.'

An hour later, Angelo came running up to Anne.

'Her name is Paula Galeta,' he said eagerly. 'She's Catherine's mother and lives in a garret on Rue Droite across from Palais Lascaris.' The boy grinned in a teasing way, then added, 'On the way home the old lady went into a pawnshop. I peeked in the window. She gave the package to the broker. He opened it, held up two spoons to the light from the window. I could see them. Silver, I think. Then he gave her some money.'

'Well done, lad. Take me back to the pawnshop.'

A customer stood ahead of them in the shop, negotiating with the broker over the price of a necklace he had offered to buy. He was a dark olive-skinned man, lean, bent, sharp-eyed. Greek or Levantine, Anne guessed.

When the customer left, the broker studied Anne and the boy for a moment, then asked, 'What can I do for you?' There was suspicion in his voice.

'I'd like to see your tableware.' She spoke in broken dialect that would mark her as from the household of a rich winter visitor. 'My mistress has sent me to shop for certain pieces that she needs. The boy will help me with your language.'

The man appeared satisfied that a sale was possible. He brought several flat boxes to the counter and opened them in front of Anne. She passed over the larger pieces and focused on small spoons, lifting them up one by one. When she came to one of Catherine's, the boy scratched himself, a prearranged signal. The spoon had the smith's mark on the back of the handle. Anne asked the price.

'A hundred livres. It's silver.'

There were four such spoons, all with the same smith's mark. Catherine's mother might have also sold others here before. A hundred livres would buy five months' rent for a garret room in central Paris, about the same as in Nice. Catherine's mother was lucky if the broker gave her twenty-five livres per spoon.

'I'll buy one. A receipt, please. If it pleases my mistress, I shall come back for the other three.'

She and Angelo left the store with the spoon in her pocket.

What should be her next step, Anne wondered, as she climbed the road up to the villa. She had instructed the boy to continue to watch Catherine's movements. Where did the maid find the spoons that she passed to her mother? Had she stolen them from Gabriella's pantry? That would have been difficult to do. Gabriella was a businesswoman who kept close account of her property. She would raise an alarm if silver spoons were missing.

Could Gabriella have given the spoons to her maid? That was highly unlikely. She was a close-fisted mistress of the household. If the spoons were an honest gift, Catherine would not have had to pass them on to her mother in secret.

Where else could Catherine have got the spoons? Finally, it occurred to Anne. The maid cleaned the houses of several winter visitors who hadn't brought servants from Britain. Could the silver have been stolen from them?

Possibly, Anne thought. She would speak to Beverly, who knew most of the visitors and could perhaps steer Anne in the right direction.

Back at the villa, dusty and tired, Anne went directly to her room, where she washed and lay down to rest. Her mind drifted over the events of the day, prompting a feeling of sadness mixed with discomfort. The maid's predicament grew clear. She stole to support an aged parent. Anne regretted having to take advantage of her desperation. In pursuit of justice she was about to grievously hurt someone who had never hurt her. That didn't seem right.

The opportunity to speak to Beverly came in mid-afternoon when she had tea in a ground-floor parlour. She held to this ritual religiously, whether anyone joined her or not. She was pleased to see Anne and greeted her warmly. A servant brought a tray of tea and currant scones. Beverly poured.

Anne buttered a scone while Beverly spoke about her health. She had recovered from the stressful aftermath of Captain Howe's death. Her breathing had returned to near normal, and her spirits had improved.

'Janice and I took a long, pleasant walk in the countryside this morning,' she reported, pointing to a vase of daffodils in the window. 'Janice picked them. The profusion of flowers in this place is extraordinary, even in the middle of winter. With a pad and pencil I taught Janice many of their names. She seemed to be pleased. If I could only learn her signs, I could be of use to her.'

'The signs aren't difficult,' Anne suggested. 'Janice and I could help you learn them. We could start tomorrow.'

Beverly smiled noncommittally. 'I'll think about it.'

With the maid Catherine's suspicious spoons in mind, Anne led the conversation toward Beverly's acquaintances among the winter visitors. 'Some of them have come here with few if any servants. Have they found reason to regret hiring help from the local population?'

'Many complain that local servants are lazy and dirty, but I don't take such remarks seriously. To be honest, I have been most pleased with Philippa, our cook, and her family. They keep themselves clean, do their work well, and rarely complain. Of course, I pay them generously.' She took a scone, distractedly nibbled on it. 'I do wonder how Mr and Mrs Howard are faring. They are both quite feeble. She often can't remember the names of her own children back in Britain or what she ate for dinner yesterday. He has failed a great deal since arriving here in early November. I can't imagine how they will make the trip back to Britain.'

'Who looks after them?' Anne's interest in the Howards grew rapidly.

'They say they don't need anyone to manage their lives, certainly not a lot of indolent, superstitious papists. "We can still care for ourselves," they claim. Gabriella Rossi, the owner of their house, sends her maid Catherine to cook and clean. Her handyman Carlo does repairs.'

'Do you know if the Howards brought any valuable items with them?'

'What *do* you mean, Anne? Sometimes I believe you are obsessed with crime. Take care. It's truly degrading.'

'Thank you, Beverly, for the warning. Crime can fascinate the mind and were it an obsession it would be unhealthy. I mean only that many local people are very poor. In comparison, we are very rich. They think we should share our wealth.

If we don't, if we pay low wages, for example, they will steal without compunction.' And why not, she added mentally.

'I see your point, Anne. Well, to answer your question, I have been to the Howards' house and have seen very fine gowns, ribbons, hairpins, and the like. He has an expensive watch. Her diamonds are paste, but her gold bracelets, necklaces, and rings are certainly genuine. She also brought to Nice a few boxes of silverware, table linen, and fine porcelain. They refuse to eat from an undressed table. You are perhaps right to be concerned. With a little cleverness and caution, one could easily steal from them.'

'Do you think we could pay them a visit, Beverly, let us say for tea?'

'Surely, Anne. I shall send them a message immediately, suggesting tea tomorrow afternoon. They are usually alone and might appreciate our company.'

Anne picked up hand puppets in her room and went directly to the kitchen. She would converse with the cook in dialect and entertain with the hand puppets. They fascinated the cook's boy Angelo, so Anne taught him how to do short farcical sketches from the commedia dell'arte.

A half-hour of Punch and Judy passed pleasantly, then Anne asked where Grimshaw had gone. He often took part in this recreation.

'It's nearly Saturday evening,' Philippa remarked. 'He usually has business in town.'

'Oh,' Anne said, her curiosity piqued. 'What kind of business could he have on a Saturday night?'

Philippa shook her head. 'It's not what you're thinking. A group of collectors gather at Palais Lascaris, eat together, show their ancient coins and medallions, smoke and drink.'

Anne suddenly saw an opportunity. Grimshaw would be away from the villa for the evening and probably wouldn't return until late at night, at the earliest. The servants would be in their rooms in the basement. No one else would be on the second storey but her. There was an hour of daylight left.

She opened his door with her hatpins and locked it behind her. Over the past two years, her husband's adjutant, Georges Charpentier, had taught her not only how to pick locks but also how to search a room. She must not leave any trace of her presence behind. That was the first and foremost rule. So she moved carefully through the study, scanning the shelves and the tables for a diary, account books, letters, or other papers that might offer clues to his secrets and the hidden recesses of his character.

The room revealed that Grimshaw was a remarkably precise and orderly man, which Anne had already surmised. He also smoked. The room reeked of tobacco. She saw nothing that could implicate him in wrongdoing, much less in the murder of Captain Howe. So, she wondered, where would he hide his secrets?

She cautiously entered his bedroom, as if there might be a trap within. The furnishings were simple: a bed, chairs, table, washstand. He kept his clothes neatly in an armoire and a chest of drawers. Nothing hidden there.

The wardrobe adjacent to the bedroom was locked, a likely place to hide things. In a minute Anne had it open. A window to the south admitted the early evening light. Shelves of ancient pottery and artefacts covered the walls – perhaps borrowed from Parker for purposes of study. The maid was probably not allowed to clean in this room.

Anne quickly fingered through boxes of maps, plans, and sketches – many of them dated to the last century, when the villa was built. There wasn't time to discern their significance. She was about to put the last box back in its place when she noticed a discrepancy: the inside wasn't as deep as it should be. With careful prying, the false bottom came out, exposing a small account book and several letters.

The account book recorded Grimshaw's weekly payments to Captain Howe over the past few months. The sums were small at first but grew gradually to reach a total of some six hundred livres, about what a skilled artisan would earn in a year in Paris. Was that enough to motivate a murder? Anne supposed it might be, especially if Grimshaw feared that the size of the payments would continue to increase. The account book didn't indicate the purpose of the payments. So, strictly speaking, they didn't prove extortion.

The letters were written in a script too tiny for the naked eye. Anne borrowed one of Grimshaw's magnifying glasses, sat down at his desk, laid the letters before her, and began to read. They were from Madame Lebrun to Grimshaw concerning her imprisoned husband. Passages were sometimes cryptic. In the earliest letter she acknowledged receiving Grimshaw's account of the trial. Later letters at intervals of several months or years contained references to Lebrun's situation and included messages to him from his wife reporting the death of their son and other news of the family. Madame Lebrun's last letter to Grimshaw, dated only November 1787, hinted at a crisis. In the enclosed message to her husband she hoped to see him again.

Anne stared at the letters. They revealed a side of Grimshaw that she could not have imagined. Then she recalled Paul's letter reporting Grimshaw's suspicious visit to the naval prison. When passing through Toulon, he could have contacted the prisoner and aided his escape, even hid him at the villa.

Anne recalled now with clearer understanding the commandant's failed search of the villa almost three weeks ago. If Grimshaw himself had concealed him there, he had also warned him of the search in time to escape.

It was hard to imagine that Grimshaw would risk being caught and imprisoned himself, unless for friendship's sake. To what lengths would he then go to protect the fugitive?

Grimshaw could have killed Captain Howe, not only to protect the vulnerable Janice from his lecherous hands, but also to safeguard Lebrun from being inadvertently exposed by the rogue as he probed for a hidden treasure trove.

Anne asked herself if she should report her discovery to the Comte de Maistre. No, she thought, she had better wait a few days and discuss the matter with Paul. She no longer trusted the count to do the right thing. His preoccupation with shielding his son had warped his judgement. He might unfairly pursue Grimshaw as he had the Comtesse de Joinville.

Suddenly, Anne became aware that more than an hour had passed. It was growing dark in the room. She feared that if she lit a candle she might be discovered. So she arranged the boxes as she had found them, and locked the doors on the way out. She would have to do another search later, when there was more time. Still, the account book and the letters indicated that she was on a promising path into the mystery surrounding Jack Grimshaw.

143

Eighteen

A Maid's Confession

Sunday, 17 February

At mid-afternoon Anne and Beverly arrived in a mule cart at the Howards' house on the road to France. The lonely, elderly couple had welcomed Beverly's suggestion and had gladly extended an invitation to tea. Anne hoped on this occasion to find out if her small silver spoon matched any of theirs. She might also learn if the suspect Catherine had access to their silverware.

The house appeared to be three or four years old. Typical of the new buildings erected for the winter visitors, it was a square, single-storey structure with white-stuccoed walls and a red-tile roof. A terrace at the rear of the house offered a delightful view over a garden of fruit trees, vegetables, and flowers that extended to the pebble beach and the sea.

A young female servant met them at the door.

'Mary Kelly,' Anne exclaimed. 'I didn't know that you worked here.'

'When Mrs Howard has guests for tea, she borrows me from the consul for the day. The local girls cannot meet the lady's standard for service.' She curtsied to Beverly. 'And you must be Mrs Parker. I'll tell Mrs Howard that you are here.' She left them in the hallway.

In a minute, Mary was back. 'This way, please.' She led them into a parlour where a table was set with a silver tea service and English porcelain on fine linen. An elderly couple shuffled in and greeted their visitors.

Mr Howard was a tall, angular man. In his prime he must have been an imposing figure – long face, imperial nose, great chin. Now, perhaps eighty and bent, he looked feeble, inspired pity. His skin hung like loose parchment on his large skeletal frame, and his hair was thin and grey. He stared at Anne with bleary, uncertain eyes. 'A pleasure to meet you, Mrs Cartier. We know Mrs Parker from years ago.' His voice cracked and faded away. He reached tentatively for his wife's chair and eased her into it.

Mrs Howard was also tall for a woman, and rather stout. Her complexion was remarkably fresh and pink. According to Beverly, she was her husband's age, although she looked ten years younger – except for the vacant look in her eyes. She recognized Beverly but struggled for her name.

The maid poured an aromatic East Indian tea and served scones with clotted cream and strawberry preserves, then stepped back to the sideboard. While everyone applied themselves to the tea and the pastry, Beverly took the lead in the conversation. Mr Howard asked polite questions about the Parkers and other winter visitors. Otherwise, he mostly complained about his wife's distracted mind and the inconvenience it caused him. For the most part, she maintained a dignified silence, smiling inappropriately at his remarks.

In a rare moment of clarity, Mrs Howard beckoned Mary from the sideboard to the table. 'Well done, Miss Kelly. This is a true English tea, properly brewed. And your scones are delicious. I see that you have also polished the silver. I shall commend you to Mrs Green.'

Mary bowed, murmured, 'Thank you,' and stepped back. Mr Howard and Beverly resumed their conversation. Mrs Howard's mind drifted away.

In the midst of the conversation Anne discreetly turned her spoon over. The smith's mark was the same as the one in her pocket. She cast a swift glance at the maid. Her eyes met Anne's, then darted away; her throat tightened.

Mr Howard noticed his wife's head was now drooping. 'Kelly,' he asked, 'would you be so kind as to help my wife to bed? A nap would do her good.'

Anne seized the opportunity. 'I would be happy to help Kelly.'

Before Mr Howard could voice a different opinion, Beverly said to him, 'I'd like to see your garden. Mrs Cartier will join us in a few minutes.' He hesitated but a fraction. 'Yes, that would be lovely.'

Like the gallant gentleman that he once must have been, he offered Beverly his arm. She took it graciously. His eyes brightened with pleasure. He shed years from his gaunt, withered appearance.

145

When they left the room, Anne and Mary brought Mrs Howard to her feet, moved her shuffling to her bed in an adjacent room, and laid a light cover over her. She quickly dozed off. On tiptoes, Anne and Mary returned to the parlour. Anne surveyed the table, idly playing with one of the spoons.

'You noticed, didn't you?' Mary hugged herself, staring at the table. Her lips quivered.

'Yes, I did. When Mrs Howard complimented you on the silver, you looked as if someone had struck you. I believe that I know why. But I want you to tell me.'

The maid remained silent and turned away. Her shoulders began to heave with sobs.

'Don't cry. I'm sure you didn't do it.'

Face wet with tears, Mary stared at Anne. 'How did you find out?'

'I've been observing the thief.' Anne pulled a small spoon from her bag, laid it next to one of the spoons on the table. 'They match.' She turned them over. 'See, the same silversmith's marks. I know the location of three more of the missing ones and who took them.'

Mary seemed confused but relieved. 'I knew how many spoons the Howards had brought from England. They had hired me to serve several teas when they arrived in early November of last year. Every time I polished the spoons, I carefully counted them. Always a dozen. Today, when I opened their case, only six were left. I'm afraid I'll be blamed.' She cocked her head, puzzled. 'But you said you know the thief. How is that possible? The tableware is locked in a cabinet, and only Mr Howard has a key. I had to ask for it.'

Anne put the spoons back in place. 'He must have earlier mislaid the key, the thief found it and had a copy made.'

Mary's brow furrowed with thought. 'Only one or two persons could have done it. They work here at times when only Mrs Howard is at home and she's—'

Anne raised a hand to interrupt her. 'That's right. She's demented. But it's too early to confront the thief. The spoons are involved in the investigation of a much more serious crime. I want you to put the spoons away and say nothing about the missing six until I tell you. This matter will soon be resolved.'

Mary nodded, then reached toward the table. 'I'll wash them now.'

Anne picked up the spoon that she had brought with her. 'I'll need this one for a little while longer.'

The mule cart took Anne and Beverly back up the hill to the villa. After indulging in scones slathered with clotted cream and preserves, Anne would have preferred to walk, but they had dressed for the tea and were wearing thin silk shoes.

'Did you learn anything of value?' asked Beverly when they had seated themselves comfortably in a ground-floor parlour.

'Yes, as we suspected, the Howards are being robbed. Mary Kelly discovered that six spoons are missing. For the moment, we must say nothing about the theft to the Howards, or anyone else, for fear of alarming the thief before we are ready to act. In the meantime, please try to persuade Mr Howard to hire a reliable servant to look after them and their property. I suggest borrowing Kelly for the remaining month or two of the winter season. The thieving would cease.'

'Why not bring the problem to the attention of the Comte de Maistre?'

Anne shook her head. 'The situation is very delicate. The thief is someone whom I believe to be a decent person, who steals to support a poor elderly ailing mother. I must move cautiously so as to avoid making their situation worse. But I shall use my knowledge of the thief's guilt to persuade her to tell what she knows about Mario de Maistre's involvement in the death of Captain Howe. That will be very difficult for me, very risky for her. For the time being I should not reveal any more about the matter. Please regard what I've said as confidential.'

'I'm pleased that you've trusted me thus far, Anne. I'll help you whenever I can. I'll also speak to Mr Howard and the consul's wife about hiring Miss Kelly to live in the house and care for them.'

Anne next went to the kitchen and asked Philippa if her son Angelo had left a message for her.

'Yes, he has,' replied the cook. 'He said you should meet him at the Croix de Marbre.'

That meant going back down the hill to the city. The large

147

marble cross on the road to France was the principal land-mark of the new quarter where the visitors lived. Anne dressed for work and set off.

Angelo was waiting for her. 'The maid Catherine will visit her mother this evening. One of the boys working in the kitchen told me.'

Anne thanked him, praised his cleverness, and sent him home. She should deal with Catherine alone. For a short while, Anne waited opposite Gabriella Rossi's house. Then, Catherine passed through the gate with a covered basket on her arm, and walked rapidly toward the city. Anne followed her into the cathedral. For several minutes she knelt in a busy side chapel, ablaze with lighted candles. When she rose to her feet, Anne approached her.

'Catherine, I must speak to you, privately, in a quiet place.' At that moment Anne sensed that she was being spied upon and glanced over her shoulder. A figure hurried away toward the exit.

The maid stared at Anne, eyes wide with alarm. 'Who are you?'

Anne introduced herself. 'Be calm. I'll try to help you and your mother. But first, we must talk about the missing silver spoons.'

'Oh!' Catherine began to sway, as if about to faint. Anne held her under the arm, led her into a deserted side chapel.

'A few hours ago,' Anne said softly, 'I had tea at the Howards' house and discovered that six small silver spoons were missing. I have recovered one of them at the pawnbroker's shop.' She took the spoon from her bag and showed it to Catherine. 'Three more spoons like it are still in the shop. Two are missing. Yesterday afternoon, I saw you give two spoons to your mother in Saint-Gaetan and observed your mother selling them to the broker.' Actually Angelo had made the observation.

The maid stammered something in dialect that Anne couldn't understand.

'Speak slowly and clearly.'

'Madame Howard gave them to me.'

A cunning excuse, Anne thought. Mrs Howard wouldn't remember whether she had or not. 'But how could she? Mr Howard keeps the key. Do you wish me to lay this issue before him?'

Catherine cast her eyes down, shook her head.

'What would happen if I told the Comte de Maistre what you and your mother have done?'

She replied too softly. But Anne caught the word 'prison'.

'If you do what I tell you, I shall keep you and your mother from prison. Listen carefully. I want you to tell me exactly what happened early that morning when Captain Howe was murdered.'

It was dark when Anne and Catherine reached the home of Dr McKenzie. He was startled to see them. 'What in God's name brings you here at this hour?'

'A very serious matter, Doctor. May we come in? I want you to witness Catherine's testimony. You understand the dialect much better than I.'

They gathered at a table. The doctor laid out a clean sheet of paper and dipped his pen in ink. 'Proceed,' he said.

Anne met Catherine's eye. 'Tell the doctor what you told me in the church.'

She took a deep breath and began to explain. Mario had arrived at Gabriella's house at about two o'clock on Monday morning, his clothes wet, stinking. He said he had fallen into a pile of dung, then tried to clean himself in a horse trough. Gabriella told him to take off his clothes at once and give them to Catherine to be washed. He stripped on the spot.

When Catherine looked closely at the sleeves, she noticed that blood had stained them. He was naked, crying, and acting crazy, but she could see no wounds on his body. She thought that her mistress should know, so she pointed out the blood. Up to that point, they hadn't heard about the captain's murder.

Madame Rossi seized Mario by the shoulders, shook him, demanded to know what had happened. Finally he admitted attending the festival and then the ball at the villa – against his father's orders. Late in the evening he agreed to meet Captain Howe in the arena to settle a gambling debt.

'When I arrived,' Mario had said, 'I found the captain lying on the ground, as if he were asleep. I shook him, but he was already dead. Then I saw the blood on my sleeves. People would think I killed him. So I came here. You've got to help me.'

As she spoke, Catherine was reliving the incident, her face

taut with concentration. She described Madame Rossi staring at Mario like she didn't believe his story. Suddenly, her attitude seemed to change. She ordered Catherine to wash the clothes and keep her mouth shut about the incident.

Catherine looked anxiously to Anne then to Dr McKenzie. 'I could see that Madame Rossi was sorry that I had seen Mario and heard his story.'

McKenzie produced a copy of the maid's words and read it to her. 'Is that the truth, Catherine?'

'Yes.' She nervously worked her lips.

'Then sign your name there.' McKenzie pointed to the spot. 'Madame Cartier and I shall sign as witnesses.'

The signing was quickly done.

The next matter was the maid's theft from the Howards. 'You must return the spoons, Catherine. Eventually Mr Howard will discover that they are missing. He will become angry and prosecute you. The longer you delay, the worse your situation will become. Do you understand?'

She nodded.

'I can account for four of the six. Where are the other two?'

The maid retreated again into herself, averted her eyes. She wasn't a good actress, Anne thought.

'Am I to understand that you still have them?'

She nodded stiffly.

'And what will you do with them?'

'Return them,' she replied softly. Perspiration was gathering on her brow. 'But I can't return the four that I sold. My mother and I together haven't enough money to buy them back.'

'We will try to make an arrangement with Mr Howard. He seems to be a humane man. The broker must sell them back for no more than he paid. If he refuses, he could be charged with receiving stolen goods. Dr McKenzie and I will speak to him.' She glanced at McKenzie with a teasing smile.

'Yes,' he agreed. 'I'm sure we can work out a suitable arrangement.'

Anne probed Catherine further. 'Before we finish, I have a question. I've been told that even before this matter of the bloody garment you disliked Mario. Tell me why.'

'When my mistress is away, he comes to the house and . . .

annoys me. When I fight him off, he threatens to use his father's power to hurt me.'

'I'm not surprised,' Anne remarked, glancing at McKenzie.

'Mario exaggerates his influence over his father,' said McKenzie to the maid, weighing his words carefully. 'The commandant isn't a complete fool. He doesn't trust his son and won't do his bidding. Still, Mario's a dangerous enemy. Use tact in fending him off.'

Anne rose from the table. 'Catherine, it's time that we leave the doctor. He should rest. Say nothing to Madame Rossi or Mario about what we've done here. Until I tell you otherwise, it must remain secret. Your life may depend upon it.'

Nineteen

A Plan Unravels

Monday, 18 February

As was her habit, Gabriella awoke at the crack of dawn, stretched, made a quick toilette, drew on a housecoat, and rang for breakfast. She was never one to linger in bed. There was too much to do, even when she and her husband shared the housing business. Now she did it alone. Mario was no help, at least not at work. But he was a pleasant distraction when the daily routine became tedious and a handsome companion when she had to show herself in society.

Lately, however, she had wondered more than once whether her relationship with the young man was causing her too much irritation. Exactly a week ago, he woke her up, pounding on the gate, filthy and hysterical. He claimed he hadn't killed the British captain, had only discovered his bleeding body. 'Everyone will say I did it,' he whimpered. 'They'll point to our loud quarrel in the street, and to all this blood on my clothes. What shall I do?'

She had taken him at his word, despite an uneasy feeling that he might be lying. She reassured him, had his clothes cleaned, related his story to the count, his father. For a while, her suspicion lifted from the young man. He and she went on with their promenades on the seaside terrace, intimate dinners, amorous pleasures. But doubts and worries gradually arose that she couldn't banish from her mind. What if Mario had in fact killed the captain? Like a child, he would lie without compunction to avoid punishment. If she were too closely associated with him, his crime might taint her reputation. The winter visitors would think ill of her, perhaps shun her. She couldn't afford to lose their money.

And what did the Comte de Maistre really expect of her? He appeared to want her to provide his son's alibi, regardless of the consequences to her. She must not alienate such a powerful man. Thus far she had kept her doubts to herself.

But for how long? In the market and on the terrace people whispered when she and Mario walked together. Intendant Marco de Spinola passed them without a greeting or a smile. Madame Cartier and many winter visitors continued to suspect Mario, even while they considered other suspects.

A knock on the door interrupted Gabriella's anxious musing. 'Come in!' she shouted.

The handyman's wife entered. 'I brought your breakfast tray.'

'Something wrong with Catherine?'

'Yes, indeed, and I think you should know. She came home late last night.' The woman laid the tray on a table by the window.

'Well, what of it? Get to the point.' Gabriella really disliked this woman. Her long, pointed nose, black beady eyes, and malicious grin reminded her of a rat.

'She had been talking with Madame Cartier in the town. Then they went to Dr McKenzie's house.'

'How do you know this?'

'Madame Cartier and a boy from the villa have been watching you. So I thought I should watch them. Catherine's been acting strangely.' She waited, hands clasped, head tilted expectantly.

For a long moment Gabriella pondered what she'd just heard. Finally she said, 'You may go. Continue to report whatever looks suspicious. Send Catherine to me.'

* * *

Catherine was washing dishes when the handyman's wife entered the kitchen. The maid shuddered. The woman had an evil reputation for snooping into the affairs of servants.

'The mistress wants to see you, Catherine. You had better let me finish the dishes.' Her voice had a threatening tone.

Catherine wiped her hands, tucked a stray lock of hair into her cap, and set off for what she feared might be a reprimand. The affair of the spoons had distracted her. She must have forgotten an errand she was supposed to do.

Mistress Gabriella was seated by the window, drinking coffee. For a moment, Catherine felt relieved. She had been called to take away the tray. Then she noticed the dark cloud on her mistress's brow.

'Catherine,' said the mistress softly, 'come here.' She pointed the maid to a chair facing her. 'I must ask you some questions. Did you meet Madame Cartier in the cathedral last night?'

The maid hesitated, realizing that she had been spied upon. 'Yes, I did. She came up to me while I was praying.'

'And what did you talk about?'

Catherine couldn't bring herself to confess the theft of the silver spoons. 'She wanted to know about Mario returning to the house that night a week ago. I told her his clothes were messy and I washed them. That's all.'

'Did she ask about the blood?'

'Yes, but I said I didn't know where it came from.'

'And then you went with her to Dr McKenzie's house. Why?'

Catherine's chest was tight. Her face felt hot. What should she say? She couldn't mention the paper she had signed. At that moment, there was a knock on the door.

'Come in,' said Gabriella.

The handyman's wife walked in, a wide grin on her face and a hand behind her back. 'Look what I found in Catherine's room!' She gave a small loosely wrapped package to Gabriella, who studied its contents, frowned, then held it up for Catherine to see.

Two small silver spoons! Catherine felt faint. The room seemed to whirl around. She lost consciousness.

The Comte de Maistre got up from his writing table and walked to the window to view the Mediterranean. From this distance, the water looked calm, a tapestry of blue as far as the eye could reach. The sight usually healed his spirit, removing the cares that came with maintaining order among thousands of poor, ignorant, quarrelsome, and sometimes violent men and women. He opened the window and breathed deeply of the fresh air. It worked like a tonic, braced his nerves.

A clerk opened the door and announced, 'Madame Rossi and her servant to see you, sir.'

Gabriella had sent a messenger ahead, asking for this visit. Said she had important matters to discuss. The count had found it prudent to maintain a mutually beneficial relationship with Gabriella, a capable, intelligent woman, one of his best connections to the winter visitors. She also offered an indispensable alibi for his son Mario in the case of the murdered British captain.

Merely thinking of Mario disturbed the count's calm. With a sigh he left the window and adopted an official stance behind his writing table. Despite a strong effort of self-control, his hands trembled. He held them behind his back and told the clerk to admit the visitors.

Gabriella swept into the room, her black eyes blazing. 'Monsieur le Comte, I believe we have a problem.' She threw a withering glance at the maid Catherine standing by her side. The maid stared at the floor.

The count seated the two women and himself, then asked, 'What has happened?'

Gabriella explained that Madame Cartier had cleverly persuaded the maid to admit to the theft of several silver spoons from the Howard household. With the threat of revealing the crime, Cartier had pried loose from the maid a detailed account of Mario's panicked visit to Gabriella's house shortly after the captain's murder. 'Madame Cartier and Dr McKenzie know that Mario had been at the scene of the crime and had come to my house, his sleeves all bloodied. What's worse, they have that knowledge in writing with Catherine's signature, and verbally from Carlo the handyman.'

The count felt the colour drain from his face. This revelation made his son at least as likely a primary suspect as the French countess. Like her, Mario had a strong motive to kill the captain, and he had blood on his clothes. But Mario was physically more capable of the deed, for he was young and strong. True, he lacked courage. It was hard to imagine him attacking Captain Howe.

The count also clung to the fact that his son had not admitted to killing the captain, only to finding the body shortly after the crime. But that admission was too incriminating for comfort. It must be concealed from Intendant Spinola. If he were to report it to the count's enemies at the royal court in Turin, Mario might be charged with murder. Under rigorous interrogation or the threat of torture, he might confess to the crime, even if he hadn't committed it. His character was so pitifully weak and changeable. Only a bold and vigorous defence could save him – and the family's honour.

'I thank you, Madame Rossi, for looking after the interests of my son and for promptly bringing this matter to my attention. Now listen, this is what we shall say really happened. Contrary to the maid's misleading account, my son had not been near the captain's body and had no blood on his garments.' The count glowered at Catherine. 'She's unlettered and ignorant, and didn't understand the document that she was asked to sign.'

'What could be Madame Cartier's motive for this deception?' asked Gabriella.

'It was her zeal to shield the Comtesse de Joinville, one of the winter visitors, that moved her to shift blame to a local person, unfortunately, my son. To preserve goodwill, as much as possible, I'll order the return of the spoons to Mr Howard with an apology from the government. I'll assure him that Catherine and her mother will be held here for trial, promptly convicted, and severely punished. I will also arrest the pawnbroker for trafficking in stolen goods. Finally, I'll speak to Madame Cartier and Dr McKenzie and bring them to a better understanding of the case of Captain Howe.'

Gabriella appeared anxious, doubtful.

The count elaborated. 'To gain sympathy, Catherine told a clever lie about my son that she thought Madame Cartier would like to hear.' He met Gabriella's eye, put a little ice in his voice. 'Do you have any more questions?'

She shook her head.

'Good! Then we understand each other.'

The count summoned guards, who led a stunned and

weeping Catherine away. She hadn't said a word and probably hadn't understood half of what the count said. She did appear to realize that she and her mother were going to prison. The count congratulated himself that his version of the case would prevail.

'Madame,' he addressed Gabriella formally, 'I expect you to do your part. When speaking with the visitors, correct any false rumours and explain what really happened when Mario went to your house.' He rang for his clerk. 'You may leave now, Madame Rossi, but remain nearby. Let my clerk know where you will be. I'll send for Mario. When he arrives, I'll summon you. Together, we'll bring him around to our new, corrected version of his movements a week ago.'

She smiled to reassure him, but he sensed that he hadn't fully convinced her.

At a cafe across the square from the palace, Gabriella sipped a lemonade. She had time and a pressing need to think. With every passing hour, she grew more fearful of her future. The count's concern for his son and his own honour had warped his judgement. He could not so easily fool Madame Cartier and other winter visitors as he seemed to believe. They would resent his deception. If he persisted on this course, Intendant Spinola would report him to the royal government and he would come to a bad end. Gabriella determined not to fall with him.

By the time the count's clerk came for her, Gabriella had regained a measure of calm. She found the count pacing the office floor.

'Have a seat, Madame Rossi. My son will soon be here.' The count was striving but failing to conceal his irritation. 'After three hours of searching, my men found him in a gambling den in the old town, a short walk from the palace.'

A few minutes later, Mario sauntered into the office, clearly in a light-hearted mood. He appeared surprised to see Gabriella, but gave her a warm smile and a deferential bow. Then he addressed his father in almost a mocking tone. 'Sir, your men rudely insisted that I go with them immediately. They should have shown more respect. I hated to leave the betting table, for I had Lady Luck with me. I'd already won five hundred livres and was looking forward to celebrate in the evening

156

with friends. So, please tell me, sir, why did you send for me?'

He took a seat at the writing table across from the count, crossed his legs, and waited comfortably for an answer.

'There has been a serious turn of events, my son. Madame Cartier and Dr McKenzie have attempted to gather evidence that you murdered Captain Howe. The maid Catherine fell into their hands, signed her name to a story that implicated you in the crime.' He described Madame Cartier's discovery of the missing spoons and the hold that she gained over the maid.

While the count narrated the events leading up to the maid's incarceration, Gabriella observed Mario with mounting concern. His nonchalance quickly evaporated. A storm of anger gathered on his brow. When the count finished, the young man could hardly contain his feelings.

'Madame Cartier be damned! She dares to accuse me of treacherously stabbing the captain in the dark of night. She dishonours me. I would have gladly killed the captain, but only in a fair duel in daylight. She must be taught never again to insult a gentleman.'

Gabriella would usually have smiled at Mario's youthful excess. But this outburst chilled her and she shivered. Beneath his bombast and bravado she sensed the serious intention to harm Madame Cartier. Should she be warned of the danger?

The count appeared not to have noticed his son's changed attitude. 'You must listen carefully, son. This is what happened early last Monday morning. You were angry with the captain and intended to confront him after the ball. But you couldn't find him in or around the villa, so you decided to walk down the hill to Madame Rossi's house. Unsteady on your feet from too much wine, you fell and soiled your clothes. Madame Rossi saw to their cleaning. End of the story. No one can contradict it, except Catherine, who is now silenced in prison. Carlo, the handyman, now agrees that it was too dark that night to have recognized blood on your clothing.'

The count stopped speaking and stared impatiently at Mario, whose body was rocking slightly back and forth to an inaudible inner beat. He had paid little heed to his father's discourse.

'Do you understand, son?'

The young man ignored the question, studying instead the

table in front of him, eyes half-closed, teeth clenched. He seemed absorbed with his own dark thoughts.

'Do you hear me?' the count demanded, struggling to regain control over the young man who had drifted out of reach.

Mario nodded, not to what his father had asked but to a mysterious voice from within himself. An expression of resolve came over his face. His features hardened. Gabriella nearly cringed with fear.

Exasperated, the count gave up, waved the young man out of the office, and bade Gabriella a curt goodnight.

On the way home, Gabriella grew deeply troubled. 'The count's deception is too clever by far,' she muttered to herself. 'His own son gives it little credence and charges recklessly forward on a path of destruction.' She feared that the count's concern for family honour and for his son had become irrational, an obsession.

Madame Cartier had the maid's written statement that confirmed Carlo's testimony. Who were the winter visitors going to believe? The royal intendant usually kept himself well informed. What would he report to the government in Turin?

In her mind's eye a fiery pit opened up before her. She teetered on the brink.

At the villa, late in the afternoon, Anne and Dr McKenzie sat on the terrace drinking cool lemonade. She had grown fond of the beverage since arriving in Nice, where it was both delicious and inexpensive. The doctor was discreetly probing into the circumstances that had brought Anne and Paul together.

'I was living in England,' she explained gladly, 'when Paul brought news to me that my stepfather had killed himself and his mistress in Paris. I couldn't believe he would do such a thing, so I went to Paris to investigate. Paul and his adjutant, Georges Charpentier, helped me discover the true killer and clear my stepfather's name. And we became friends. One thing led to another and—'

A servant interrupted Anne's story. 'A message for you, madame.'

Anne opened the letter, scanned it, then turned to McKenzie. 'It's from Marseille. Paul and his colleagues have just solved a twenty-year-old murder and have arrested the victim's stepson. The fugitive convict, who de Maistre thinks has hidden in Nice, is almost certainly innocent and should never have been sent to prison.'

'Amazing!' McKenzie exclaimed. 'Does he say more?'

'He says that I should keep this news confidential. It's too early to celebrate. The law considers Lebrun to be guilty, until the other man is convicted. Before the news gets out, Paul wants to question Grimshaw. Paul will explain more in detail when he arrives in Nice. Last Sunday he was going to sail from Marseille. With fair winds he should arrive here tomorrow afternoon.'

After supper, Beverly and Janice retired to their rooms. Anne was seeing Dr McKenzie to the door. Suddenly, the boy Angelo appeared out of the darkness, breathing heavily. He must have run up the hill.

'I have news, Madame Cartier.' He stopped, stared at McKenzie.

'The doctor should hear it, too, Angelo. Come into the parlour.'

When Anne had closed the door behind them, the boy blurted out, 'They've arrested Catherine and her mother this afternoon. Locked them up in the palace. The guard said they're thieves. No one can talk to them. I asked, "What did they steal?" He told me to mind my own business. "Go home," he said, "or I'll lock you up too." '

'The devil's luck!' exclaimed Anne. 'Poor Catherine and her mother.' She turned to the doctor. 'I see de Maistre's hand in this, trying to suppress evidence that implicates his son in the murder of Captain Howe.'

'How did he find out?'

'I'm sorry, I'm at fault,' Angelo broke in. 'The boy who works in Gabriella's kitchen must have betrayed me. I have been asking him questions about the maid Catherine.'

'Things sometimes just go wrong. You've done well.' Anne patted the boy on the shoulder. 'Carlo's wife probably followed me.'

'What shall we do now?' wondered McKenzie.

'We shall wait,' Anne replied. 'I believe the Comte de Maistre will get in touch with us tomorrow.'

Twenty

Reunion

Anne woke up tired, having slept restlessly. The anger and
regret she felt at the arrest of the maid Catherine and her
mother had mixed with feelings of guilt. Before falling asleep,
she had tossed in bed for an hour or more, imagining the two
unfortunate women languishing in prison. She asked herself,
what could I have done differently?

She admitted that she should have watched out for spies
more carefully. Gabriella had to protect the alibi she had
given. So she would engage someone like the handyman's
wife to keep an eye on Carlo and Catherine. But otherwise
Anne felt vindicated. Her implied threat to expose Catherine
for thieving was the only way to get her to tell the truth.

Anne's mind told her that she needn't feel guilty. Someone
else, if not her, would have noticed that the spoons were
missing. The maid's thieving was desperate, inept. She and
her mother were destined to end in prison.

Nonetheless, while dressing, Anne resolved to remember
Catherine and her mother. An opportunity to help them might
arise. By the time Anne ate breakfast on the terrace, her sense
of failure had receded and her thoughts turned to her husband.
Yesterday's message from Marseille said that he would arrive
by ship as early as this afternoon. Anne hoped that the sea
would be gentle.

Shortly after breakfast, Anne and Beverly walked a short
distance to the monumental ruins of the Temple of Apollo.
Covered by a makeshift roof, the building had served for
centuries as a barn. Beverly had invited Anne to meet a
newborn donkey.

As Anne opened the door, the scents of rural life – oiled
leather, manure, hay – awoke fond memories of her grandfa-
ther's farm in Hampstead, near London. She had left her horse
in his care when she married Paul last year and moved to

France. Mignon was the horse's name, a fine-boned black thoroughbred. Anne yearned to ride her again.

Inside the barn, Anne's eyes adjusted slowly to the darkness. The only light came from a few high windows. But after a minute, Anne detected the little donkey already standing on thin, shaky legs.

'She's a charming creature,' said Beverly.

'And as beautiful as she should be,' Anne added, drawing on her slender fund of ancient history. 'With Apollo as her patron, she has an auspicious future.' Anne recalled Grimshaw's description of this building in Roman times. Thin slabs of polished marble once cloaked the thick, lofty brick walls and a broad arched vault covered the interior. The sun god Apollo, god of beauty, must have been pleased to dwell there. In its present decrepit state the building was better suited to shelter farm animals.

A messenger found them still in the barn, petting the donkey.

'Anne Cartier?' he asked, his voice uncertain.

Anne reached for the message. 'That's me.' She opened it and read:

The Comte de Maistre, Commandant in the County of Nice, wishes to speak to you in his office at eleven o'clock.

With a grimace but without comment, Anne showed the message to Beverly.

She read it and handed it back to Anne. 'The count will go to great lengths to protect his son Mario. I fear for the Comtesse de Joinville. She may be guilty, but she still deserves a fair trial.'

'And as fair a trial for the maid Catherine and her mother. In some measure I've caused their misfortune. I sense that my visit with the count will not be pleasant. Thus far, he has shown me his gracious side. Now I expect to see the other.'

At eleven o'clock promptly, Anne presented herself at the Comte de Maistre's office door in the royal palace. A servant in livery announced her and let her in. The count sat perfectly composed at his highly polished mahogany writing table, free of clutter. As she approached, he rose and bowed, greeted her formally, and gestured to a chair facing him.

When they had both seated themselves, he began, 'I think

161

we must come to an understanding, Madame Cartier, concerning the investigation of Captain Howe's murder. In brief, I am in charge. If I need your assistance, for example to question the deaf Miss Janice Parker, I shall request it. But I cannot allow you independently to investigate possible suspects, such as my son Mario. Nor may you seek out and question possible witnesses. By threatening to expose the maid Catherine's theft of silver spoons, you and Dr McKenzie cajoled her to give erroneous testimony concerning my son's involvement in the captain's death.'

Anne sensed that this wasn't going to be a free or even-handed exchange of opinions. So when the count paused for a moment and before he could resume his remarks, she seized the opportunity to speak her mind.

'With all due respect, sir, I object to your charge that we cajoled the maid. We raised the issue of the spoons in order to persuade her to return them, thus freeing her from the threat of prison. She then gave unfettered, truthful testimony concerning your son's appearance when he came to Madame Rossi's house that night. Need I add, the maid did not accuse him of the crime.'

If the count was impatient or irritated with her, he didn't show it. His expression remained courteous, but also unyielding. It was obvious that nothing she might say would change his attitude. She was simply to cease investigating the case and leave it all to him. And if she refused . . . ?

That question was understood by both of them, but it was neither raised nor answered. She imagined that his soldiers would simply pack her off the scant few miles to the French border. The Comtesse de Joinville as well as Catherine and her mother would have to fend for themselves, with little hope of receiving justice.

Back in her room at the villa, late in the afternoon, Anne anxiously awaited her husband. She had kept herself occupied up to now by instructing the cook's boy Angelo in simple English. He was a quick, bright, enthusiastic student. Janice had also come to her, ostensibly for more training in proper articulation, but really in order to unburden herself of frustration. Her infatuation with Captain Howe seemed to be subsiding, but her tension with Beverly remained strong. She was also impatient with her difficulty in communicating with

162

hearing people. They could understand her better than she could understand them.

Janice had just left, when Anne heard a commotion outside. She rushed to the window to see Paul step out of a sedan chair, pay the porters, and send them off. A donkey carried his luggage. Anne hurried downstairs and met him at the front door. For a moment they gazed at each other, then warmly embraced. He had been gone less than two weeks. Yet so much had happened that his absence seemed much longer.

Beverly and Janice arrived to greet Paul, then they all gathered for tea and biscuits in the parlour. His trip in a large felucca had been quick and pleasant, the sea moderate, the winds westerly. He said nothing about his mission for the Baron de Breteuil but described scenes in Marseille, especially its busy harbour. Men, women, and children of every race mingled on its quays and in its narrow streets.

Anne was pleased that he chose to sit opposite Janice, so that she could more easily read his lips. And he often signed while he spoke. Janice responded with lively interest and a lovely smile.

Paul surveyed his friends. 'So tell me what has happened while I was away.'

Anne smiled inwardly. He knew about the captain's murder, since she had kept him informed. He must think he could learn something from the retelling of the story.

Beverly started off with a brief description of the Cimiez festival, followed by the ball at the villa, and then the discovery of the captain's body. Anne added a few general remarks about the subsequent investigation, ending with the arrest of the Comtesse de Joinville.

Little of this could be news to Paul, but he asked, 'Who are the possible suspects?'

Janice blurted out, 'Mr Grimshaw.' Her articulation was measured and clear, her eyes narrowed and cold. She might grieve less for the captain, but hadn't forgiven the man she believed killed him.

Paul raised an eyebrow at her vehemence, but didn't chide her.

Anne added Mario to the list of suspects.

'And Louise?' he asked.

'Possibly,' Anne replied. 'She once attacked him with a

knife. After his death, the commandant's men found blood on her gown.'

Beverly then led the conversation to the beautiful weather and other less grim topics.

After tea, Anne and Paul walked outside. 'I'd like to see the arena,' he said, 'the scene of the crime.'

A few minutes later, they stood there, recalling what might have happened. With sticks and stones, Anne laid out the position of Howe's body.

'I simply cannot imagine,' mused Paul, 'how the Comtesse de Joinville could have stabbed Captain Howe at night and in this place. Granted that the moon was nearly full, the sky was clear, and the arena was free of shadows. She could have recognized him. But was there enough light for her to have thrust the knife precisely at his throat?'

'Probably not,' replied Anne. 'Louise went to the arena without a lantern. Also she had drunk heavily during the festival and the evening ball – unless, of course, she was only pretending. After midnight, if truly drunk, she couldn't have walked a straight line. Her eyesight would have been impaired and her hand unsteady. Drink might also have disarmed her caution when she discovered the body. She apparently threw herself on to him in a fit of remorse and cradled his body. Hence the bloody gown.'

'The count could reach the same conclusion as we. Why hasn't he?'

'He wants a scapegoat and thinks that Louise is the best candidate. His son Mario and Jack Grimshaw are in fact stronger suspects.'

'Though we dislike Louise and believe her capable of murder, if not under these circumstances, we must make every effort to ensure that she is treated fairly.'

'Unfortunately, Paul, I may have compromised her cause.'

He stared at her. 'How is that?'

She described the investigation she carried out with Dr McKenzie into Mario's flight from the scene of the crime. 'The testimony of Gabriella's handyman and her maid Catherine agreed on the point of his bloodstained clothes. We also discovered that Catherine was stealing silver spoons from Mr Howard. While we were searching for a way to return them, the count arrested her. He has spies everywhere. He believes we were trying to implicate his son in Howe's murder and demands that we cease our investigation.'

'Don't feel badly. You did well. The count has great power in the County of Nice, since he's in charge of the military and the police. It's very difficult to work against him. I couldn't have done better. It's unfortunate that his concern for his honour and for his son is corrupting his judgement. In other respects he's an enlightened commandant. But we must do what we can for Louise. The baron expects no less.'

'Would he care if she were an artisan's daughter?' asked Anne, irritated by yet another reminder of noble privilege. With undisguised irony she answered her own question. 'We cannot stand by, arms folded, while the baron's daughter is tried and hung! We must find the captain's killer, the Comte de Maistre notwithstanding.'

Paul smiled tolerantly and didn't comment.

The sun was setting now, throwing strange shadows into the ruined rows where spectators had once urged gladiators to kill each other.

Paul waved a hand over the arena. 'This place reminds me that there is yet another potential suspect, Mr Grimshaw, a man familiar with brutal Roman customs and perhaps touched by their violent spirit. If he wished to settle accounts with Captain Howe, what more appropriate place could he choose?'

'That's true,' Anne said. 'What did you learn about him on your trip?'

'First, I'll mention a hidden connection to the escaped convict Lebrun that I would never have imagined, a friendship reaching back more than twenty years.'

'I'm not surprised,' Anne remarked. 'While searching his wardrobe, I found letters from Madame Lebrun indicating that he kept her informed about her husband.'

'And at Barrett and Sons, his bank in Marseille, Georges and I learned that he probably supplied Lebrun with the money to escape from the naval prison at Toulon.'

'Then is Grimshaw facing arrest?' Anne asked. 'Will de Maistre extradite him to France for trial?'

'Well, I'm not sure,' said Paul. 'For Lebrun shouldn't have been in prison in the first place. With help from others, Georges and I discovered another man who committed the murder for which Lebrun was convicted. Should Grimshaw be punished for freeing an innocent man?'

'I should say not! But magistrates might think otherwise, sad to say.' She paused, sighed. 'What else did you learn?'

'At Barrett and Sons we found a considerable sum in Grimshaw's bank account. But that was money he had saved over many years. His strongbox contained interesting personal papers and a few gold and silver coins. If he has a treasure trove, he must have hidden it elsewhere.'

'I know a likely place.' Anne described the cave that might lead to a hidden Mithras sanctuary. 'In his wardrobe, I also discovered his secret account book, indicating that he paid extortion to the captain, presumably to keep his treasure a secret from Mr Parker.'

'His papers in Marseille reveal yet another motive to kill Howe.' Paul described the passages in Grimshaw's diary concerning his daughter's suicide and his failed attempt to kill her seducer, a certain Captain H . . .

'Captain Howe, of course! Now I better understand the intensity of Grimshaw's hatred for the captain.'

'Do you see in Grimshaw a mind to murder him?'

Anne nodded. 'I can imagine Grimshaw shifting his feelings for his daughter to our Janice. To protect her and to avenge his daughter would blend into a potent, overwhelming desire to kill Captain Howe.'

'A plausible theory,' Paul remarked. 'Still, we have no evidence to prove that he actually killed the captain.'

'We may yet find it,' Anne said. 'In the meantime, let's look for his treasure trove tomorrow, beginning in his cave. Now it's time for supper. You must be hungry, Paul. There's a delicious lamb ragout waiting for us.' They embraced again, linked arms, and left the arena.

Late at night, Mario entered a wine tavern in the old town, with money in his pocket. This evening, luck had been with him in the gambling dens of Nice. He looked over the men crowded around small tables. The place stank of spilled wine and acrid tobacco smoke. Loud shouts and bursts of raucous laughter assaulted his ears. The clientele was the human refuse of Nice. The majority were smugglers, pimps, or petty thieves.

Neither surprised nor offended, Mario had come here before when he needed men for work that was either dangerous or illegal or both.

His eyes began to smart. He couldn't get used to the foul air. Finally, he saw them, two men whom he had hired previously and could trust. He had a job for them.

He caught their eye, then spoke to the barman. Yes, the back room was available. Mario put a coin on the bar and beckoned the men. They rose and followed him.

Wineglasses cupped in their hands, the three men huddled over a table as if fearing to be overheard through the thick, tightly closed door.

'Here's half your wages in advance. You'll receive the rest when you complete the job.' Mario handed each man a coin. 'I want you to follow the winter visitors Madame Cartier and Dr McKenzie. Report to me where they go, what they do. I intend to prepare a surprise for each of them, beginning with the woman.'

Twenty-One

Out of the Depths

Wednesday, 20 February

A rush of frightening images woke Anne from sleep. Barely conscious, she saw herself in a long, low chamber. Paul was at her side. Their flickering lanterns cast an eerie light on smooth, polished white marble walls. At the far end, a nude youth gripped a bull by the head and plunged a knife into its throat. Blood spurted from the wound. Suddenly the floor shook, the walls collapsed, and the ceiling fell in upon them. Trapped in a tiny space in total darkness, they gasped for air. Panic seized her. She opened her mouth to scream.

'Anne! Wake up! What's wrong?' Paul was leaning toward her, his hand on her shoulder, his brow furrowed with concern. They were in bed. A thin, early morning light slanted through the windows.

'I've been dreaming of Grimshaw's cave. Dr McKenzie's tales about Mithras have infected my imagination.'

While dressing, they discussed possible complications in the investigation of the cave. It began to look like a dangerous expedition. If there was a sanctuary beneath the hillside, they didn't know its condition. The walls *could* collapse and trap them.

Anne wondered what the Comte de Maistre would think of this investigation. He would probably argue that it violated his injunction against her investigating any aspect of the captain's death without his permission. Nonetheless, until she could trust his judgement again, she intended to ignore him. She would investigate Grimshaw but be cautious.

Anne went to Beverly's room for breakfast. After a casual exchange of views on the health of the Howards and other sickly visitors, Anne remarked, 'If anyone were to enquire about Dr McKenzie, Paul, and me today, you could say that we are going out to amuse ourselves in the countryside. We plan to take a lunch with us.'

'How delightful.' Beverly seemed disappointed at not being invited to share in their pleasure.

Anne smiled gently. 'Today's hike will be rather arduous. You shall join us another time when we take a more leisurely walk and picnic in the country.' Anne lacked confidence in Beverly's discretion. If told that they would explore the cave in the hillside, she might inadvertently betray the secret to Grimshaw.

'By the way,' Anne said, as she was leaving the room, 'where is Mr Grimshaw?'

'He just left for the city on various errands. He should return late this afternoon. Did I need anything, he asked. I gave him a short list.'

This news lifted Anne's spirits. She had imagined him suddenly confronting them at the cave.

At midmorning, Anne, McKenzie, and Paul left the villa in sturdy walking shoes and rustic clothes. They had armed themselves with hidden pistols and stout walking sticks. Anne wore her riding breeches rather than a dress. A donkey carried their lanterns, food, and other supplies.

They took a roundabout route to the cave to allay suspicion. Grimshaw might have told his assistant to keep an eye on them. Their progress was slow. The hillside was rocky and thick with bush. Paths were narrow and uneven. And McKenzie tired easily.

As they approached the cave, they scanned the hillside. No one in sight. No sounds but the wind rustling in the trees. They tethered the donkey to a tree off the path behind thick bushes and entered the cave. Anne shovelled the cover of dirt from the stone lid, then with Paul lifted it and set it aside. With trembling hands, Anne held a lantern over the hole and they peered in. A few feet below, there was a landing, from which stone steps descended into the darkness. As far as Anne could see, the landing was clear of debris. Grimshaw's work, no doubt.

Before setting out from the villa, they had studied again McKenzie's drawing of the typical layout of a Mithraic sanctuary, so they would know what to expect. They had anticipated that Grimshaw might have set out traps for unwary, unwelcome visitors. Therefore they had come with a long coil of rope. McKenzie would remain above ground, guarding the cave, while Anne and Paul went below. Anne would take one end of the rope, McKenzie would hold the other. They agreed on a few signals – two quick jerks meant an emergency.

Paul went down first, holding on to the edges of the hole until he had tested the landing, then he helped Anne down. They lighted the lanterns and surveyed the stairway. It was circular, built entirely of cut stone, and in good condition. Paul tested each step, as well as the walls and ceiling. Anne followed him, holding the rope and counting the steps. After the thirtieth step, they came to a bottom landing. She calculated that they were about fifteen feet below the surface.

In front of them was a small, low, stone door. 'Probably thin marble,' Paul said. 'The hinges have recently been oiled.' He gingerly lifted a simple latch and pulled the door toward him. 'Definitely marble, polished on the inside.'

Bent double, they squeezed through the opening and held up their lanterns. They had entered the apse. In front of them was a free-standing altar and behind it a large expertly sculpted marble relief of young Mithras and the sacred bull. Mithras wore a loose blouse, long pants, and a Phrygian cap. A short cape billowed out behind him.

His left hand pulled back the animal's head. His right hand held the knife that he had just plunged into the bull's neck. A serpent slithered up to drink the gushing blood. A crab seized the animal's genitals.

Studying this ritual in books hadn't troubled Anne. But now in the sanctuary, staring at this ghastly picture, she felt mentally soiled, profoundly revolted. What kind of men had drunk the bull's blood or poured it over themselves? she wondered. They must have been depraved. Then she recalled the arena where Captain Howe had died. Centuries earlier, the men who worshipped here had also sat in the amphitheatre and urged gladiators to spill their blood on the same ground.

She forced her eyes away from the apse and examined the rest of the sanctuary. Marble still covered the interior walls. The tile floor was clean. Debris had been gathered in neat piles near the walls. Grimshaw must have partially restored the sanctuary or at least cleaned it. Anne and Paul walked down three steps into an area for worshippers, rather like the nave of a Christian church. Stone benches stretched along the side walls. At the far end of the nave they climbed four steps into a vestibule. A half-dozen more steps and they came to a plain stone wall.

Anne tapped on it. Solid and thick. 'On the other side must be the entrance hall that Grimshaw called a shrine to Mercury. I was misled. The wall sealed off the sanctuary when the cult was abandoned.'

They turned and looked back toward the apse. The space was smaller than in Anne's dream. She imagined fifty men, mostly soldiers, worshiping here by lantern light under a low ceiling.

Then she gasped – a man was lying on a stone bench against a wall. A canvas cloth covered him, except for his unshaven face. He appeared to be sleeping.

She brought a hand to her mouth to stifle a scream, nudged Paul, and pointed.

He drew his pistol, half-cocked it.

She whispered to him, 'Who is he?'

'I can guess.' He moved closer to the stranger, held his lantern high.

At that moment the man awoke, eyes dazed, uncomprehending. Then he moaned and covered his face with his hands.

Paul moved the light away from the man's eyes. 'Monsieur Jean Lebrun, I suppose.'

The man slowly nodded.

Paul uncocked his pistol, lowered it. 'Then I bring you good news. You are nearly a free man. Madame Duclos has recanted her testimony against you and implicated her son Henri Duclos in the murder of his stepfather. The police have arrested Henri. The magistrates will soon put him on trial, and they have begun to review your conviction.'

Lebrun remained silent, staring at Saint-Martin and at Anne. Finally he asked, 'Who are you?'

Paul identified himself and Anne. 'My adjutant Georges Charpentier is overseeing your cause in Marseille. He knows you better than anyone. For weeks he searched for you in Paris, met your wife – who is well. Together, he and I reopened the investigation in Marseille, persuaded Madame Duclos and her maid to tell the truth.'

While Paul spoke, Lebrun threw off the canvas cover and sat up. His legs were bare to the knees. Anne gasped when she noticed the broad red welts on his ankles, the marks of the shackles.

'A souvenir of Toulon,' he remarked, as his spirits revived.

Paul holstered his pistol. 'I recently visited the naval prison and enquired after you. A cruel place, a human hell. I regret, more than I can say, that our system of justice put you there for the best years of your life.'

'The first year I spent in despair. Toulon is indeed a human hell. But then I discovered a goal, a purpose for my life there – to escape. My skill with wood and with writing ingratiated me with the officers. I carefully studied the failed attempts of other convicts. When my opportunity came, I seized it.'

His face lit up. 'I can hardly describe the feeling of being free, even as a fugitive.' He met Paul's eyes. 'You called the prison a cruel place. That's true, but in a way it's also necessary. A few of my comrades in chains are truly monsters, and had raped, robbed, and killed without compunction. Given the opportunity, they would gladly repeat their crimes. Toulon is the right place for them. Like wild beasts, they must be strictly confined.' He rubbed his wrists. A habitual gesture. They, too, were marked.

171

He went on. 'For most convicts, Toulon is too cruel. They are simple men: thieves, poachers, deserters, who caused far less harm to others than tax farmers, corrupt magistrates, or self-serving royal ministers.' He paused, smiled wryly. 'Pardon my complaints. I do appreciate your kind words. It's rare to hear anyone in authority say they are sorry for the evils that they or the system have done.'

'How long have you hidden here?' Anne asked.

'Four weeks. A few weeks earlier, Grimshaw had discovered the entrance in the cave above us, had opened up the sanctuary, and had begun to explore it. He hired me to help look for treasure. I lived in the barn and got food from the kitchen.' He gazed at Anne. 'I used to watch you from a distance and try to recall the image of my wife. Someone at the villa told the police that I was on the domain. Before they could find me, Grimshaw hid me here, brought food from time to time. I have fresh water from a spring.' He pointed to a far corner of the sanctuary. 'There's another way to the outside, a vent for fresh air. Grimshaw gave me a rope and I often climbed up to lie in the sun, hidden by the bushes.'

Anne was puzzled. 'Why didn't Grimshaw turn you in? He could have collected a reward.'

'We are actually friends. Years ago we met in Marseille. I fled to Nice, hoping to meet him. One day he noticed me in the marketplace and brought me here. Even now I fear that he might be punished for helping me.'

'You have reason to be concerned,' said Paul. 'The law sometimes acts in perverse ways. I'll do what I can for him.' He paused, glanced at Anne. 'I think it's time we leave.' She nodded. They began to walk toward the exit and the circular stairway. On an impulse, Paul turned to Lebrun and asked, 'Did you find anything of value here?' He was thinking of the treasure trove that Grimshaw was suspected to have discovered and hidden somewhere.

Lebrun appeared uncomfortable. 'I would rather let Grimshaw answer you.'

'Then we shall return to the villa. I can think of no reason why you should continue to hide here. I must inform the Comte de Maistre that you are in my custody. He also needs to know what has happened in the Duclos case in Marseille.

He should no longer threaten you, though he may raise questions concerning the treasure. To whom does it legally belong is the issue, assuming that it exists.'

An hour later, the Comte de Maistre arrived at the villa. Anne and Paul were waiting for him in the parlour. Lebrun was resting after a bath. McKenzie had returned home.

'The *galerien*. Tell me about him.' The count sat on the edge of his chair, sceptically glancing first at Anne, then at Paul.

Anne replied, 'A few days ago, while enjoying the countryside to the north of the olive grove, I chanced upon a cave. This morning, for amusement's sake, we set out to explore it. We discovered an ancient underground sanctuary and a hidden man, the escaped convict Jean Lebrun.'

Paul added, 'I've taken him into custody until the magistrates in Provence formally determine his status. We discovered in Marseille that he's not guilty of the crime for which he was convicted.' He handed de Maistre a police report signed by Captain Barras and Lieutenant General Clary.

'Could I see Lebrun?' asked the count, a look of irritation on his face.

'He's resting,' replied Paul.

'Then later. In the meantime I would like to visit the sanctuary. According to rumour, a treasure trove was found there.'

Anne and Paul led the count to the cave and down the steps into the sanctuary. He stared at Mithras and the bull with a grimace of disgust. His expression changed to wonder as he examined the marble walls. Then he collected himself. 'I wish to see where you found Lebrun.'

They moved to the area for worshippers and Anne pointed to Lebrun's bench.

The count stared at the bench, lifted the canvas cover, turned around and surveyed the sanctuary. 'This isn't an easy place to find.' He seemed puzzled, then he asked, 'How could he live here?'

The count's question wasn't addressed to anyone in particular, so it hung in the air for a few moments. Finally, Paul suggested, 'Mr Grimshaw might know. He's perhaps the person best informed about the villa's property and its inhabitants.'

The count pursed his lips. 'Where might I find him?'

173

'Somewhere in the city, sir,' Anne replied. 'He's expected back late in the afternoon.'

'That gives me a couple of hours,' declared the count through thin, pressed lips. 'I want to question everyone who might recall Monsieur Lebrun. Someone must know how such a notorious fugitive from the French King's justice could hide for several weeks, only two miles from my office.'

When they returned to the villa, de Maistre turned to Anne. 'I would like your assistance, Madame Cartier, to take notes and to translate for me.' His tone was almost deferential, his manner once again courteous. Anne could detect no trace of the stiff manner, the rigid reproof, she had experienced in his office yesterday.

She wasn't entirely surprised. Her skill in English and sign language could again be of use to him. Even more important was the fact that the count's attention had now shifted to Grimshaw, suddenly another promising suspect, an alternative to the count's own son Mario. The count seemed to think that Grimshaw could have killed Captain Howe in order to protect not only a treasure trove but also a reputed fugitive murderer.

Anne and the count began upstairs. Neither Beverly nor Janice remembered Lebrun, and had probably never seen him.

Downstairs, Anne spoke to the cook Philippa in the local dialect, with the count sitting to one side. Yes, she remembered the missing man. He had said very little. His few words in the dialect had a French accent. She had felt sorry for him, fed him. He looked so desperate, like a hunted animal. For a few weeks, he worked in the olive grove and slept in the barn. Then he was gone. She thought nothing of it. Strangers like him often came for a short while, then left. She rarely learned their names.

At four o'clock, Grimshaw returned from the city, surprised to discover the Comte de Maistre and Anne waiting for him in the ground-floor parlour. The count pointed him to a seat, then began asking about his work at the villa. The questions were in French, Anne taking notes. He quickly sensed that he was in trouble and became reticent.

Finally, the count leaned forward and said, 'This morning, a Mithraic sanctuary was discovered north of the olive grove.

174

Inside was hidden the Toulon convict Jean Lebrun, formerly a fugitive from the French King's justice.'

Grimshaw started, seemed perplexed. 'Formerly a fugitive?'

Anne spoke up. 'Yes, my husband says that the police in Marseille have arrested another man for the murder of Lebrun's master. Lebrun should soon be exonerated.'

Grimshaw's eyes widened in disbelief. He opened his mouth to speak. But the count pressed on. 'Can you explain how Lebrun came to be in the sanctuary?'

Anne closely studied Grimshaw's eyes and detected the working of fear.

'Several weeks ago,' Grimshaw replied, 'I discovered the sanctuary, but kept it secret while I searched it for precious objects. There was a danger of looting. Having found nothing of great value thus far, I decided to prepare the sanctuary to show to Mr Parker, who leases the property. In the market I hired a labourer to clean the floors. The name he gave me was Jean Leblanc, French, I thought.'

Grimshaw was concealing his friendship with Lebrun. Why? Anne wondered. He knew exactly whom he hired.

The count scowled. 'At some point you must have discovered that he was a fugitive from justice. You should have turned him over to me. I would have taken him back to France. If the French authorities had discovered that he was innocent of the crime for which he was convicted, they would have released him. Instead of following the law, you led me and my men on a fool's errand when we searched the villa and the domain. Why didn't you report him then? It makes me angry to think that you treated me like a common simpleton.'

Grimshaw remained calm. 'I believed that the man was innocent, wrongly convicted. It appears that I was correct. I didn't trust the French authorities to do the right thing. After all, they had held him in prison for twenty years. I regret that I had to mislead you. I meant no offence.'

Grimshaw's reply failed to mollify the count. 'Colonel Saint-Martin has told me that there are gold and silver Roman coins in your strongbox at a bank in Marseille.'

Grimshaw seemed stunned at the reference to his bank box.

The count went on, 'I believe you found a treasure trove months ago, of which you put a few coins in the box. Where is the rest of it? Had Captain Howe discovered evidence of your newly found wealth and demanded a share of it?'

'He had seen me with a gold medallion that Mr Parker could have claimed for himself. The captain wrongly concluded that I had discovered a hoard of gold and silver and had hidden it. I paid him when he threatened to tell Parker. But I did not kill him. I'm not a murderer.'

'We shall see. Nonetheless, I'm going to arrest you now on suspicion of killing Captain Howe and hiding a treasure trove that legally belongs to the Sardinian King. You will be kept in a cell in the royal palace for further questioning.'

The count rang for his men and they took Grimshaw away.

Anne glanced up from her notes. The count had a look of satisfaction on his face.

Saint-Martin was in Lebrun's room, having a friendly conversation with the former fugitive, who was trying to adjust to a more normal life than he had in the Toulon prison or the underground Mithras sanctuary. Even a simple smile proved difficult.

Then Anne came to report the count's arrest of Grimshaw. 'De Maistre,' she opined, 'felt insulted and allowed his pique to influence his decision. The count also placed too much credence in Grimshaw's treasure trove. It's no more than a figment of Howe's imagination or a maid's fantasy.'

Paul countered, 'But it serves as another excuse to make Grimshaw, like Louise, a scapegoat for Mario. Still, Grimshaw might in fact be guilty. We know that he had ample motives to kill the captain.'

'Motives aren't enough,' Anne rejoined. 'The count has to find evidence. In the meantime, Paul, the count wants you to bring Monsieur Lebrun to the parlour for questioning.'

Paul turned to Lebrun. 'Are you ready?'

'Yes, Colonel,' he replied. 'I feel better now that you are going with me.'

As Saint-Martin walked with Lebrun into the parlour, he felt increased pressure at his temples, a sure sign of anxiety's onset, triggered by the room's oppressive atmosphere. A pair of wall sconces gave off a pale, fitful glow. The count sat rigid and unsmiling, his back to a window illuminated by a late afternoon northerly light. Eyes narrowed with suspicion, lips curled with distaste, he studied Lebrun from head to toe.

The former fugitive had shaved and bathed. His hair had been trimmed. Dressed in a clean brown suit, he looked like a respectable, middle-aged craftsman, who had gained some of a master's self-assurance. But when he saw the count, he stiffened. Fear returned to his eyes.

De Maistre began. 'You should know, Lebrun, that I've arrested your protector Mr Grimshaw on suspicion of killing a certain Captain Howe ten days ago. I also suspect him of illegally taking certain treasure out of the country. What, if anything, can you tell me about these crimes?'

'On his visits to the sanctuary, Mr Grimshaw used to give me the latest news from the villa. He told me about the murder and that he was among the suspects. He had an alibi, he said, but wouldn't use it unless forced to. He wouldn't speculate on who had committed the crime.'

The count waved a threatening finger at Lebrun. 'I warn you, if you try to lie to me, you will soon find yourself back in irons and in a prison cell. Now, tell me, did Mr Grimshaw discover a treasure trove in the sanctuary?'

Lebrun replied to the count's question in a remarkably calm voice. 'If he discovered a treasure, he did so in the weeks before hiring me. He told me to be sharp-eyed. When I cleaned or made repairs, I might find coins, jewellery, or precious stones.'

'And did you find anything of value?'

'A few pieces. I gave them to Mr Grimshaw. He never told me their worth or what he did with them.'

'I have no more questions, Lebrun.' The count examined him closely. 'You might be innocent of the crime for which you were convicted, but you spent many years in very bad company. That's bound to have left a black mark on your character. I would prefer to keep you in detention for as long as you remained in Nice. However, Colonel Saint-Martin has agreed to be responsible for you.' De Maistre bade goodbye to Saint-Martin, nodded to Lebrun, and left the room.

Saint-Martin put a hand on Lebrun's shoulder. 'Your road back will be bumpy. Men of ill will, like the count, will vex you. Still, you have a clean conscience, a craftsman's skilled hands, and the support of loyal family and friends. Have courage.'

Late in the afternoon, Saint-Martin went to the office of Intendant Spinola in the royal palace. A clerk showed him in. The intendant rose from his writing table. 'Welcome back, Colonel. Please take a seat. I've been looking forward to your return and to a vigorous game of tennis. Was your visit to Toulon and Marseille as useful as you had hoped?'

'Useful indeed. I followed the trail of the notorious fugitive Jean Lebrun from Toulon to Marseille and back to Nice.'

The intendant raised an eyebrow.

'Yes,' Saint-Martin continued, 'my wife and I found him a few hours ago in a Mithras sanctuary near the villa.'

'Well! That *is* news!'

Saint-Martin gave the intendant a brief version of Lebrun's story. 'I'm confident that, this time, the magistrates will exonerate him and convict the guilty man. I shall be responsible for Lebrun until his status is officially determined, assuming that the Comte de Maistre has no objections.'

'Why should he object?' the intendant asked, inclining his head in a gesture that encouraged Saint-Martin to explain what he was hinting at.

'As you might know, I'm at odds with the count concerning the detention of my cousin the Comtesse de Joinville. I don't wish to interfere in the criminal justice of a sovereign foreign country. I have no official standing here. I act only on behalf of the family and not the French state. So it is with all due respect that I suggest that the commandant appears to use her as a scapegoat to divert attention from a much more likely suspect in the murder of Captain Howe.'

Spinola's expression became guarded.

Saint-Martin then ventured to describe de Maistre's bias in favour of his son, which led him to suppress the incriminating testimony of the maid Catherine and the handyman Carlo.

'The Kingdom of Sardinia,' Saint-Martin observed, 'is known to follow the rule of law. Would a sound jurisprudence allow a magistrate to lead the investigation of a capital offence in which his son was among the chief suspects?'

The intendant hesitated to reply. He was surely aware of

178

Mario's notorious behaviour, as well as the father's failure to control him. The intendant also had to know that Mario was a potential suspect in the murder case. Still, he needed to use great care in speaking about a colleague to an outsider.

'Colonel, I share your concern for integrity in the law. But I'm not in an official position to challenge the Comte de Maistre. Nonetheless, after careful reflection, I might bring the issues you raise to the attention of the proper higher authority.'

'Sir, that is all I can ask of you.'

Late in the evening, Anne, Paul, and Dr McKenzie sat down to supper with Beverly and Janice. The Mithraic sanctuary became the topic of conversation.

'It's the first to be found in this region,' said McKenzie, the leading local amateur authority on archaeology. 'But that's not remarkable. Evidence of similar sanctuaries have been found in neighbouring French provinces. What is unusual is that this sanctuary was so well built and well hidden.'

Paul agreed, 'It's in remarkably good condition after fourteen hundred years.'

The doctor went on to ask Paul, 'If the treasure trove exists, to whom do you think it rightfully belongs – to the Sardinian King in Turin, to the property owner, to the leaseholder Mr Parker, or to the man who discovered it, Mr Grimshaw?'

'I believe the King's lawyers would prevail on the legal principle. But, if the treasure were found in France, they might not succeed in persuading the French authorities to send it back, especially if the Comte de Maistre insists on prosecuting the Baron de Breteuil's daughter. But this discussion is moot. I believe that this treasure either doesn't exist or will remain hidden for the foreseeable future.'

Anne noticed Janice trying to enter the discussion. 'What do you think, Janice?'

Her expression was grim. 'The treasure trove is the key to solving a horrible crime. It was the reason Mr Grimshaw murdered Captain Howe.' She leaned back and crossed her arms defiantly.

Beverly had listened to Janice with mounting displeasure in her eyes. At the mention of the murder of Captain Howe, Beverly raised her voice in shrill protest. 'For goodness' sake,

Janice, let us not hang Mr Grimshaw without evidence of his guilt. There's nothing to prove that he killed the captain, only conjecture.'

The two women glared at each other. Then Dr McKenzie moved the conversation to another topic.

Anne sat back, struck by the vigour of Beverly's defence of Grimshaw.

Twenty-Two

A Warning

Thursday, 21 February

Early in the morning, Gabriella finished her coffee and turned immediately to the business of the day. There was a great deal to do. The winter visitors were a demanding lot, insisting on perfect service. Many were ailing, had too few servants of their own, and could do little for themselves. Since Catherine went to prison on Monday, Gabriella had been unable to find a suitable replacement. She would have to do much of the cleaning, cooking, and other chores herself. Few of the local girls could understand more than a word of English or were at all familiar with English ways.

The usual complaints were pouring in. The new maids were dirty, lazy, and stupid. Paying them was like throwing good money away. Gabriella sighed. Clean, hardworking, and efficient Catherine had pleased the English.

With regret, Gabriella recalled Monday's visit to the count's office when he charged the maid with theft. He should have simply ordered the spoons returned with an explanation, an apology, and some compensation. The Howards – gentle, reasonable people – would have been satisfied. The count appeared anxious that Catherine might incriminate his son, so he shut her up in solitary confinement. Since then, Gabriella had found herself wondering what the count's intentions were toward *her*? Like Catherine, she had also seen the bloody costume, heard Mario's story. Did the count suspect her loyalty? Would he turn against her? Suddenly, Gabriella felt very vulnerable.

And the count wasn't her only worry. Since Captain Howe's death, Mario had become a changed man. Or, she admitted to herself, he had begun to show a less pleasing side of his character. He was spending more time with his gambling companions, dissolute young rakes, than with her. When she reproached him, complained of his neglect, he replied that he wasn't her pet any longer. Lady Luck was now his mistress and treating him kindly. And, he remarked, his father was showing him more respect.

The count's attitude made Gabriella wonder if he were at his wits' end, failing to control his son but afraid to take stern measures that would provoke even worse behaviour.

Well, no point worrying any more about matters that she couldn't control. She had a business to take care of and needed a young woman to fill Catherine's place. A family in the city had a daughter who might be suitable. Gabriella's hopes rose. She would visit the family now.

On the way, Gabriella noticed Mario seated with two evil-looking companions at a table outside a cafe. She glanced about. Yes, the boy Angelo was following her. He worked for Madame Cartier. She beckoned him. He appeared confused and embarrassed. She gave him a friendly smile this time and beckoned again. He approached her gingerly.

'I don't mind at all that you follow me, young man. I like to think you are one of my admirers. Now you can do me a favour. See those men?' She pointed to Mario and his companions. 'I want you to sneak up to them and listen to what they say. Come back and tell me. You can tell Madame Cartier too.'

The boy shrugged, nodded, then set off. He scrunched down behind a low wall within a few feet of the men's table. They had begun to lean toward each other like a band of conspirators. Gabriella hoped they spoke loudly enough for the boy to hear. The companions handed something over to Mario, but he refused it. Finally, they nodded to each other and left in different directions. The boy hastened back to Gabriella.

'The two villains are smugglers. The man called Mario told them that the count's soldiers were laying a trap for them in the mountains above Cimiez. The smugglers offered him money. He said, "Not this time. Instead, I want you to do something for me." They agreed. Then he said, "Find Madame Cartier. Cut her up so she feels pain. Make it look like a robbery. I'll pay you extra." They said they would try.'

Gabriella was stunned. Her anxieties about Mario and his father peaked and rendered her momentarily incapable of thinking. The boy stood in front of her, waiting for a coin or an order to leave. 'Shall I go, madame?' he asked.

'Not yet, I may need you.' She finally gathered her wits; she couldn't go to the count. He seemed unreliable, but she couldn't allow this cruel assault to happen. She spoke again to the boy. 'Tell Madame Cartier what you've heard. It's very important. She must be warned. And tell her I'd like to talk to her.'

Angelo was hurrying up the road to Cimiez and was about halfway to the villa when he heard someone walking behind him. He glanced over his shoulder. It was the man called Mario. The boy became fearful, looked for help. The road was empty. He started to run. The man ran after him. For a moment, Angelo thought he was doomed. The man was almost close enough to grab him. Then the man staggered, stopped, and bent over, clutching his chest. He was out of breath. Angelo trotted on. At the top of the hill near the villa, Angelo looked back. The man was standing in the road, shaking his fist.

Anne was in the parlour strengthening Janice's pronunciation of the word *out* when a maid announced that the boy Angelo had an important message and needed to tell it to her himself. 'Could he wait?' Anne asked, reluctant to annoy Janice, who was sensitive to any perceived slight.

The maid appeared to understand Anne's predicament but insisted nonetheless. 'I've asked him. He says it's a matter of life or death.'

Janice had been following this exchange. 'You had better listen to him, Madame Cartier. He's a sensible boy and wouldn't make up a story like that.'

Angelo was admitted and gave Anne the message he had overheard. She was at first most upset that Mario had chased the boy up the hill. Someone must have seen Angelo spying on Mario and warned him.

Anne said to the boy, 'We must keep Mario and his companions at a safe distance. Gabriella wants to see me, you say.' Hmm, Anne murmured to herself, if she wants to talk about Mario, the wayward son, I might find myself straying into the count's forbidden territory.

Anne sent the boy off to the kitchen for dinner. 'When you've finished eating and have had a rest, I'll have an errand for you.' Then she turned back to Janice, who had observed this incident, wide-eyed, for she had grasped the gist of it.

'Aren't you afraid, Madame Cartier, that Mario's men will hurt you?'

'Janice, it's time that you call me Anne when we're alone. I think we have become friends.'

The young woman seemed embarrassed, but smiled gratefully. 'That would please me.'

'To answer your question, I'm seldom really afraid or paralysed by fear. When I was a girl, even younger than you, my stepfather Antoine taught me how to walk a tightrope, starting only a foot from the floor and gradually raising it to a great height. Eventually, I even danced on the high wire at Sadler's Wells and enjoyed the thrill of it. I had grown confident, had learned the limits of my skill, and lost all fear of heights. In a similar way, my husband Paul and his adjutant Georges Charpentier have gradually taught me how to deal with evil, dangerous men. They don't frighten me, just make me a little more cautious, alert. I truly enjoy matching wits with them and take great satisfaction in defeating them.'

'Could you show me how to walk on a tightrope? I'm too often afraid that I'll fail because I'm deaf, then people will laugh at me.'

'Before I mastered the rope, I often failed. If I fell, a net would catch me. Eventually, I didn't need a net.' Anne stepped back and studied the young woman. She had a slender, well-proportioned body, moved with natural grace, and had danced well at the festival ball. Her only health problem appeared to be an allergy to the damp, foul air of London. After a few months in Nice, she seemed to breathe normally. Physical exercise could only benefit her.

'We'll start training tomorrow and begin to discover where your talents lie. The servants will prepare a room and make you a proper costume.' The young woman's face turned bright with expectation.

Anne took her hand. 'Now let's have something to eat.'

Early in the afternoon, Anne sent Angelo with a message to Gabriella for a meeting to discuss certain pressing issues. Gabriella sent him back with a reply:

> *Meet me at six o'clock in the evening at the Howards' home to consider the maid Catherine's fate, and other matters. Don't tell anyone.*

That last sentence forced Anne to reconsider her plans. She realized that the count's spies were everywhere. Mario also must not know her movements. Intendant Spinola had called Paul to his office. Otherwise he would have accompanied her. She had told him about Mario's threat but added that he should not be concerned. It would be daylight and safe on the road when she set out for the meeting. For the trip back to the villa in the dark, she would find a trustworthy person to accompany her. She would also take her pistols along, just in case. Still, as she walked down the hill toward New Borough on the road to France, she felt her chest tighten. A small inner voice warned her that this could be a trap.

By the time she reached the Howards' house, she felt reassured. Gabriella was inside, waiting for her, visiting with Mr Howard. He bounded to his feet to greet Anne. Then they sat down to tea and biscuits. He was fully alert, his voice enthusiastic. The opportunity to discuss a serious issue with two attractive women seemed to rejuvenate him.

Gabriella opened the conversation by offering her free service to the Howards until a suitable maid could be found. Mr Howard thanked her graciously but said he had engaged Mary Kelly, the consul's maid. Gabriella then enquired if he had received the missing spoons.

'Yes, they arrived late this afternoon, with a letter of apology in French. I could probably pick out the meaning, but since I knew you were coming, I waited to ask you to read it for me.' Gabriella gestured to Anne, who took the letter from Mr Howard. She read the relevant passage aloud:

184

Please accept my deepest apologies for the criminal behaviour of the maid Catherine. Herewith I return the silver spoons that she stole. Be assured that she will be severely punished, as will her mother, who profited from the theft, and the pawnbroker, who knowingly accepted stolen property.

Anne returned the message to Mr Howard with an expression that invited him to respond. He remained silent for several moments, pondering what he had heard. 'I have made a few enquiries among the British visitors for whom the maid had also worked. She had not stolen anything from them. They agreed she was a woman of good character. Her mother was an invalid, a penniless widow.'

Gabriella added, 'And I have learned that the pawnbroker, to whom they owed money, proposed the idea of stealing silver spoons and suggested your collection as the most suitable target.'

Mr Howard fell silent again. Finally, he said, 'I believe that excessive leniency in these matters encourages thieving. Yet I fear that the punishment that the count intends is much too severe. He will have the maid stripped then whipped to a bloody pulp. She and her mother will be imprisoned in a workhouse for years. I don't know what will be done to the pawnbroker. Nor, frankly, do I care, for I believe that he is the true villain in this piece.

'The count seems to feel that he must be severe to these unfortunate women in order to reassure us, the British winter visitors, that we should never have to fear for the safety of our lives and property in the County of Nice. If they were asked, some of my acquaintances here would agree with his sentiments. But I do not. I would feel very distressed if those two women were destroyed because of my silver spoons. Furthermore, I believe the count's measures would repel more of us visitors than they would please. He should calculate the cost to the local economy.'

He turned to Anne. 'I would like you to help me write a petition in good French to the count to mitigate their punishment. No whipping, please. Perhaps Catherine could do a year of useful work for the poor. The count fancies himself an enlightened man. Let him devise an enlightened resolution to this affair.'

Anne had come to this discussion with much apprehension, for she didn't know Mr Howard well. She was feeling better as she began writing his sentiments in the form of a petition. It was neatly done in an hour. She translated it for him, then he signed it.

He poured small glasses of port and offered them to his guests. 'Let us drink to the success of this petition. May it convince the count's mind and win his heart.'

He saw the two women to the door and said good night.

Outside, in the small front garden, Gabriella said to Anne, 'This is a safe place. I'd like to continue our discussion.' She led Anne to a bench under an orange tree near the house, checked everywhere within earshot. 'Good, we can speak freely here.' They sat down and began to talk about Mario and the count.

Anne asked, 'Why is Mario plotting to attack me?'

'He sees you as the person most responsible for making him a prime suspect in the death of Captain Howe. For you have argued for the innocence of the Comtesse de Joinville, and you have persuaded the maid Catherine to witness against him. In his eyes you have become a powerful, hateful enemy. Think of it, your husband is a major French police officer whose patron is the Baron de Breteuil. At the present time, you seem to be the only serious obstacle to Mario doing his will. Out of fear of losing honour and respect the Comte de Maistre is indulging his son's folly, hoping that he may come to his senses. The count's attitude may change but unfortunately not before Mario does something spectacularly evil.'

'Like maiming or killing me,' Anne added with a wry smile. 'Then the count will lock him up in a fortress.'

'Since Captain Howe so rudely disgraced him in public, Mario has changed for the worse. He thinks that his father won't allow him to be charged with Howe's death or with any other crime. So he flaunts his immunity and acts recklessly, as if daring his father to stop him. He has money now. They say he gets it from smuggling French silk into the county. And he keeps bad company.'

'How does he treat you?' Anne asked.

'I don't see him anymore. He's no longer one of my admirers. I think he resents that I saw him so shamefully dirty and distressed after the captain's death. If he were to suspect that I'm speaking to you, he would become angry. I wouldn't feel safe.'

'Is there any way to bring him under control before it's too late?'

Gabriella slowly shook her head. 'I don't know of any.'

After bidding good night to Gabriella, Anne engaged a mule cart and driver on the road to France. 'To the villa in Cimiez,' she ordered. Though it was now dark, and the road almost deserted, she felt safe with the driver, a robust, honest-looking man who had driven her before. She was also reassured by her pistols, concealed in a bag at her side.

At the point where the road began to ascend the hill, the driver got out of the cart and led the mule. Soon the road was empty. Anne grew alert, especially where olive trees stood close to the road and offered cover to would-be assassins.

So she was ready when, halfway up the hill, two figures sprang out of the shadows. One of them seized the reins and threatened the driver with a club. The other man dashed toward Anne, brandishing a long knife. Anne drew a pistol and shot him from a distance of two paces. As he fell, she drew the other pistol and aimed it at the first man. 'Give the reins and your weapon to the driver and put your companion in this cart.' She stepped out on to the road and picked up the fallen man's knife, then told the driver, 'Continue on to the villa.'

She walked alongside the cart, her pistol cocked and pointed at the back of the uninjured villain in front of her. At first her legs felt numb with shock. She feared they might collapse beneath her. Her heart was pounding so hard she thought it would burst. But by the time she reached the villa, her body had returned to normal.

An incredulous servant opened the door and cried for help. Paul was home from the city and came running. He blinked when he saw the scene before him. With the driver's help he tied up the healthy villain. Servants took him to a strong room in the barn. The injured man was carried into the villa and Dr McKenzie called. The mule driver was persuaded to stay overnight as a guest.

'Well done, Anne,' said Paul when they were finally together in their room. He had been to the barn to question the uninjured bandit. 'Were you frightened?'

187

'Not really. I had the pistols. The mule driver is a stout, trustworthy fellow. Did you learn anything from the villain?' She opened a window, took a breath of fresh night air, gazed at the stars.

'No, I tried my French and Italian on him but in vain. He just stared at me like an idiot. Speaks only a dialect, or so he pretends.' Paul joined her at the window.

'You should have called me. I might have understood him.'

'You needed to rest. Besides, he simply wouldn't cooperate with either you or me. I'll send for the count tomorrow morning. We'll see whether he can persuade him to talk.'

'What is Dr McKenzie's verdict on the injured man?'

'He's unconscious, shot through the chest. The wound is serious but probably not fatal.'

Anne turned to face Paul. 'Did you take Angelo to look at these men? Are they the ones he overheard yesterday speaking to Mario?'

'Yes, he identified them.' Paul took her hand and kissed it.

She caressed his cheek. 'Tomorrow, then, we'll learn what de Maistre makes of this incident. At least he can't accuse me of meddling in his business. I wonder if he will find that his son was involved.'

Twenty-Three

A Conspiracy?

Friday, 22 February

Early the next morning, when Anne awoke, images of the night's attack crowded into her mind. While she slept, the rogue's knife had grown longer, sharper, more lethal. His face broke into a hideous grin. Her body began to tremble. For a minute or more her nerves seemed out of control, then gradually calmed down. This was a humbling experience. She wasn't quite the model of self-mastery that she had presented to Janice.

In response to a message from Paul, the Comte de Maistre

arrived at the villa late in the morning with several soldiers and settled into a parlour. Anne and the mule driver reported to him what had happened on the road during her return from the Howards'. She didn't mention Gabriella's warning nor blame Mario for having ordered the assault. The count would accuse her of meddling again and spreading unreliable, second-hand tales.

'Rather late for a woman to be out alone,' remarked the count, an inscrutable expression on his face. 'Men might wonder about her character.'

'The two men who attacked me, sir, were in no doubt about my name or my character.' The count's remark had irritated her. He seemed to blame her for the incident, as if the two men had mistaken her for a loose woman. She had to restrain herself, then added, 'I wasn't alone. An honest mule driver was with me.'

For a moment, de Maistre stared at her without comment, then announced that he would take the two men with him. The wounded one would go to a hospital. The healthy one would be interrogated at the palace where someone could be found, if needed, to translate for him. Without further ceremony, the count ordered the soldiers to gather the two rogues and they marched off to the city.

As Paul watched the count's entourage depart, he remarked to Anne, 'De Maistre didn't express concern for what might have happened to you. I'm sure he saw the hand of his son in this attack.'

Early in the afternoon, Dr McKenzie came to the villa for tea and reported that news of the incident had prompted lively discussion in the markets. As Anne and Paul had expected, the two men claimed that they had seen a lone woman on the road to France, late at night. When she engaged the mule cart, they concluded she was on her way to an assignation in Cimiez. They had shared a bottle of wine and were in a playful mood. So they tried to intercept her, intending only to frighten her. They were surprised by her violent reaction. Women in Nice did not ordinarily carry pistols. Nor, if they were respectable, did they go out alone late at night.

McKenzie concluded with an exasperated shake of his head. 'I saw Mario and his companions spreading their tale to anyone who would listen.'

'How did the crowd receive the news?' asked Paul.

'Unfortunately,' replied McKenzie, 'many of the common sort of people seemed guardedly sympathetic to the rogues. It was a pity, said many, that one of the men was badly injured. No one appeared to object that the other man was released with only a reprimand and a warning that he would be severely punished for a second offence.'

'Their painful experience may make them shy of lonely women in mule carts late at night,' Anne remarked. 'But I'm sure that Mario can hire two different rogues for another attempt.'

'I don't like the mood of the people,' said Paul. 'They resent wealthy winter visitors even while they covet their money.'

'True,' echoed the doctor. 'When they speculate on the killing of Captain Howe, they focus on the foreigners who are accused of the deed, Mr Grimshaw and the Comtesse de Joinville, and ignore the commandant's son.'

'I hope,' said Paul, 'that the leaders of the people come to their senses. The winter visitors bring wealth to Nice, as would become painfully clear if they were frightened off.'

McKenzie added, 'If the Comte de Maistre can't control his own son, he shouldn't be in charge of public order in this city.'

Paul rose from the table. 'I'll pass your opinion on to Intendant Spinola. In an hour, he and I will play tennis. Perhaps I'll also find out his view of the attack on Anne.'

Saint-Martin and Spinola played until the late afternoon light from the high windows began to fail them. It was an even match. The Frenchman was the younger and had the advantage in power and accuracy; the Italian had played more recently and displayed greater finesse. When they came off the court, they relived the game, discussing lost chases and memorable serves. Paul enjoyed his opponent's spontaneous, almost youthful delight in the sport.

In the privacy of the dressing room, Spinola's expression began to change. Paul sensed that he had news to tell. His eager voice took on a conspiratorial tone.

'I regret what happened to your wife last night,' he began. 'The government is taking steps to ensure that similar incidents shall not happen again.' He paused, then continued with studied composure. 'This evening, the commandant will announce his retirement, effective on Monday, when he will leave Nice for his estate in Savoy. His replacement, the Comte de Bogino, is on his way from Turin and should arrive by Monday. He has experience in police work and will deal promptly with the case of Captain Howe.'

'What a surprise! You have kept the secret well. I assume that this change has been under discussion for some time.'

'Yes, over a period of a few months. The decision was taken a week ago, when it became clear to the government that Mario de Maistre was a primary suspect in the murder of Captain Howe and that his father wouldn't recuse himself from the case. And this latest incident, the assault on your wife – certainly the young man's handiwork, confirms the government's wisdom. The count is unwilling or unable to control his son. That's intolerable in a civilized society.'

Saint-Martin shook the intendant's hand. 'I commend the government's action. We must meet for tennis again soon.' He left the palace with the guarded hope that the mystery of the captain's death would now be solved fairly and rationally. Hopefully, the new commandant would also put a stop to Mario's dangerous follies, and Anne would be safer.

Early in the evening, while Paul was still in the city, Anne went to Beverly's room to visit. They hadn't spoken much to each other, yesterday or today. Beverly had seemed preoccupied with her own thoughts. To judge from her downcast mouth, she was more unhappy than usual.

Anne wondered what the reason might be. It didn't seem to be Janice. She was busy with her speech training and her new interest in the slack rope. Nor did Beverly appear to miss her husband. She rarely mentioned Mr Parker. And if she did, it was never with affection. Perhaps she wasn't feeling well. Anne decided to comfort her.

Beverly's maid told Anne that her mistress had just left the room. 'She's probably gone to the terrace.'

And that's where Anne found her. She stood at the far edge, looking out over the ruined Roman city. The set of her shoulders, her inclined head, everything about her spoke clearly of a dejected woman. At first, Anne thought she shouldn't disturb Beverly's private misery. But it wasn't making the woman happy or likely to resolve whatever depressed her. So, Anne called out, could they chat for a while?

Beverly turned, forced a smile, and beckoned. The two women then watched silently as shadows slowly crept over the ruins.

'I long for him. It isn't fair.' Beverly didn't look at Anne as she spoke.

Anne let these enigmatic words hang in the air. Someone who didn't know Beverly and saw her wedding ring might assume that she was referring to an absent husband. But Anne realized after living in the household for several months that her cousin did not long for Mr Parker. Then for whom?

Beverly glanced over her shoulder to make sure that they were alone. 'Jack . . . Jack Grimshaw. Since November, we have been close friends. When Parker left, we became lovers.' She stared at Anne. 'Are you shocked? Or just surprised?'

'Surprised. Both you and he have hidden your feelings rather well. And I haven't noticed any indiscreet behaviour. Does anyone know?'

'My maid, but she's totally loyal to me.'

'Does Mr Parker know?' Anne added mentally, would he care?

'I don't think so. He has never brought up the matter. Nor should he.' Her voice took on a sharp edge. 'As long as we've been married, he has had mistresses. He's most likely dining with the latest one as we speak. I doubt that he has ever really cared for me, other than as lady of the house. As you know, my family were successful silversmiths and provided a large dowry. Mr Parker was also rich, but greedy for more.'

Anne gazed at Beverly's refined features. She was uncommonly beautiful, a jewel of a woman that Mr Parker must have coveted.

'Jack and I have been careful. He rented a charming cottage, ten minutes from here. The maid and I often walked there and met Jack. The maid stood guard. He and I made love. In the villa we played our proper, assigned roles.'

'Did you know about the stranger in the sanctuary?'

'Yes, Jack told me. Lebrun is his friend, wrongfully imprisoned. Jack intended to hide him until the police gave up the search.'

192

'Have you and Jack thought ahead to the future of your relationship?'

'We've often said that, one day, I would leave Parker. Jack has saved enough money for us to live on for the rest of our lives. Maybe in Naples, where Jack could work and the air is fresh and warm, like it is here.' She paused, looked away to the ruins. 'We were dreaming, of course. Now he's in prison and I'm . . .'

'Do you think Jack killed Captain Howe?'

'I know he didn't. He was with me all the time. At midnight during the festival ball, we slipped away to my room. There's a hidden stairway.'

'Now I understand. He won't use that alibi because it would disgrace you.'

'Yes, if exposed, our affair would taint my character, as they say, and offer grounds for Mr Parker to divorce me. I feel chained hand and foot to the British society in which I was raised. Therefore, I'm afraid to pursue that dream of endless bliss in Naples. I also know nothing of Italy or the Italian language, and have no social connections there. The British community in Naples would probably shun me. What would I do? Bask in the sun all day?'

'But if you don't step forward and give him the alibi, he may be convicted of the captain's murder.'

She shook her head vigorously. 'Regardless of the consequences to me personally, I shall not allow him to be convicted of a crime he did not commit.' She studied Anne's face. 'Would you and your husband advise me if and when I should tell the authorities?'

'I can promise for both of us.'

It was late at night before Anne and Paul had an opportunity to speak in the privacy of their room. While preparing for bed, Anne sat at a mirror in her shift and brushed her hair, Paul stood to one side in shirtsleeves and described his visit with Nice's intendant and their conversation about the Comte de Maistre's retirement.

When he finished, Anne breathed a sigh of relief. 'That's encouraging. We now can hope that the new commandant will be more detached, more fair-minded than the old one.' She stopped brushing for a moment. 'And I have something to tell you.' She went on to report on her conversation with Beverly. 'Unless she changes her mind, she will clear Grimshaw of suspicion in the captain's murder. He still faces questions concerning the fugitive Lebrun and the alleged hidden treasure.'

Paul was silent for a few moments, reflecting, a grave expression on his face. 'If I were to take a magistrate's point of view, I would ask, "Did Beverly and Grimshaw conspire to kill the captain?" She has admitted paying extortion money to him, lest he reveal his earlier affair with her. That's a sufficient motive to see him dead. And she would gladly lie to protect her lover, Grimshaw. Passion moved him to avenge the seduction of his daughter and her subsequent suicide. My imaginary magistrate, therefore, would conclude that the two lovers must have cooperated in the murder. Her part was to provide Grimshaw with an alibi, if he were suspected.'

Anne was disappointed, for she liked Beverly, and Grimshaw as well – to a certain degree. But she acknowledged the force of Paul's argument. This wouldn't be the first time that two lovers violently removed a person blocking their path to happiness. Anne recalled Beverly's repeated defence of Grimshaw, her unhappiness in the marriage with Mr Parker. In this light, Parker could regard himself as fortunate that the victim was Howe rather than him. Anne sighed, resumed brushing her hair. The solution to the mystery of Howe's death seemed as elusive as ever.

Twenty-Four

Father and Son

Saturday and Sunday, 23 and 24 February

On Saturday morning, Paul and Anne left the villa to call on Louise in her cell at the palace. It had been several days since Anne's last visit. Paul hadn't seen her in weeks. Led by the warden's wife, they approached Louise with apprehension. For a woman accustomed to a worldly, dissipated, self-indulgent, and disorderly life, her ten days in nearly solitary confinement would be an entirely new, and unsettling, experience.

Worse, it could seem like systematic torture. No card playing or gambling, no trash literature, no dancing or theatre, no gossip or other distractions that had previously filled her days. And, finally, at Anne's request, she was denied strong spirits, especially brandy, to which she was addicted. Her only alcoholic beverage was a glass of wine with dinner.

Anne had made arrangements with the warden to provide Louise with simple, healthy meals at regular hours. Aside from daily exercise, she had little else to do for ten days but to reflect. The count had questioned her briefly. Otherwise, she was alone with the crucifix on the wall above her bed, with the New Testament and the *Introduction to the Devout Life* by Francis de Sales. Anne had earlier brought her pen and paper. The guards were kind but spoke only a few words of French.

At Anne's request, supported by a suitable payment, the warden's wife had kept Louise under close observation. In such altered circumstances, she might attempt suicide. In fact, according to the warden's wife, Louise did suffer bouts of depression, anger, self-pity, regret, and uncontrollable weeping, especially during the first six or seven days. 'Lately,' the woman said, 'she's been more peaceable.'

The warden's wife peered into the cell through a small window in the door. 'She's ready to receive you,' said the woman and unlocked the door, let them in, then locked it behind them. Louise stood to receive them, head erect, gaze steady. Anne was pleased to see that she was not a broken woman. Extra chairs had been brought in. With a gracious gesture she invited them to sit.

Gradually, Anne perceived other differences. First and foremost, her eyes. Gone was the nervous, mocking expression, previously so characteristic of her. Instead, Anne saw anxiety mixed with resignation. Her voice seemed to have a kinder tone. But her hands trembled slightly.

Paul opened the conversation. 'Have you heard that the Comte de Maistre is retiring to Savoy?'

Louise shook her head. A puzzled expression appeared on her face.

'That's a hopeful development,' Paul continued. 'De

Maistre's replacement as commandant will arrive on Monday. In conversations with the intendant, I gathered a favourable impression of the new man. He should investigate the captain's death more competently than his predecessor. You have grounds to expect that you might leave the prison as a free woman.'

'How sad!' she remarked. 'Just when I was beginning to enjoy the place.' Her irony, Anne thought, was almost good-natured.

'Has Captain Howe been properly buried?' Louise asked. 'I did love him once.'

Anne replied, 'The cemeteries in Nice are reserved for Catholics. As best I could determine, the captain was not a religious man and belonged to no church, though probably baptized in the Church of England. Dr McKenzie and I saw to his burial in a private plot of land for non-Catholics. His grave overlooks the sea.'

Louise murmured her approval.

'How have you been treated?' Paul asked.

'Better than I expected.' She glanced at Anne. 'I understand from the warden's wife that I have you to thank. In the beginning it was hard to do without brandy morning, noon, and night. I felt like crawling out of my skin. But now I'm much better. My head is clear for the first time that I can recall. Still, I'm worried that if I return to Paris, I'll fall back into my old bad habits.'

'That's likely,' agreed Paul. 'You might think of remaining in Nice in Dr McKenzie's care, until you feel stronger.'

'I shall consider your suggestion, Paul.'

During this conversation, Anne observed Louise carefully. Although her pride of class remained undiminished, she had become more serious, more reflective, and less flighty. A stronger person. But not a friendlier one, at least not toward Anne, whose presence she merely tolerated. In her expression Anne detected envy and resentment, and that had to do with Paul. Louise saved her charm for him, her distant cousin and social equal, as well as a handsome man her own age.

Anne sighed inwardly, tempted to regret what she had done for Louise. But she concluded that she owed it to herself to do the decent, humane thing, even if Louise's response wasn't what it ought to be.

Later, when they had left Louise and were walking on the seaside terrace, Paul took Anne's arm. 'I'm proud of you,' he said. 'It wasn't easy. The arrangements you made for Louise were exactly what she needed. She's still a flawed person, but there's at least a glimmer of hope for her.'

Anne gave him a smile for the compliment. 'Do you think it's at all likely that she killed Captain Howe?'

'I can't rule out the possibility. At the time, she was unstable, angry, and prone to violence. She had the opportunity. But she appeared to be drunk and virtually incapable of such a well-placed thrust to the neck as the captain received. The blood on her gown could indeed have come from throwing herself on his dying body. If the new commandant is a reasonable man, he might give her the benefit of the doubt and release her. Then again he might believe that she wasn't drunk, merely pretending.'

'Grimshaw is a more serious suspect, is he not?'

'Yes, he and Beverly together, I fear. He passionately hated Captain Howe. His diary describes how he once intended to murder the captain, whom he blamed for his daughter's suicide. Grimshaw was also familiar with the Roman dagger and capable of using it expertly, as Louise was not. If pressed, Beverly would give him a false alibi. I couldn't even guess what the new commandant would conclude. The evidence against them is circumstantial. We must wait and see.'

Anne and Paul continued their promenade under a gentle midday sun. But a cloud of sadness darkened her spirit. Too much human misery on her mind. For relief she caressed Paul's hand, drank of the love in his eyes. They turned toward the sea. Side by side, they gazed at the waves rolling endlessly on to the pebble beach.

It was teatime when Anne and Paul returned to the villa. After leaving the terrace, they had stopped at the Maccarani Theatre for costumes. Tomorrow was the third Sunday in Lent and another festival. Anne had little inclination to join in herself. The festival ball that ended in Howe's murder had spoiled her taste for merrymaking. But she had overheard Janice and Angelo wishing they could take part. So, at the theatre, Anne had borrowed two costumes for them from what was available.

At tea with Paul and Beverly, she asked for Janice.

'Probably in the kitchen,' Beverly replied with disapproval. 'She's taken a fancy to the boy Angelo.'

Anne suspected that they had recently become friends. Janice was teaching Angelo to sign, a source of mutual amusement. Anne excused herself and went looking for them.

She found them together in the barn. They had put up a slack rope in an empty stall and laid thick piles of clean straw on the floor. Janice was walking the rope barefooted, her face screwed up in the effort of concentration. Her hand rested on Angelo's shoulder for balance. For a few minutes Anne stood in the shadows, watching. Slim and well coordinated, Janice performed quite skilfully for a beginner.

Then they switched roles, Angelo walking the rope, leaning on Janice. He was physically as suited for the sport as she. They did in fact appear to be a congenial pair. Then Anne thought of the social distance between them. He was a poor Italian boy, while she was a wealthy English girl, and deaf as well. Miracles nonetheless happen. Anne thought of her own experience. She and Paul were also a social mismatch.

'Come to the villa,' Anne said when they paused to rest. 'I have your costumes for tomorrow. Try them on.'

They embraced each other with delight and rushed to the villa.

The Harlequin costume fitted Janice, and the Punchinello suited Angelo. Anne gave them conventional instructions on good behaviour, then added, 'While you are enjoying the music, the food, and the merrymaking, please keep your eyes open for Gabriella and Mario. If you notice anything unusual, report to me and my husband. We will be on the seaside terrace, either walking or at an outdoor table of a cafe. Tomorrow is the last day that the Comte de Maistre wields power in Nice. I expect something dramatic to happen.'

Late in the afternoon on Saturday, Mario hurried to the commandant's office in the royal palace. He had come from a cafe where everyone was talking about his father's sudden announcement. A clerk showed Mario in.

The Comte de Maistre sat at his writing table, reading an official document. He looked up as his son approached and gestured to a chair facing him.

'I'm about to retire, son, as of Monday. I'll settle down in the family chateau in Savoy. Do you want to come with me?' The tone of his voice was flat, without feeling. This was not a warm, heartfelt invitation.

'Why go back to Savoy?' Mario replied. 'That's where you came from. The chateau is little more than a big draughty hovel. Society consists of surly peasants and rustic gentry. You could return to Turin. It's not London or Paris, but at least it offers decent food and drink, tolerable conversation, a few beautiful women, gambling dens, parks to ride in, company in which to shine.'

'I do not have a choice, son. The government is sending me to the chateau. I am condemned to stay there. This is the end of my career. You see, the intendant has regularly reported your misdeeds and my failure to prevent them. The miscarried investigation of Captain Howe's death was the last straw.'

De Maistre rose from his writing table and began to pace the floor, his hands clasped behind his back. With a baleful glance at his son he continued his discourse. 'In a cell on the ground floor of this palace I have placed a French countess, daughter of the Baron de Breteuil, the most powerful minister in the French King's government. She's my principal suspect but was too drunk that night to have stuck a pig, much less a professional military officer who had disarmed her once before. I put her in prison chiefly because she insulted me. I can't believe I was so foolish.'

He shook his head in self-reproach, cleared his throat, and went on. 'In the cell next to her is my other serious suspect, a British scholar and archaeologist, who was making love to Mr Parker's lady at the time of the murder. At least that's what her maid has told me. Not that it matters. If need be, Madame Parker would give Grimshaw an alibi. He could actually have killed the captain – he has the mettle for it.'

The count's pacing grew rapid, his gestures agitated. 'In the view of our government in Turin, I am an idiot who needlessly jeopardized the County of Nice's greatest economic resource after olive oil, the winter visitors. The government must placate them, or they won't come back next year.'

He glanced again at his son. 'The suspect whom I should have detained, of course, is you. I have always doubted that you had the courage for such a horrendous deed. But you

199

could have somehow tricked the captain, killed him dishonourably. Frankly, I don't know if you are guilty or not. And I don't care to find out.'

The count wagged a finger at his son. 'In any case, if you are wise, you will leave Nice before my replacement arrives on Monday. I'm sure he is well informed about the murder investigation and will act quickly to set it right. You will be at the centre of his attention. Now I have other matters to think about. Good day to you.' He walked to the window and stared out at the sea.

Mario understood that he had been dismissed. Dazed and numb, he left the palace and went to the cafe in the old town where he usually met his companions. They were at a table in the corner. When he entered, they turned their backs to him. They had heard of his father's announcement and realized that he could no longer supply information to them or offer protection.

He fled from the cafe out into the busy street. Suddenly, he felt a strange chill, though the evening air was mild. A scene welled up from his memory. A small boy alone at his mother's grave. The others had left the churchyard, had forgotten him. He had wailed but no one heard him. Now in the middle of this narrow, bustling street, without friends, or parent, or money, he was again utterly, desperately alone.

At another cafe, where he wasn't recognized, Mario sat drumming his fingers on the tabletop, an empty coffee cup before him. For hours he had pondered his alternatives, whether to leave Nice or to stay. With the end of his father's protection, the city seemed increasingly dangerous. Enemies who previously feared to attack him would now be emboldened. Those who resented his privileged position would now rejoice if he were to stumble and fall. He would be exposed to ridicule.

On the other hand, how could he live outside Nice? He had only the money in his pocket, he had saved nothing. He also had no connections abroad, no easy, palatable way to earn a living. As an outcast, a fugitive, he wouldn't have an assured status or respect anywhere.

This debate continued to rage in his mind through the evening, while he roamed from one gambling den to the next, playing at cards and at dice. But Lady Luck no longer favoured him, and by midnight he was deep in debt, and the gambling dens wouldn't lend him any more money or give him credit.

Alone in his room, despondent, he thought of Gabriella and felt a surge of hope. Unfortunately, she was no longer dependent on his father's goodwill. Still, he had once pleased her. Intimately. He had also once been a *cicisbeo* in her entourage. Against all odds, Mario thought she might still offer him protection and support. She enjoyed respect in the community. Yes, he would speak to her.

Sunday morning, he went to church and saw her from a distance. Several young men he knew attended her. She looked so beautiful and gracious. Increasingly confident, he encouraged his imagination to run wild. She would certainly take him back. They would become passionate lovers again.

From the church he followed her out into the city. A festival for the third Sunday in Lent was soon in full swing. She and the men of her entourage had put on black half-face masks and marched behind a band of musicians through narrow, boisterous streets into the large square in front of the palace. Mario had also donned a mask. Now he summoned his courage and approached Gabriella. She had stopped at a wine merchant's table and ordered drinks for her young men.

'May I join you, gracious lady?' Mario put as much confidence in his voice as he could muster.

'And who are you?' She peered at him through her mask. The noise from the crowd was so loud that they could barely hear each other.

Instantly, her young men gathered round, on guard.

Mario raised his mask.

She jumped back a step, alarmed. 'Mario! Are you mad? I want nothing to do with you. My maid Catherine and her mother are in prison because of you. How dare you try to join my entourage!'

The faces of her young men took on a menacing aspect. Mario had forgotten that Gabriella had a hot temper. She now loosed it upon him, called him vain, treacherous, cowardly, and, at a peak of fury, 'assassin in the dark of night'. The young men echoed her and shook their fists at him. An excited murmur spread throughout the crowd.

'Get out of my sight,' shrieked Gabriella. Her young men

seized Mario, pummelled him, and cast him from the square.

Red-faced and dishevelled, weeping, he stumbled down a narrow side street, lost his balance, and fell. As he scrambled to his feet, two masked costumed characters stared at him. The one with a parrot's nose, Punchinello, cocked its head and asked in dialect, 'What's the matter?'

Nearly blinded with rage, Mario staggered away, muttering, 'I'll have my revenge, I'll kill the bitch.'

Late in the evening, Gabriella returned home from the festival, leaving her young men to their own devices. She went to the kitchen and sat at the table with a glass of wine and her account book. The house was quiet. The servants had the night off for the festival. She opened the account book, idly fingered its pages, and let her mind drift back.

An uneasy feeling had grown upon her since the confrontation with Mario. She regretted her outburst of temper almost as soon as her young men had returned from chastising him.

Then, an hour or so later, two masked persons had approached her. One of them, a tall woman, raised her mask – it was Madame Cartier. She had said softly in French, 'Gabriella, beware. A short while ago, Mario de Maistre said he would kill you. He meant it. Tonight is his best chance. Trust us.'

'What shall I do?' she asked, her throat tightening with fear.

The other masked person had also raised his mask – it was Colonel Saint-Martin. 'Go home, Gabriella. We shall follow you at a safe distance, then join you and devise a plan for this evening.'

Suddenly, the clock on the kitchen wall chimed nine, shaking Gabriella back into the present moment. She closed the account book and took a deep drink of her wine. Now reflecting on that plan, she concluded sourly that most of the risk seemed to fall on her. The silence of the house began to feel ominous. She shuddered. Then she heard a sound in the garden, like a foot treading on the gravel path.

The storeroom off the kitchen was small and windowless, the air stuffy. Anne stretched out her arm until it touched Paul's shoulder. He took her hand and kissed it. They were hiding among Gabriella's store of onions, herbs, dried fruits, and vegetables. Through louvres in the door Anne could survey the dining area of the large kitchen. Gabriella was sitting at a table, her account book spread open. Her back was rigid, her hand trembled as she lifted her glass. Persuading her that the plan would work hadn't been easy.

Peace of mind would be her reward. As long as Mario was free, even in exile, she would have to live in fear. He could slip back into Nice and kill her, or he could hire assassins to do it. She would be safe only when he was dead or imprisoned in a fortress for life.

Anne recalled with pleasure when Janice and Angelo had found her and Paul in a terrace cafe. Breathless with excitement, they reported having followed Gabriella and her young men through the festival crowd. They had drawn close enough for Angelo to hear her scathing rebuke to Mario. After the young men punished him, Janice and Angelo witnessed his threat against Gabriella.

Anne thanked the two young people and allowed them to enjoy the festival until dusk. Then they should return to the villa. They agreed with visible reluctance.

The clock on the kitchen wall struck nine. Anne touched her pistol gingerly. It was half-cocked and had to be handled with care. She whispered in Paul's ear, 'Perhaps he won't come. His fear of getting caught might have won out over his anger.'

'Wait, I think I hear movement outside the kitchen door.'

In the rear of the house was a garden of vegetables and fruit trees. Surrounded by a low stone wall, it was the most likely way into the house for a man who would not want to be seen on the street or by the handyman and his wife.

'Good evening, Gabriella,' Mario said as he entered the kitchen. His voice was strained. His eyes had a wild look, as if small fires burned in them. He was wearing a festival costume and a black half-face mask that he had lifted to his brow. 'I have come to persuade you to forgive me and take me back into your favour.'

'So you climbed over the wall, crept through the garden, and entered by the kitchen door.' She looked at him askance.

Uninvited, he sat opposite her, laid his hands on the table, nervously tapped the surface with his fingers. 'I knew that Carlo wouldn't let me in. I realize that I haven't *earned* your favour. I seek it from your goodness and from the memory of better times.'

'And if I refuse?'

He reached into his shirt, pulled out a dagger, and pointed it at her throat. He said nothing, just stared at her, a malevolent grin on his face.

Anne grew tense, raised her pistol.

With a surprisingly calm voice, Gabriella asked, 'Is that how you settled accounts with Captain Howe? Frankly, I thought you couldn't have done it. You *are* clever, but he was such a strong, alert man, skilled in the use of weapons. No one ever dared challenge him to a duel.'

Mario lowered the knife. His eyes seemed to shift to a distant scene. 'The captain never had a chance to use his strength or skill. For hours I practised on a tailor's dummy, feinting and then thrusting with a knife. During the ball in the villa I told him I would meet him in the arena and settle my debt. He looked sceptical but he agreed. At the appointed time, he was there. I approached him, held out my right hand as if to shake his. He hesitated, confused.

'In that brief moment, while he was staring at my empty right hand, my left hand drew the knife and stabbed him in the neck. I had correctly figured that he wouldn't immediately recall that I'm ambidextrous. What I hadn't planned for was the blood. It spurted from the wound and soiled my shirt-sleeves. I couldn't go back to the villa, so I smeared dung on the bloodstains and went to you.'

He paused, stared at her. 'I can see that you will not take me back.' The wild look returned to his eyes. He rose from the chair and raised the knife. 'If I thought that you had ever truly loved me and would keep my secret, I would spare you. But even while we were in bed together, I meant no more to you than the gold bracelet on your wrist or the embroidered gown you wore. So prepare to die.'

Before he could thrust, Paul burst from the storeroom, pistol pointed at Mario's head. 'Drop the knife!' he shouted.

For an instant Mario seemed stunned and unable to move. In the meantime, Anne also rushed forward with a pistol. Mario let go of the knife. It clattered on the floor. He collapsed in a chair, sobbing.

While Paul trained a pistol on him, Anne bound him hand

and foot, then sent the handyman to call the guard. She kept her pistol ready. There was danger that Mario might have had accomplices outside the house. Only when a captain and a detachment of the guard arrived could she attend to Gabriella, who was leaning over the table, breathing heavily.

Anne caressed her, applied a damp cloth to her forehead, gave her a sip of brandy. 'You were magnificent, Gabriella. That was a bravura performance. Relax now. It's all over.'

One of the guards remained with Anne and Gabriella. The rest left with Paul and their prisoner. 'No point waking the Comte de Maistre,' said Paul to the captain. 'It's nearly Monday. You can hand this rogue over to the new commandant.'

Twenty-Five

A New Start

Monday, 25 February

Late in the afternoon, Saint-Martin mulled over last night's dramatic events. He was waiting outside the palace office of Amadeo de Bogino, the new commandant, and was still surprised that Mario had attempted to kill Gabriella and had in fact killed Captain Howe.

Mario had seemed to lack the necessary courage and resolve. Though loud, his anger had previously been impotent. It had usually dissolved into futile weeping. His reputation for knife play also was intended merely to frighten others. He hadn't actually stabbed or cut anyone, though he had hired the two thugs to attack Anne. His threats had weight mainly because his father stood behind him.

Previously, Gabriella had curbed Mario's wayward, destructive impulses. That control had recently eroded, allowing Mario to act as he wished.

Bogino's arrival interrupted these reflections. 'Sorry to be late,' he said, lines of fatigue etched in his face. 'I've just had a hair-raising journey through a late winter snowstorm on the mountain pass at Tende. Please allow me a little time to settle into my office.'

Within minutes a clerk summoned Saint-Martin.

The new commandant sat at his table. The two men introduced themselves. A slender man with a high, intelligent forehead, Bogino had a keen way of listening that inspired confidence. He also spoke English, as well as Italian and French, and understood the local dialect. In the army he had earned a reputation for diligence and efficiency. Saint-Martin felt at ease with him.

'What can I do for you?' Bogino asked.

'My first item of business,' Saint-Martin replied, 'concerns the capture of Mario de Maistre.'

The commandant leaned forward, fully alert. 'I heard the news upon arriving at the palace.'

'You also need to know that, in the presence of three witnesses, including myself, the young man confessed to the premeditated killing of Captain Howe. Your guards lodged Mario in a ground-floor cell.' Saint-Martin handed Bogino a written report, signed by himself, Anne, and Gabriella.

The commandant studied the document, then looked up with a grateful smile. 'This makes my task easier. In due time, I shall question Mario myself. In addition to the murder, he must also answer to charges of smuggling. I see no reason why I should hold the Comtesse de Joinville in prison any longer. May I release her into your custody? I might need to speak to her later about the case.'

'I'll vouch for her. Will you continue to hold Mr Grimshaw?'

Bogino tapped a file that lay on his desk. 'My predecessor contends that Grimshaw should have surrendered the fugitive Jean Lebrun to the police. However, the French authorities are no longer searching for Lebrun and have charged another man with his crime. Frankly, the issue is moot. However, the Comte de Maistre also charged Grimshaw with hiding a treasure trove that he had discovered on the villa's domain. It is said to be in a Marseille bank. My colleague the intendant believes that the treasure may belong to our royal government and was taken out of the country without permission. Mr Grimshaw should remain in prison until these legal issues are resolved.'

'Could they be resolved quickly?' Saint-Martin asked. 'I

have in fact recently searched that bank, Barrett and Sons, and found no treasure. Grimshaw's deposits at the bank are reasonable for a man who has bought and sold antiquities for decades. It seems unfair to imprison him on the basis of mere hearsay.'

'You've thrown new light on the matter. I'll urge the intendant to resolve his concerns immediately.'

'Finally, sir, I would like you to consider the fate of the maid Catherine and her mother, Paula Galeta, charged with stealing silver spoons from a winter visitor.' He described their crime and their arrest by de Maistre. 'He threatened them with the full rigour of the law and put them under strict confinement in one of the palace's strong rooms.' Paul drew a paper from his portfolio and handed it to the commandant. 'This is a petition from Mr Howard, owner of the spoons, requesting humane treatment of the two women. Prior to this incident they had a spotless record. Poverty and the tricks of an unscrupulous pawnbroker led them to this crime.'

Saint-Martin paused to allow the commandant to scan the petition, then went on, 'Catherine could serve as a key witness to Mario's crime. She washed the blood from his sleeves. The Comte de Maistre has held her in solitary confinement to prevent her from incriminating his son.'

Bogino glanced at the report and the petition. 'I shall move forward on these matters, Colonel. The government fully appreciates the winter visitors' contribution to the prosperity of this city and tries to make their stay as rewarding as possible.'

As Saint-Martin left the office, he sensed that the commandant's concern for the winter visitors was politic, but it also seemed genuine.

Meanwhile, in Louise's cell on the ground floor of the palace, time passed at a snail's pace. Anne stared out the window into the courtyard, waiting impatiently for Paul. Several officers were bowling. Their shouts and laughter echoed off the walls. Louise sat stiffly at the table, staring at her hands folded before her. She had little to say. And Anne couldn't bring herself to force a conversation. The tension between the two women was palpable and uncomfortable. They had almost nothing in common except for their rival interest in Paul.

Anne was relieved to hear a key turning in the lock. The door opened and the warden's wife entered, together with Paul. He smiled at Anne, then went up to Louise, put a hand on her shoulder, and said softly, 'Louise, you are free to leave. The new commandant believes that you had nothing to do with the death of Captain Howe. The warden's wife will arrange to move you back to your house.'

She remained still for a moment, then she looked up with teary eyes. 'Paul, I'm grateful for all you've done.' She glanced at Anne by the window, 'And to you as well.' She sounded sincere. Anne acknowledged to herself that nearly two weeks in prison, suspected of murder, must have been trying.

When Louise had gained a measure of calm, Paul met her eye and said, 'The commandant has placed you in my custody. You are to remain in Nice until he decides you are no longer needed in the investigation. He couldn't say how long that might be, since he has only today arrived in the city.' Paul hesitated, then said, 'I must have your word that you will comply with his condition.'

For an instant, Louise's eyes sparked with anger. 'I wish I'd never set foot in this city!' But her expression quickly softened. 'Don't mind me, Paul. At this point in my life, I might as well be here. There are fewer distractions than in Paris. The weather is much better. It's a place where I can think more clearly. Yes, I promise that I will comply. I wouldn't wish to cause you grief.'

Anne made a heroic effort to hide her dismay at Paul's 'custody' of Louise. That *was* an opportunity for mischief. Anne caught Paul's eye and flashed her misgivings. He smiled back sheepishly.

As Anne and Paul walked on the seaside terrace and enjoyed the sun setting below the horizon, he reported on his conversation with the new commandant. 'He should free Grimshaw within a few days.'

Anne smiled wryly. 'And you will become responsible for him, I suppose, as well as for Louise and Jean Lebrun. Remember, sir, you came here to rest and to improve your health.'

Twenty-Six

Finale

Monday, 31 March

At midmorning on a warm spring day, Anne and Paul and their friends gathered at the entrance to the villa to say goodbye. More than a month had passed since Captain Howe's murder had been solved. The Senate of Nice had recently condemned Mario de Maistre to life imprisonment in a royal fortress. The maid Catherine and her mother were treated gently, as Mr Howard had requested.

Beverly and Jack Grimshaw now openly lived together. They appeared to be happy. A few days ago, their future had taken a curious turn. With his attention fixed on his mistress and his business in London, Mr Parker had lost interest in the villa and its estate and had offered the leasehold to Grimshaw. He was inclined to accept. Under his management, the estate's olive groves, vineyards, and orchards could produce a profit. At least for the time being, Parker did not seem to care what his wife was doing.

Janice and Angelo were still friends, enjoying not only rope walking but also acrobatic tricks and puppetry that Anne had taught them. Janice's future was uncertain. If it were her choice, she would probably return to Braidwood's school in London.

For the foreseeable future, Louise would remain in Nice with Dr McKenzie to improve her health. They were culti-vating a garden together at her house.

In the weeks since Jean Lebrun emerged from the sanc-tuary, he had begun his recovery from years in prison and months as a fugitive. The Parlement at Aix had vacated his sentence. His way home was now legally clear. His friend Grimshaw gave him work cleaning ancient artefacts and replacing rotten timbers in the barn. He also made himself useful in the villa. But like a hurt animal, he spoke little and withdrew from the company of others. Anne was concerned how he would adjust to married life in Paris. She and Paul had invited him to travel with them to the capital.

He bid a touching, warm farewell to Grimshaw, then boarded the small, simple coach, and it pulled away from the villa, clattered down the hill to the coastal road, and set off for France.

In Marseille, they joined an informal reception at the Abbé Gombert's house. Georges Charpentier approached Lebrun with outstretched arms.

'Jean, I looked all over Paris for you, got to know your wife. Fine woman. When she hadn't heard from you in months, she dreamed that you had died, hidden in a deep, dark chamber. She asked me to clear your name and to bring your body home. I agreed to try. Well, she's getting more than she asked for. Your good name is restored and you are going back to her alive.' The two men embraced.

'I thank you all,' said Lebrun with tears in his eyes.

Paul shook his hand. 'In a sense, you earned your freedom with your daring escape. You might otherwise have suffered in prison to the end of your life.'

For the rest of the trip to Paris, Paul rented a larger, more comfortable coach. Georges and Lebrun rode outside to enjoy the view and the fresh air and to watch out for bandits.

Inside the coach, Anne turned her eyes to her husband, who was examining a map of Provence. The lines of worry had disappeared from his forehead. He breathed easily, without wheezing or coughing. The sun and air, the scenic beauty of coast and countryside had restored his health. Still, even while on vacation, he had managed to accomplish a great deal of good. Without his work in Toulon and Marseille, Lebrun might still be a fugitive.

Anne recalled with satisfaction her part in his redemption. Her investigation of Jack Grimshaw's suspicious behaviour had uncovered the hidden sanctuary of Mithras where Lebrun was hiding. She helped return him to society and correct an old injustice.

By the time they reached Paris, it would be spring and a new beginning for them all. The coach rumbled on. Anne began to think of Lebrun's painful transition to normal life. From outside came a burst of hearty laughter, then another. Anne leaned back and relaxed. Georges's company might be just the medicine that the former Toulon convict needed.

AUTHOR'S NOTE

Mr Parker's villa in Cimiez is based on the historical Villa des Arènes two miles from downtown Nice. The Gubernatis family of Greek descent built the villa as a country home in the seventeenth century and owned it at the time of this story. Today, beautifully renovated, it is the location of the Musée Matisse.

Cemenelum was the administrative centre of the Roman province of Alpes Maritimae. It owed its third-century prosperity to its strategic location on the Via Julia, the principal east–west road between Italy and Gaul, as well as to its port of Nicaea. Its garrison also guarded the empire from incursions by the barbarian mountain tribes to the north. With the decline of the empire in the West, the city was abandoned about the year 500. Its population moved to its more defensible port in the shadow of a lofty citadel.

The ruins of the Roman city of Cemenelum are more visible today than in the late eighteenth century. Then, much of the site was still covered with olive trees, gardens, and vineyards. The most visible monuments were the amphitheatre and the great northern baths, known then as the Temple of Apollo. Amateur archaeologists and treasure hunters, like the fictional Jack Grimshaw, frequently mined the area for ancient Roman artefacts and occasionally found treasure troves.

Twentieth-century scientific excavations in an archaeological park just south of the villa have exposed the considerable remains of the ancient city's baths and other public buildings and principal streets. A modern museum adjacent to the site displays artefacts, weapons, jewellery, and many other vestiges of the city's prehistoric and Roman past.

The Mithraeum in the story is fictional, based on the hundreds that have been discovered in the lands ruled by Rome. At least up to this point, none has been found in Cemenelum, though the preconditions existed – the presence of soldiers and foreign merchants.

In the late eighteenth century Nice was the principal city of the County of Nice in the Kingdom of Sardinia. The city's population of about 20,000 was similar to that of ancient Cemenelum at its high point in the third century. Except for a brief period of French rule, 1792 to 1814, the county was historically Italian. In 1860 its population voted to join France.

Nice was part of a centralized, authoritarian monarchy on the French model, governed from the capital, Turin. Under a royal intendant's close financial supervision, the county enjoyed a modest measure of self-government. A governor represented the King and a commandant controlled the military garrison and maintained law and order. The Senate of Nice, appointed by the King, administered criminal and civil justice.

Nice's first influx of wealthy winter visitors, *les hivernants* in French, began with the British author Tobias Smollett in the 1760s, who touted the region's remarkably mild, sunny climate and natural beauty in his *Travels through France and Italy* (Oxford, 1979). See also Arthur Young's *Travels during the years 1787, 1788 and 1789* (London, 1889). Finally, the American representative to the French court, Thomas Jefferson, recorded his impressions of southern France and Nice in his letters. See George Shackelford, *Thomas Jefferson's Travels in Europe, 1784–1789* (Baltimore, 1995).

At its peak in the late 1780s, the tourist industry at Nice attracted about five hundred visitors, mostly British, including servants. It was second only to the exportation of olive oil in its significance to the local economy. The French occupation beginning in September 1792 brought tourism to an end. It revived in the early nineteenth century following the Napoleonic Wars and greatly expanded after mid-century with the advent of the railroad.

Deeply rooted in popular traditions of the Middle Ages, Carnival in Nice evolved by the eighteenth century into the elaborate festivities of Mardi Gras, including Shrove Tuesday on the eve of Lent, as well as the various feasts on the Sundays between Ash Wednesday and Easter, which the Church regarded as outside of Lent. Though elaborate, these festivities were still local. Since the late nineteenth century Carnival has grown into an international spectacle.

With improved facilities but a still harsh regime, the Toulon naval prison functioned into the mid-nineteenth century, when it was replaced by overseas penal colonies such as Devil's Island. Among it best-known inmates is the fictional Jean Valjean in Victor Hugo's *Les Misérables*. Malcolm Crook's *Toulon in War & Revolution . . . 1750–1820* (Manchester, 1991), offers a modern account of the French naval prison.